The Lightning Queen

The Lightning Queen

LAURA RESAU

SCHOLASTIC INC.

ISBN 978-1-338-03294-9

12 11 10 9 8 7 6 5 4 3 2 1   16 17 18 19 20 21

Printed in the U.S.A.   40

First Scholastic paperback printing, April 2016

Book design by Abby Dening

For Bran, who lights up my world

Table of Contents

CRACKLE

Mateo

THE HILL OF DUST,
OAXACA, MEXICO

Present Day

TUG OF MAGIC

*A*t the brink of every summer, something yanks me toward the Hill of Dust. Something like fishing line, spooling out from the heart of the hill, across Mexico and all the way up to Maryland, zipping through cul-de-sacs, searching me out, trailing bits of magic all the way. It doesn't even matter if I'm holed up in our basement rec room, lost in Xbox with my buddies . . . somehow the string finds me and ties itself to a place smack in my center.

Then it reels me back in.

Its pull is strong on the first airplane, even stronger on the second, and stronger still on the bus bumping its way into the mountains. And at the foot of the Hill of Dust, the pull is so strong, my sneakers barely touch the ground, and I'm nearly floating up the dirt path to the very tip-top. Finally, I lurch straight into its heartbeat.

Which is where I am now, sitting on a small wooden chair across from Grandpa Teo in his healing hut. I'm missing Xbox already, but mostly just buzzing from the journey. Mom's right across the muddy courtyard, inside the adobe kitchen, catching up with her great-aunts and great-uncles. You'd think a robotics engineer might feel out of place here, but she always settles right in. After all, this is where she grew up with Grandpa and Grandma before she went to college in Maryland, before she married her American boyfriend, before they had me.

Since Dad has to work, it's usually just me and Mom who come here. Every visit gives me that swooping, soaring feeling, like a Ferris wheel ride. And somehow, this space here—Grandpa's small, old healing room—is the hub.

It's dark, cave-like, and mostly empty except for an altar covered in ancient things like tin-framed saints, and fresh things like white flowers, and glowing-sweet things like candles. It all feels outside of time—the packed dirt floors and clay walls and film of incense smoke coating everything. I bet I could've been sitting here fifty years ago and it would've felt the same.

Grandpa and I stare at each other, which is both weird and not weird. It's like looking into a mirror, seeing myself when I'm old, only subbing an Orioles cap for his palm hat, and a Ravens jersey for his white collared shirt. All my gray-haired relatives say he was my spitting image when he was twelve, especially the crazy-thick eyelashes.

"Mateo," his voice rumbles, deep as the engine of Dad's old pickup truck. His eyes widen, like he's been waiting all year for this moment. "I need your help."

Whoa. My help? This is new. I just got here and we usually have small talk first. School, soccer, and guitar lessons on my end. Corn harvest, baby goats, and weather on his end. "Sure, anything, Grandpa."

He takes something from his shirt pocket, raises it in the candle's glow. It's some sort of necklace . . . a string of coins. Coins that flash here and there, kind of shimmering like far-off city lights.

I peer closer. The coins are freshly polished but old, the stamped faces worn smooth, the words foreign, nothing like Spanish or English.

He holds the necklace before me, letting it swing back and forth. I wonder if he's mesmerizing me like one of those old-fashioned hypnotists with pocket watches.

Sure enough, with every sway of the coins, the heartbeat of magic grows stronger, louder, ringing in my ears, booming through my blood. "Um, what's going on, Grandpa?"

His face beams like a little kid's, all fresh and new. "It's a long story," he says. "A path paved in wonder. A path that stretches to long, long ago." He speaks Spanish, which I know, thanks to Mom, but his words are so much different from hers. Hers are about car pools and errands, while his are lines that sound snatched right from poems and songs.

He leans closer, the coins shining spots of light onto his face like a field of fireflies. "Mateo, can you believe in the impossible?"

The pulse is growing louder, moving lower, then higher, practically a full-blown melody now. A picture of swirling, silver ribbons pops into my head. Something's happening, and it's awesome and crazy . . . but mostly awesome, I think. *Can you believe in the impossible?* I ask myself.

"Open your hand," he says, and lets the necklace spiral into my palm.

And now my heart's really thudding because sure, I've seen magical stuff here, just more like glimpses from the corner of my eye. But these coins crackling in my hand—well, this is something different. Sparks are jumping into my palm, zooming through my arm like tiny fireworks, and exploding in my chest.

Now sweat's dripping from my cheeks and an earthquake's rolling through my bones. I manage not to freak out, just barely, because Grandpa Teo's voice is comforting, like syrup streaming over pancakes, promising something delicious to come.

"Now turn away from the movie of your own life, Mateo. And look at the movie of mine."

As he speaks, his words somehow beam light onto an imagined screen, flooding the room with people and places from long, long ago. "*Mijo*, you are about to embark on a journey of marvels. Of impossible fortunes. Of a lost duck, three-legged skunk, and blind goat—all bravely loyal. Of a girl who gathered power from storms and sang back the dead. Of an enchanted friendship that lifted souls above brutality."

He pauses, tilts his head. "Perhaps there will even be an intermission or two. But as of yet, there is no end. That, mijo, will be up to you." He winks, clears his throat, and begins.

"There was once a girl called the Queen of Lightning . . ."

I hang on to the humming, zapping necklace, and just before I slip completely into his movie, I wonder: *Okay, just what kind of help does Grandpa Teo need?*

RUMBLE

Teo

THE HILL OF DUST,
OAXACA, MEXICO
Long, Long Ago

SECRET PATH

*E*sma, Queen of Lightning, rolled into my life like the first wild storm at the end of dry season. Her caravan wound up the mountain in four horse-drawn wagons, kicking up clouds of dust all the way through the valley. I watched it with the other children, all of us parched as the earth, thirsty for . . . *something.*

"Who is it?"

"Are they coming here?"

"All the way out here?"

"But why?"

The who, we soon discovered, was the Gypsies.

The why was uncertain; no visitors came here, just the occasional patient hoping to be healed by my grandfather. Yucundiachi—the Hill of Dust—was a cluster of adobe and wood huts surrounding a single stone cathedral, perched on the peak like a lonely bird, waiting. Our village was not on the way to anywhere. And there was little reason to seek it out.

Yet by some miracle, the Gypsies must be headed here. Like fate, the road led only here. There was simply nowhere else to go.

On bare, calloused feet, we ran toward this ribbon of dust snaking up, up, up to our village. The closer we came, the more the caravan's colors shone through the haze—royal greens and golds and reds, painted blooms and swirls—a brilliant relief to the dry, cracked grays and browns that life had become. I drank them up, these Gypsies who came like sparkling raindrops, a thrill of colors and flowers, a pulsing promise.

They didn't look like us, not Mixteco, or like other country Oaxacans. They didn't even look like the city Mexicans I'd seen . . . no, these visitors were something else entirely. The women were walking gardens, wearing long, flowered skirts, flowered shirts, flowered scarves in their hair. And the men glinted, sporting gold necklaces, coins galore, and mustaches as large as small animals.

But that's not when I first noticed Esma, Queen of Lightning. It was that night, the night of my first movie, when I truly saw her in all her electric glory.

And nothing was ever the same again.

That night, the projector beam sliced through the air as if a square had been snipped in the sky, channeling light from some secret place, as if these Gypsies knew of a hidden tunnel straight to the stars. The beam stretched to the side of the cathedral, where a makeshift screen of white sheets was hung, illuminated and dancing in the breeze. The clicking of the projector accompanied the chirping of crickets and flutter of moths. The generator hummed and croaked like a giant toad.

My entire village had gathered in the dusty plaza—the adults on wooden chairs they'd carried from their houses. The women shone in their nicest *huipiles*, woven with red zigzag patterns, and the men wore gleaming white shirts and pants, their freshly washed faces bright beneath palm hats. Children darted around, wild with anticipation. I sat in the dirt, hugging my knees, watching it all, thinking of secret paths to the moon.

"Teo!" my cousin Lalo shouted at me. "Come sit back here with us!"

I pretended not to hear. I wanted my front-row view, away from the silliness of my cousins. I was only eleven, still young enough for silliness, but the events of the past year had made me weary. My cousins called me a few more times, then gave up.

A Gypsy man my grandfather's age stood before the crowd. He twirled the tip of his massive mustache, patted the waterfall of glittering coins tumbling across the lapels of his ragged suit jacket. Once all eyes were on him, he removed his strange, tall hat with a flourish and gave a deep bow. "May I introduce myself to you, kind people. I am Ivan, Master of the Traveling Cinema, Duke of the Impossible Caravan. And we shall bestow upon you, dear friends, magic beyond your wildest dreams."

That was the gist of it, at least. His thick accent made his Spanish words as garbled as turkey squawks. Since most adults in the audience spoke only Mixteco and barely understood Spanish, his meaning was lost on many. But the words didn't matter because the dramatic curves of his mustache were enough to enchant us. It was as sleek as a muskrat, an elegant creature perched on his lip with a graceful life of its own. As the mustache danced over the Duke's mouth, two other men attended to the projector, and the Gypsy women wove through the audience, collecting our fifteen centavos. For those of us who had no money, which was nearly everyone, they kindly accepted freshly woven hats or baskets as payment.

The Duke bowed again, and we clapped and whistled in anticipation. He pulled something from his pocket, a white orb—an exotic fruit, maybe—and munched on it as he breezed back to the projector. A sharp, biting smell pierced the air.

Now came voices, crackling from the speakers, then words on-screen that few of us could read. Hardly anyone had gone to school, and those of us who had only attended for a short time. Six years ago, a one-room schoolhouse had been built in a nearby town, but along with it had come a beautiful, cruel teacher. She'd scared off every child on the Hill of Dust within a year. Although I'd lasted longer than most, I could only pick out a few easy words here and there on the screen. It didn't matter; soon enough, the story started and swept me away.

My pulse raced and I tried not to blink so that I wouldn't miss even a second. It was my first-ever movie, *Nosotros los*

Pobres—We the Poor. It starred Pedro Infante—whose neat little mustache didn't hold a candle to the Duke's—and his spunky daughter, Chachita, and the dramas of their village, far more exciting than our Hill of Dust.

During the songs, a girl's voice joined the actors'. A real girl's voice, from somewhere in the back. No one from my village, I was certain; it had to be a Gypsy. Her voice sounded surprisingly *right*, completing something that had been missing. At the funny parts, her laugh rose above others, a cackle of wild abandon.

I looked back, squinting through the beam of light. A girl stood beside the projector, mouthing the words, every single one. Her face mirrored the expressions on the actors' faces, only hers were even more dramatic, the way she flung her braids, raised her proud chin, widened her eyes. The night breeze caught her headscarf, made it flutter like wings lifting into flight.

I hadn't seen so much . . . *aliveness* . . . in a long time.

After the movie, the rest of my village was abuzz, wondering what film we'd see tomorrow, because rumor had it the Gypsies would stay two more nights! Parents ushered children back home, some half-asleep on their shoulders, some holding hands. I missed the cozy nighttime feeling of someone's hand in mine. My sister's. My mother's.

I would never touch my sister's hand again. And probably not my mother's. My mother wasn't dead, not exactly, but she was one of the only people who'd stayed at home that night. For nearly a year, she hadn't been interested in having fun or holding hands. She wasn't even interested in the *possibility* of ever being interested again. As usual, my grandfather stayed with her, worried to leave her alone. I wished he had come, too. This past year, he was the only person who made me feel at ease.

"Let's go, Teo," my aunt Perla said, half-heartedly trying to herd me with Lalo and my other cousins, but I drifted away to the edge of the milpa. Through head-high cornstalks, I watched the lingering Gypsies. Soon, all the other villagers had left. But I wouldn't let the aliveness of the night end, not yet.

The Duke was busily tending to the long spiral of film, while the projector's beam tunneled light through darkness. And the girl—she left the projector and ran toward the screen in a strange, loping gait, carrying a violin with one hand. Standing before the sheet, she tossed up her arms and let them swoop down in a deep bow, then raised her violin and eked out a melody at once mournful and cheerful. She held the bow and moved her fingers over the strings in an odd way, slightly lopsided, the same way she ran.

She belted out a song in her language, an impossibly huge voice for a small girl. She looked no older than me. Her voice was a storm, rolling in low, gathering strength, spinning and swirling into something high and keening with a life of its own. It was beautiful and wild and a little scary, as if she were channeling all the power of rainy season at once. I sucked up her raindrop notes like a half-shriveled plant.

Afterward, she took another deep bow and, in perfect Spanish, announced, "*¡Gracias!* I am Esma, Queen of Lightning!"

The other Gypsies paid her no heed; she could've been a moth fluttering around for all they cared. They were talking among themselves, carrying the equipment toward their camp. But I lingered in the shadows, soaking her in, wishing I had even a drop of that aliveness inside me.

It wasn't until the next morning that I would discover the fate of the Queen of Lightning was already woven into my own. For life.

FORTUNE

efore dawn, I awoke at the rooster's first cries. For a moment, I lay there on my *petate,* rubbing my thumb over the woven palm, listening to early birds chirping and my aunts slapping tortillas in the kitchen hut. My mother snored lightly by the far wall. Had last night been a dream?

Uncertain, I crept outside, into the darkness. Half-asleep, I stumbled toward the Gypsies' camp by the river. Yes, they were there, asleep inside their circle of wagons around the ash-filled fire pit. A spontaneous smile broke out over my face. It felt strange; my mouth hadn't arranged itself like this for a long time.

All morning, along with every other child on the Hill of Dust, I followed the group of Gypsy women and children as they walked from house to house. My eyes kept landing on that girl, the one from last night who'd shot electricity right through me.

We discovered they were offering to tell fortunes in exchange for food—small bags of beans or corn or eggs. When they made it to our house, I was almost bursting. My cousins and I quieted our dogs, shooed away our turkeys and chickens, darted ahead to clear a path for the visitors.

Standing in the center of our dusty courtyard, the girl spoke to us in bold and perfect Spanish, just as she'd addressed her invisible audience the night before. "Amigos, I am Esma, Queen of Lightning." She raised her arms dramatically, speaking with the confidence of a true queen. She wore her dark hair in two thin braids, woven with tiny shells and ribbons and draped over her shoulders, while the rest of her hair was tucked back in the blue-flowered scarf. A fringe of bangs framed her forehead, and around her neck hung strands of beads, shiny brown and black and red seeds, sprinkled with glittering coins. She exuded queenliness.

Chin high, she announced, "May I present to you my royal court."

The blank expressions of the other Gypsies made me realize they didn't understand her words in Spanish. They simply nodded, then continued chattering among themselves in their own language.

With a flourish, Esma motioned to the eldest and largest woman. It looked like a field of wildflowers had blown away and stuck to her skirt and blouse and apron and headscarf. "My grandmother, Roza, Mistress of Destiny!"

The woman's nose filled most of her face, as if it were in the spotlight, and the other features—squinty eyes, shriveled lips, brown-spotted cheeks—were all forced into the shadows. The nose was a mountainside, shadowing the rest of her face, with crevices and nooks and caverns of its own. It twitched in a kind of greeting.

"And my ladies-in-waiting," Esma continued, motioning with her chin to four women who looked in their teens or early twenties.

They nodded, and, in broken Spanish, mumbled, *"Buenos días."*

"Amigos, I shall serve as your translator this afternoon, as the Mistress reads your fortunes from her magical cards, passed down for generations. Now, in exchange for this rare opportunity, we only ask for food in return—what you see fit as payment for this once-in-a-lifetime opportunity . . ."

Esma rambled on as I murmured the translation in Mixteco. Language had always come easy for me, and my family on the Hill of Dust turned to me to translate on the rare occasions we had visitors. I'd learned Spanish the first years of my life, back in my father's village, closer to Mexico City. Stubbornly, I'd held on to the language. It was the only piece of my father left.

As Esma talked, she began looking straight at me. Blushing, I looked back, and found I could almost guess her next sing-song word before she said it. Soon we were engaged in a strange dance with words, her in the lead, and me following without thinking, simply letting speech flow from her mouth to mine.

It was as if our words moved to music only the two of us could hear.

I could have gone on like this forever, but the other young Gypsy women were growing antsy, shifting from one leg to another and muttering among themselves. Clearly, they didn't understand Esma's words. And they didn't care.

At the limits of her patience, one of the women smacked Esma on the head. Another scolded her. The others grumbled in agreement.

Esma, Queen of Lightning, scowled.

So these were not her ladies-in-waiting. Just the opposite. And it appeared they only put up with her for her language skills.

The Mistress of Destiny gave a thunderous snort and, in a raspy voice, hushed the others.

Esma raised her chin and asked us, "Are you interested, amigos?"

As this was the most exciting thing that had happened in our village since—well, since ever—my aunts and uncles and cousins all nodded eagerly.

Grandfather studied our visitors with eagle eyes, being the only one who hadn't fallen completely under the Gypsies' spell. He spoke little Spanish—mainly Mixteco—but he'd come to rely on me as his translator for out-of-town patients. This had its advantages, he'd told me. When you don't know the language others speak, you watch their faces, their eyes, their movements—all of which say worlds more than flimsy words.

To my surprise, instead of setting out chairs for our guests in the courtyard, Grandfather escorted them into his healing hut. "*Por favor,* come in," he said in choppy, Mixteco-accented Spanish.

The Gypsies looked surprised as well. As we walked inside, the Mistress of Destiny said something to Esma, who translated softly. "Thank you. Most places we go, no one invites us in."

When I passed her comment to Grandfather, he crinkled his eyes at Roza. "Most outsiders don't show our people respect. To them, we're backwards *indios*. Indians who know nothing. Yet you treat us as royalty. So we, in turn, will treat you as such."

"Most outsiders distrust us," Roza replied, meeting his gaze. "To them, we are sneaky thieves. But you treat us as royalty. So we, in turn, will treat you as such."

While Esma and I murmured translations, Grandfather and Roza locked eyes, as if they shared a secret joke. As if their faces, so very different, were somehow mirrors.

The adobe hut barely fit us inside—about twenty people, pressed shoulder-to-shoulder, all the way back to the altar at the far wall, where beeswax candles flickered. As always, the earthy, sweet scents of copal incense and pine filled the dark room. The dirt floor was cool on my feet, a welcome relief from the relentless sunshine.

Slowly, with old-man movements, Grandfather dragged an empty table to the center of the room. I helped him carry several chairs from along the wall to the table. He offered them to the women, who nodded politely and sat with toddlers piled on their laps.

Roza, Mistress of Destiny, spread a shiny cloth over the table—red silk with coins and gold beads sewn into the fringe. Ceremoniously, she placed a deck of worn cards in the middle.

Once I looked past the central feature of her face, I saw that her eyes were similar to Grandfather's—watching carefully, picking up tiny details that slipped by those of us focused on words and obvious things like noses. Her gaze slid over every item in the healing hut—the colorful pictures of saints and Virgin Marías, the green bundles of herbs, the golden candles, the clay incense burners . . . and over my entire family.

My entire family except for my mother, that is, who was most likely staring into space in the kitchen.

Meanwhile, my youngest aunt, Perla, returned with cups of steaming chamomile tea and set them before our guests.

Esma said, "Amigos, who will go first? Who has a question for the Mistress of Destiny?"

I did. I had questions that had been growing and whirling like a dust storm inside of me. A year earlier, when the water had swept away my sister, it had also stolen a piece of my soul. The piece that felt happiness. In its place was an empty space— cold and dark and fearful. *Will I find that piece? Or grow a new piece? Will I ever feel alive again? Will life ever feel strong and good again?*

But the words wouldn't form on my tongue.

Meanwhile, my aunts were tittering and whispering among

themselves. My uncles elbowed each other, urging each other on. Finally, Aunt Perla volunteered. She asked shyly, "Will I marry soon?"

The Mistress of Destiny seemed to expect this question. She motioned for my giggling aunt to deal out cards. From her pocket, Roza pulled out a gleaming black pipe and wedged it into her mouth. She didn't light it, only chewed thoughtfully on its stem. Peering at the cards, she aahed and hmmed, huffing deeply in and out of flared nostrils, and finally speaking in a voice as gruff as a man's.

Aunt Perla held her breath as Esma translated to Spanish easily, like a spool of thread unwinding, and I, in turn, spun the words into Mixteco. "Dear girl, within the year, you shall be married to a strong and handsome man with eyes the color of the finest brown horse. He shall have ample hair, the color of the blackest night."

My aunts squealed. Of course, everyone in my village had black hair and brown eyes; every man was strong from working in the fields all day; and handsome was in the eye of the beholder.

"And that's not all!" The Mistress of Destiny placed a finger at the side of her nose, apparently lost in a trance. "Within the following year, you shall have a beautiful baby, a boy with big brown eyes and black hair."

A round of giggles broke out, and Aunt Perla rocked with so much glee she nearly fell off the chair. "I'll give you an entire chicken for that fortune!"

And on it went, marriages and baby predictions for the younger women. For the older ones and the men, vague predictions like, *You will have a run of bad luck followed by marvelous luck, so keep your faith.* Or, *You will make a deal with someone that will bring you good fortune.*

By the time it was my turn, over an hour had passed, and everyone else was buzzing with their own fortunes and not terribly interested in mine.

Esma smiled at me—a dazzling smile of white, even teeth. "Your turn! The boy who translates like the wind!"

I blushed, looked down as I walked to the chair.

She asked, "Do you have a special question for Roza, Mistress of Destiny?"

I'd been going over my questions for the past hour, and distilled them down to one. *Will I ever feel alive again?*

I willed myself to speak it. But no, I couldn't, not in front of everyone.

"No special question?" Esma prompted.

I shrugged. "Anything is fine."

"Now what is your name, amigo?"

"Teo," I replied softly.

"Teo," she repeated. "The boy with the eyes."

I lowered my gaze, embarrassed. My eyes were like two mud puddles encircled by long, dark, thick reeds of lashes. That's how my sister had described our eyes; she'd had the same. A trait we got from our father, whose face I barely remembered now, except for those lashes.

When I lifted my gaze to meet Esma's eyes again, I saw that hers were the color of rain, silvery and flashing, like mica-flecked stones after a storm.

"Deal the cards, Teo."

I obeyed. They were well-worn around the edges and looked like they'd been chewed on, drooled on, and spit out by children and animals over the decades. Each featured a hand-painted scene—a majestic lady, a gold goblet, silver swords, a black cauldron, a yellow sun, a white horse, a red heart.

Esma watched Roza respond to the cards. Her nose twitched. To the right, to the left, and then did a lively dance. Her nose had not made this particular series of moves before.

I looked beyond, at her eyebrows, which were pressed together in confusion. Her shriveled lips stuck out in a puzzled pout. She blinked and squinted at Esma, Queen of Lightning. Then she squinted at me, gnawing at the stem of her pipe. My pulse sped . . . something big was coming, I was certain.

The others—Gypsies and villagers alike—were chattering and didn't notice the strange reaction; it was only me, Esma, and my ever-observant grandfather.

Finally, Roza shook herself like a dog in the rain, took a breath, and gave my fortune. As Esma translated, she seemed disappointed, and failed to conjure up any drama. With a sigh, she said, "You are kind and gentle and stronger than you know. If you do something bold, you will be rewarded."

My heart sank. Just another vague fortune.

At the prompting of my cousins, I translated, my voice flat. I turned to Roza and, with a weak smile, said, "Gracias." Then I stood up to fetch her payment.

Grandfather put his hand on my shoulder, pressing me back down. He looked at the fortune-teller, past her nose and into her slits of eyes. Still watching her, he murmured, "Teo, ask her your true fortune."

I looked at him, confused.

"Go ahead, son."

I swallowed, then said to Esma, in my most polite voice, "Excuse me, señorita, my grandfather would like the Mistress of Destiny to tell me my true fortune."

Esma's right eyebrow shot up, straight into her bangs. "Your true fortune?"

I nodded. "My true fortune."

TRUE FORTUNE

*E*sma gave me a sideways grin, then translated my request to her grandmother. My true fortune.

In the shadow beneath the Mistress of Destiny's nose, a smile spread, revealing two crooked teeth above and three below. The pipe was clenched firmly between them. Her eyes crinkled and she nodded at Grandfather in a gesture of respect before speaking.

This time, as Esma listened, her eyes sang. She translated, swiftly, with trembling excitement. "I will tell you what I truly saw, but I will also tell you that it is impossible. That is why I . . . *adjusted* the fortune. There are such things as false truths and honest lies, my friends."

I was on the edge of my seat now. I wiped my damp palms on my pants.

Roza continued, dropping her voice to the lowest rumble, the purr of a mountain lion. And as the Mistress of Destiny spoke, Esma's jaw fell open. The Gypsy women stopped their chattering and tea sipping and stared at Esma. Then at me, then back at Esma. With expressions of disbelief, they shook their heads, muttering a harsh word that bounced among them.

Finally, Esma raised her chin, drew in a breath, and climbed, in her lopsided way, onto her chair. Standing tall on top of it, she towered over us.

"According to the always-accurate prediction of the Mistress of Destiny's cards, this boy—what's your name again?"

"Teo."

"This boy, Teo, and I, Esma, Queen of Lightning, are on the path to being loyal friends for our long lives!" She paused to let this sink in. And then she continued, eyes wildly alive. "And if our friendship lasts, we will save each other when no one else can. This is our destiny!"

For a moment, my heart stopped. Then I stammered a translation for Grandfather, whose face lit up brighter than a sunrise. He gave a nod of approval to Roza, Mistress of Destiny.

My aunts and uncles and cousins were exchanging doubtful looks. "Impossible," they murmured, most in Mixteco, a few in Spanish. It was probably the same word the Gypsies were murmuring. *Impossible.*

Esma, on the chair, bellowed, "I, Queen of Lightning,

specialize in the impossible!" She smiled at me, held out her hand, and declared, "Join me, Teo, my new friend for life!"

I stood motionless, all eyes on me. I didn't take her hand, because what if she pulled me up there? What if she was crazy? What if *crazy* was the word her people were muttering?

Then I whispered, "I'll be back in a minute." Legs shaking, I stumbled out into the sunshine, then across the patch of dirt, and into the dark kitchen.

There by the hearth fire was my mother, hair messily unbraided, huipil filthy, and expression vacant. Draped over her head, a black shawl hid her eyes in shadows. She held a sweet potato in one hand and a knife in the other, unsure what to do with them. A year ago, she would have been dashing around the kitchen, shooing out the chickens that were now pecking around her still feet. I looked at her, wishing she would look back at me. She didn't.

I took three of my circles of goat cheese to use as payment and wrapped them in banana leaves. On the way out the door, I paused. "Mother, if I told you I'd be lifelong friends with a Gypsy girl, what would you say?"

She looked at me blankly, as if I were speaking another language. Impossible to understand. For her, after what had happened to my sister last year, everything was impossible. Getting up from her petate in the mornings, making tortillas, doing the simplest of chores. The smallest task, like talking to her son, was impossible. Even if she could answer my question, I knew her response. *Impossible.*

I left her in the kitchen and headed across the patch of dirt, through the squawking cluster of chickens and turkeys, and back to the healing hut. My cousins and aunts and uncles were just leaving, still giddy, while the Gypsies were putting away their things.

The Impossible Caravan, that was the name of this troupe. Did *impossible* describe the incredible wonders they'd brought all the way out to the Hill of Dust? Or did they—the Queen of Lightning in particular—hold the magical key to making the impossible happen?

Esma was humming a lively tune as I walked over and handed her the payment. "Cheese," I said, "from my goats."

"Gracias, querido amigo," she said, radiant.

Tingles crept over my skin. Dear friend, she'd called me. Where my mother was emptied of life, this girl was overflowing.

"Gracias, gracias, gracias," she sang.

I nodded. "Gracias to you."

She locked eyes with me. "It's not impossible, Teo."

I paused. "They think it is," I said, motioning to her people and mine.

She scoffed. "*They* just accept things how they are. *They* would say we're only staying here one more day and we might never come back and Romani girls aren't friends with boys of any kind and Rom aren't friends with *gadjé* and if I am friends with a *gadjo*, then I'll be impure and they'd disown me and—"

"Gadjé? Gadjo?" I asked, trying to keep up. "Romani? Rom?"

"The Rom are us. The Romani people. Gypsies. And gadjé are you all. Anyone who isn't Romani. A gadjo."

"I see." I struggled to understand. "But how can they argue with the Mistress of Destiny?"

Esma twisted a braid around her ring-bedecked finger. "It's true, my grandmother has power, but traditions run deeper than predictions. For centuries, things have been this way. It would take more than a single fortune to change that." She paused, letting her silver eyes pierce mine. "But we'll do it, my friend!"

As Esma reached her hand toward mine, one of the Romani women snapped at her and whacked the side of her head. It was a hard slap, but not enough to damage more than her pride. The women frowned, ready to leave and waiting on her.

I had more questions, but there wasn't time. I just said, "I hope our fortune comes true."

"Teo," she said fiercely, "hope is for squash heads. You and me, we won't sit around and hope. We'll make our fortune come true. Nothing is impossible. Not for me. And not for you either, now that you are my loyal friend for eternity."

Pure craziness. Yet my unasked question had been answered. All at once, life thrummed with possibility.

I searched for what to say next, but one of the women slapped Esma's head again, and another grabbed her by the elbow and dragged her away.

From the doorway, I watched them leave. The other women trudged, except for Roza—who waddled, her hips rivaling her nose in enormity—and Esma, who danced away in a peculiar lope, as if she simply refused to walk like everyone else.

Suddenly, she wrestled her arm away, turned around, and called out, "See you soon, Teo, my lifelong friend!"

Her defiance earned her another smack.

No matter. Esma, Queen of Lightning, tossed back her head and sang out to the dust-baked mountains: "Nothing is impossible!"

DUCKLING

*Y*our mind plays tricks on you when you're alone pasturing goats, way out in *el monte*. Among the spiky agave and fanning palms and rock outcroppings, you hear things that aren't there. Voices, wails.

My sister, Lucita, used to wander el monte with me and our goats. We'd been doing it for years, nearly every day, since we were six or seven. As twins, we'd looked alike—wide faces and strong cheekbones and those muddy, reedy eyes. She'd always been the more fragile one—smaller, slighter, prone to sickness.

But what she'd lacked in physical strength she'd made up for a hundred times over in spunk and imagination and curiosity. She'd been the one who'd come up with the crazy games we'd play along the dried, cracked riverbeds. She was the one endlessly interested in the world, peering at petals of succulents and insect wings and glittering mica. She was the one who was most alive.

Until she wasn't.

Today, as always, I tried to keep my goats away from the swath of green that meandered with the river, down the mountainside, all the way past my village. Giant trees with thick, bright canopies lined the water, precious shade in the otherwise roasting-hot hills.

Despite its promise of a cool drink or a refreshing foot soak, I stayed away from the stream. It was narrow now, at the end of dry season—just an arm span wide—but I'd seen it transform into something raging and terrible in mere minutes.

That day, nearly one year ago, Lucita had yelped and sputtered, flailing her limbs, struggling to keep her head above the waves. It had been a flash flood, at the seam between dry and rainy season. Trying to save our baby goat, she'd been swept downstream. I'd leapt in and grabbed for her, but the water tore her away. The spirit of the stream pulled her under, and I tried, I tried, I tried, but I couldn't save her.

My grandfather found me unconscious on the riverbank. Hours later, Lucita's body floated up, caught on a fallen branch, lifeless.

And now, every day, her screams lived on in the rush of the stream, a reminder that I hadn't saved her. That maybe if I'd paddled harder, searched longer, I could have.

In three days, it would be her *cabo de año*—the first anniversary of her death. My family was supposed to honor her along with our entire village. The idea made me queasy. Another reminder I'd let her die.

I lowered the brim of my palm hat over my eyes, licked my dry lips. But today, instead of Lucita's wails, I imagined Esma's voice, echoing through the mountains. *Friends for life! Nothing is impossible!*

Of course, that wasn't true. Bringing my sister back to life was impossible. And being lifelong friends with a Romani girl? Even if her people didn't frown on friendships with outsiders, how do you become best friends in a couple days? And what about saving each other? I wasn't strong enough to save anyone.

My goats refused to stay away from the stream. They were thirsty and I had to let them drink. As they lapped at the water, I stood twenty paces away, just in the outer fringe of shade. Ignoring my parched throat, I scanned the bush-straggled hills for Esma. Maybe she would come out here to search for me.

A noise rose over the water's wails and the echoes of Esma's words.

Squeaking. High-pitched and rhythmic and urgent.

It was coming from the shore. I took a few tentative steps toward the river to investigate. A tiny baby duck, no bigger than my fist, was stumbling in a circle on the sandy bank. It had no true feathers yet, only furry down, brown with splotches and stripes of gold. Its shiny black beak was open wide, emitting loud cheeps. It tried walking, but something was wrong, and its legs buckled after a few steps.

Strange. I'd rarely seen ducks on this river before, and never baby ducks. I searched the brush for its mother, or siblings, but none were in sight. For a long time, from my spot high on the banks, I watched it getting up, wobbling, then falling down, squeaking the whole while. As it stumbled dangerously close to the water, I held my breath, whispering, "Move, move. Away from the water."

And then the baby bird tumbled in, and a small current engulfed its body. "Swim, swim!" I urged, but it fell over and squealed in panic. Downstream it floated like a tiny, battered twig.

Without thinking, I scrambled down to the water's edge, reached in, and pulled out the duckling. It was shivering and squeaking, and looked even tinier soaking wet. And then, realizing what I'd done, I started shaking. I wrapped it in my shirt, then sat with it, both of us trembling, waiting for its mother. She would help; she'd protect it.

Hours passed. My trembling stopped. The duck's shivering calmed. Its eyes closed and its peeping vanished and it fell asleep against my chest.

Its mother never came.

As the sun started dropping, setting the sky aglow, I thought about what to do. If I left the baby duck here alone, it would be eaten by a fox or die when the temperature fell at night. So I carried it home, nestled against my chest.

At the outskirts of town, I passed the Romani camp, where women were bent over buckets and pots, washing and preparing food, chattering loudly. Men dozed on berry-red carpets spread out in the shade. I didn't see Esma but did hear violin notes soaring above the circle of wagons, and I paused to listen, wondering if it was her. If the swirling, jeweled colors of the wagons were transformed into music, this would be it, this vibrant, spiraling melody.

The baby duck woke up and started cheeping, probably hungry. I rushed home, corralled the goats, and handed the little fluff ball to Grandfather. "Why, I haven't seen a duckling like this in years," he remarked, cupping it in his palms. "They don't often come around here, just a vagrant one, here and there. A whistling duck, I'm guessing."

"Whistling?"

He smiled. "You'll find out why in a few months."

"So we can save it?" I asked.

He examined it, feeling its wings and legs with gentle fingertips. "Nothing broken. Just bruising, soreness." He raised an amused eyebrow and pointed to my shirt. "Your reward for doing something bold," he observed.

I looked down at my shirt. Yellow-green duck poo covered the front. Reward? "That first fortune the Mistress of Destiny told me—it was true?"

Grandfather tilted his head. As a healer, he knew things, things deeper and wider than most people knew. It was as though most people saw only a small black-and-white photo of the world, but he saw what was outside the frame, too, and in full, dazzling color. That's how my mother had explained it to me once, the wisdom of her father. That was before she gave up.

"Perhaps it was true," he said. "Or perhaps you made it happen. Perhaps without the fortune, you wouldn't have saved the duck." He paused. "I know being near the river is hard for you, son. It took courage to help this creature."

I cupped the duck close, a tiny bundle of pulse and breath. I felt the aliveness contained, against all odds, in this chirping ball of fluff.

"Let's get some food in our girl!" Grandfather said.

"Girl?"

"That's my guess."

"I'm naming her Thunder," I said over her squeaking.

Grandfather laughed. "She is pretty noisy."

Together, we mixed dried, crushed corn kernels with water and fed it to her in a tiny gourd. We let her splash around at the edge of the narrow irrigation ditch that flowed between the edges of our courtyard and bean field. Then we made her a soft bed with a pile of old rags in a fruit crate.

Beyond our little courtyard, the pink sunset melted into gold, then cooled into purple shadows of dusk. I drank cinnamon-chocolate *atole*—corn mush—with my cousins by the light of the kitchen hearth fire. Then I walked with them over to the church plaza, carrying Thunder in my shirt, not trusting anyone else to hold her. She was snug in a sling I made from my sister's old shawl that had sat untouched, folded in a corner, until now. I'd tied it around my neck and stuffed in plenty of rags to capture the globs of poo that Thunder dropped every few minutes.

I also brought along a tiny gourd of atole since she squeaked for more food every half hour. I settled with her in the front row and waited for the magic to begin. Even if she made a commotion, the noise of the projector and generator and music and actors would drown it out.

The film was a western, starring Luís Aguilar, whose tiny, tame mustache paled beside the Duke's. Esma, Queen of Lightning, knew all the words and songs in this film, too. As she whooped at the exciting parts, I longed to do the same. This time, after the movie, instead of belting out an impromptu song, she walked over to where I sat. Stray bits of light flashed off her coins like lightning. "Hello, my friend for life."

"*Buenas noches*, señorita." I felt a little nervous and rested my hand on Thunder, sleeping inside the sling, right over my heart. Then, after a deep breath, I said, "Let's do it. Let's make our fortune happen."

"Of course!" she declared, matter-of-factly. "We should've started today. I looked all over for you!"

She'd looked for me? A warmth spread through me, rich and sweet as cinnamon-chocolate atole.

"Where will you be tomorrow?" she asked.

"Pasturing my goats in el monte."

Behind her, a young Romani woman was approaching like a furious whirlwind.

I spoke quickly, pointing east with my chin. "Over there. Follow the river from your camp up to the mountains. But not too close. The water's dangerous. There's a boulder shaped like a sleeping dog, just beside a big tree. I'll meet you there in the morning."

She grinned, and then noticed Thunder, who was now poking her beak out of the sling. Esma tilted her head, curious, but just as she was about to speak, the Romani woman grabbed her ear and tugged her away.

At least she didn't get smacked this time.

"Until tomorrow, my lifelong friend!" she called back cheerfully, waggling her fingers like a cinema star. "And your baby goose, too!"

"Duck!" I called out.

"Duck!" she called in return.

It felt like a handshake, the seal of a promise.

SCREAM

*T*hat night, I put Thunder's crate right next to my petate in the spot where my sister used to sleep. The little duck squeaked and rustled around and tried to jump out of the box. So I laid my hand over her, and she settled down and slept most of the night, with just a few peeps here and there.

Her noise didn't bother my mother, who slept across the room with a blanket over her face, as if it could block out the world. Since last year, she wanted to sleep all the time. She would sleep and sleep and sleep until one of my aunts came in and splashed cold water on her face and dragged her into the kitchen. It was hard to remember how my mother had been before—slapping tortillas into circles well before dawn, laughing and calling me and Lucita "lazybones" when we wandered groggily into the kitchen, greeting us with smiles and cups of steaming atole.

But if I followed my memory back even further, there was another time—when Lucita and I were five or six—that our mother had slept late and let her huipil grow stained and her hair messy. It happened after our final trip to Mexico City to sell baskets and hats with my father, the last time his hand held mine. Months later, when Grandfather found our mother all crumpled to pieces, he moved her and Lucita and me back here, to the Hill of Dust, so he could care for us and heal her sorrows.

And it had worked. After a year or so, my mother had returned to herself. Mostly.

But now, looking back, I could see that a piece of sorrow had lodged inside her, waiting for the next tragedy to swallow her whole. And try as he might, Grandfather couldn't seem to heal her this time.

The next morning, my mother slept right through the barrage of hungry squeaks that woke me. My hand was still cupping Thunder's tiny, downy back. It was good to feel something so soft and alive, so close to me all night.

Outside, in the courtyard, I fed her atole and let her play a bit at the edge of the irrigation ditch, just a trickle of water now. Then I stuck her in the sling with rags, had a breakfast of eggs and beans and tortillas with my cousins, and headed into el monte with the goats. Humming a tune, I meandered toward my meeting point with Esma, weaving a new palm hat on the way—payment for tonight's movie.

I was halfway to the rock when I heard a piercing scream. A girl's. My heart stopped and then started again, wild and panicked. Could it just be the memory of Lucita's screams? I'd relived her screams before, but they'd never been quite so loud . . . and *real*. I kept walking, my pulse jagged, nausea oozing through me. I covered my ears with my palms. *Stop, stop, stop.*

But when I released my hands, the shrieks had grown louder, tearing through the valley, coming from the stream. My head spun; black stars filled my vision. My instinct was to run away, shielding my ears.

And then, a thought: *What if it's a real girl? An alive one? What if it's Esma?*

I remembered the second part of our fortune. *You two will save each other when no one else can.* Was it my time to save my friend for life? So soon?

The fortune made me brave. I drew in a breath, scanned the river for people, but I couldn't see past the thick foliage along the banks. Cupping my hand over Thunder, I ran toward the screams. They stabbed the air like thin, freshly sharpened blades.

There, at the banks of the river, in the shade of a giant tree, was Esma, mouth open wide, screaming.

And swirling. Her long skirt spun out around her; her arms flew out and up. Her hair had burst loose from its scarf and flailed out in a nut-brown halo. Her face was uplifted, her jaw open wide enough to gulp the sky.

Clearly, she did not need saving.

I watched her a moment as my heart flip-flopped.

Then I noticed three small children near her, toddlers playing in the dappled light at the sandy shore. One had a finger up his nose, another was drooling and gaping at Esma, and the third was banging two sticks together. All the while, Esma spun lopsided, screaming in her own revolving world.

Finally, I stepped into her view, just outside the arc of her arms and skirt and hair.

Her wails stopped. She slowed and stood still, wavering, wobbling, dizzy, and then her eyes focused on me and she smiled. "Buenos días, Mamma Duck!"

"You all right, señorita?" I asked, unsure how I felt about my new nickname.

"Yes. Why?"

"I thought—I thought you needed me to save you. Because of our fortune . . ." My voice faded.

She laughed. "Oh, I don't need any saving. Never have, never will. Just interested in the loyal-friend-for-eternity part."

I blinked. What a relief. But I *had* managed to save a duckling. Maybe I *was* stronger than I realized, just like my false fortune said. Maybe someday far, far away, I'd actually save the Queen of Lightning herself.

She bugged out her eyes, then crossed them, then bugged them out again. "Why are you staring at me like that, Teo?"

I blinked again. "It's just—you were screaming like it was the end of the world."

"Oh, that. That's just what I do, Teo. See, wherever we go, I find a good place to scream. Not too close to camp. Don't want the others to hear. Near a stream is good—rushing water drowns out my noise." She tapped two dented tin buckets lying on their sides. "And it's a handy excuse—fetching water. Far upstream, where it's freshest." She gazed at the stream as if it were her second best friend.

I glared at the stream, positioned myself at a safe distance, just close enough to rescue any toddlers who might fall in. The stream was calm today, all gentle currents, and no wider than I was tall. Still, you never knew.

The kids were staring at me, curious. The girl said, "Ga? Ga?" and the boy said, "Da? Da?" and the other boy said, "Ba? Ba?"

I waved to them, then looked back at Esma, who was flushed and breathing hard from so much swirling and screaming. "Why do you scream?"

"Try it," she said. "You've swallowed plenty of screams. I can tell."

I didn't try it. Instead, I asked again, "Why do you scream?"

She picked up the rose-splattered scarf that had fallen from her hair, twirled it in the air like a lasso. "You met the *boria* at your fortune."

"The boria?"

"The wives of my uncles and father—the ones who enjoy smacking me and calling me squash head. I swallow as many screams as I can—twenty-two is my limit—and then I drag these three little squash heads away from camp—I'm in charge of them—and I let loose the swallowed screams."

I furrowed my brow, looked at the ground. "You scared me."

"Oh, sorry, Teo."

If we were best friends—or even pretending to be—there were certain things she had to know. "Last year, in that stream, my sister drowned."

Esma said nothing.

I forced myself to continue. "She screamed, but I couldn't save her."

For the first time, Esma, Queen of Lightning, was speechless. She sat down on the boulder, rearranging the scarf in her tangled hair.

I perched beside her, appreciating the cool rock beneath me. I watched the toddlers squealing and tugging on the goats' tails as they lapped at the water. "Ga! Da! Ba!" the children sputtered, mouths wide open in delight.

"You shouldn't let those kids there," I said. "The spirit of the stream could snatch them under."

Esma thought for a moment, then announced, "Teo, my screams scared away every last evil spirit. Even the slipperiest of the sneakiest."

I eyed her doubtfully.

"Look, Teo, I've been screaming like this for years now. And I can tell you, at every scream, the bad spirits turn around and run off covering their ears."

I raised my eyebrows. "You see the spirits?"

"The Gypsy Queen of Lightning can do anything!"

She *was* convincing. "Why are you called that?"

She slapped her right leg, entirely covered by her long skirt. "You've noticed my limp, I presume?"

I wasn't sure what the polite answer was. "I noticed you walk like—like you're dancing."

She grinned. "Now I can see why we're best friends for life." She whacked her leg again. "Lightning strike. The doctor said the lightning should've killed me, but I tamed it instead. I've been the Queen of Lightning ever since."

As Esma talked about her powers, Thunder began squeaking in the sling. I pulled out some crushed corn from the basket strapped to my back, sprinkled it into the gourd, added a little water, then set Thunder down to dig in. I took out the rags and washed them downstream. My heartbeat, I noticed, was not as frantic as it usually was so close to the water.

Esma watched me curiously. "Is it common in your village to carry around pooping ducks?"

"I'm the first," I said, grinning. And I told her about finding Thunder yesterday.

"You're noble, Teo," she said. "Savior of baby ducks. You should be my knight."

"But I'm a—" I tried to remember the word for *outsider* she'd used yesterday. "Gadjo," I said. "Can't only Rom be part of your royalty?"

"Nothing is impossible, my friend."

I stared at a thin string of clouds above the far mountain. What seemed impossible was that someone as bold as Esma would want me as her friend. She was lightning; I was a wisp of a cloud, a puff of dust. I couldn't imagine a time when she'd need to be saved by someone like me. I asked, "How are we going to make our fortune happen?"

Her eyes gleamed. "Well, I've been thinking. My people are supposed to leave tomorrow. That's what my grandfather says, and he's the leader."

"The Duke? Biggest mustache ever?"

"That's the one. But we have to convince him to stay longer so we can plant the roots of our lifelong friendship."

"So how do we convince him?"

She tapped her chin, thinking.

There was silence, except for the rush of the stream and the toddlers' shouts of "Da! Ga! Ba!" and Thunder's contented peeps now that her stomach was filled. She wandered around, always within an arm's reach of me, just pecking in the wet sand and pebbles. She had a little limp and trouble with balance, but seemed much better than yesterday.

Something about this little duck reminded me of Lucita. The pluckiness in its eyes. I glanced at Esma. "I wish you could come to my sister's cabo de año."

"What's that?"

"The one-year anniversary of her death. It's in three days."

She raised an eyebrow. "Is that something that would plant roots of a lifelong friendship?"

I nodded. "My sister would've liked you."

"Why?"

"Because you're so . . . alive."

"Alive," Esma mused. "Well, tell that to the boria. They call me a squash head and tell me I'm crazy and slow in the mind."

"Well," I admitted, "you are crazy—"

She reached out and lightly slapped the rim of my hat. "Hush, you squash head."

"But you're good crazy," I added quickly. "And your mind— it's faster than . . . than lightning."

She smacked her leg again, so hard I winced. "They say my mind is as lame and broken as my body." She held up her right hand. The last three fingers were curled tightly in on themselves, like unfurled leaves. "It's not just my leg."

In my translations during Grandfather's healing sessions, I'd seen all manner of injuries and illness, yet I couldn't figure out how lightning could cause these particular problems in Esma. "Did the lightning do that, too?"

She looked at her fingers, then lowered them, tucking them into the folds of her skirt. "Yes."

She stood up on a boulder, and now I could see the effort it took with her weak leg. But it didn't stop her. She straightened tall like a pine tree and spoke to the valley below.

"They said, 'You'll never be able to walk again, squash head,' and I said, 'I'll dance!'"

Pausing dramatically, she tossed a braid over her shoulder.

"They said, 'You'll never be able to hold a broom, squash head,' and I played the violin!"

She gazed at the mountaintops, like an actress on-screen. "They said, 'No man will ever pay a bride-price for you, squash head.'"

I broke in. "Bride-price?"

She looked down at me and her voice lowered, as if she were telling me a secret the valley couldn't hear. "It's what the husband's family pays to his new wife's family to make up for them losing a good worker. You know the boria? Well, they left their own families when they were about thirteen years old to get married and live with their husbands, my uncles and father."

"But why wouldn't anyone pay a bride-price for you?" I couldn't help blushing as I asked. After all, we were talking about marriage.

She seemed unfazed. "The women in our boria say no man would want me. That I'll just have to let them boss me around and call me squash head until I die."

"And what do you tell them?"

Her answer came as a bellow that echoed through the valley. "I tell them, 'Someday I will be a famous singer! I will be paid a thousand times the bride-price a man would have given. I will be loved not by one man but by hundreds, thousands! By men and women and children and anyone who hears my songs.'"

She packed every word with soul-shaking emotion. Just listening to her made my life larger, as if I were being projected onto a sheet on the side of the church right along with her. As if our story were epic, a music-drenched tale of tears and laughter and heart-swelling triumph.

Turning to me, she narrowed her eyes fiercely. "Then I told them, 'And no one will call me squash head!'"

My heart raced. She was a lightning storm so bright I had to look away. So I did, and that's when I noticed what the toddlers were doing.

"Esma," I said, cringing. "Your cousins are eating duck poo."

She jumped in alarm, then scrambled down the boulder to the children. She tried wiping the yellow-green goop from their mouths and chins.

"Oh," she muttered, "I'm such a squash head." She wrinkled her eyebrows. "Think it'll make them sick?"

I shrugged. I'd never had any duck-poo-eating patients with Grandfather.

She groaned. "My people don't like poo-covered animals, and definitely don't like their children eating poo."

"Most people wouldn't," I pointed out.

"But they have this idea about *marime*. Impure things. Ideas you gadjé wouldn't understand. Let's just say the boria would tear out my eyeballs if they knew."

Da started crying, and she patted his back. "Think the poo is making him cry?"

I was a little hurt by her comment about us gadjé not understanding. Flatly, I said, "He's just mad you made him stop eating it."

She rocked Da, and just as his cries let up, Ga and Ba started wailing. Now spit bubbles and mucus and tears were smeared over their faces, mixing with the dust, creating muddy streaks along with the poo. Not a pretty sight.

Esma looked miserable.

"Let's go to my grandfather," I said. "He's a healer. He'll know what to do."

She hesitated. "My family wouldn't like that either."

"Why not?"

She let out a breath. "You know how . . . *disturbing* it felt to watch my cousins eat duck poo?"

I nodded.

"Well, that's how my people would feel if they knew I went to a gadjé home. I mean, if I went for something other than business reasons." She averted her eyes. "They think spending time with gadjé would make me marime. Unclean."

I tried not to feel offended. Slowly, I said, "I'm . . . unclean? And being with me is like . . . eating duck poo?"

"That's how *they'd* feel," she said quickly. "Not me. Listen, Teo, I like being with you. And your baby duck, poo and all. And when my family tells me I can't do something, I do it." She stuck out her chin. "So let's go, my friend for life!"

She filled one bucket and I filled the other, and we hurried into town along the river, currents rushing, water sloshing, kids crying, goats bleating, duck squeaking, *friend for life* echoing.

And no dead sister wailing.

THUNDER'S POO

*I*t took a while to get all the goats and toddlers back to town. At her camp, Esma dropped off the buckets of water, then quickly told the boria she'd found a good spot for berry picking. She grabbed an empty red pail, and before anyone could protest or offer to come with her or smack her head, she and the toddlers were walking toward my house, supposedly to pick berries. "Not lying," she assured me. "Just creative storytelling."

By the time we reached the courtyard, Da and Ga and Ba were still fussy—maybe because it was hot and they were tired; maybe because Thunder's poo was churning around in their stomachs.

My aunts, in the kitchen, didn't see us cross the patch of dust to my grandfather, who was repairing a fence. He looked up, surprised, and greeted Esma with a handshake. In accented Spanish, he said, "Buenos días, Queen."

She greeted him back. "Buenos días, Doctor."

Then, to Grandfather, I said in Spanish, "Her little cousins ate Thunder's poo. Will they be all right?"

He surveyed the toddlers' filthy, tearstained faces, then gave me a baffled look. I switched to Mixteco and repeated myself, adding that poo made her people feel extra disturbed.

He raised a brow, then took some ears of dried corn from a pile and set them in front of the children. They grabbed the cobs, banged them against each other, open-mouthed and intent. Meanwhile, he peered into their eyes. "Tell me, Teo, was the poo fresh or old?"

"Fresh, very fresh."

His eyebrows furrowed. "More green or yellow?"

I thought about it, then conferred with Esma. "Yellow," she said nervously.

Grandfather frowned gravely. "Goopy or runny?"

Esma and I discussed the consistency. "Goopy."

A wide grin spread over Grandfather's face. It crumpled into a laugh. He shook his head and wiped his eyes, and that's when I knew Esma's cousins would be all right. I laughed, and then glanced at Esma, and she laughed, too, relieved.

"Let's all have some mint tea together," Grandfather said, patting my back. "If their stomachs are upset, the tea will calm them. They'll be fine."

Esma played with the toddlers and their corn while I gathered fresh mint from our garden. I brought the bundle of leaves into the kitchen, where two of my aunts bustled around, roasting red chilies and garlic for salsa. My mother stood in the center, holding the broom, motionless.

"Mother, could you boil water to brew this mint?"

She offered me only an empty look. Beneath the shadows of her shawl, her eyes were red and watery from the chili smoke, but she didn't bother wiping them. If the river had stolen a bit of my soul along with Lucita's, it had taken most of my mother's. There wasn't much left.

Sighing, Aunt Perla said, "I'll do it," and took the herbs from my hands.

My other aunt huffed that nearly every woman she knew had lost a child or two, and they didn't use it as an excuse to laze around.

Ignoring her, Aunt Perla patted my back, then kindly offered me *panela* to sweeten the tea.

I bit the inside of my cheek and waited for the water to boil. After the tea had brewed and cooled a bit, I joined Esma and Grandfather and the toddlers outside, where we sat and sipped from chipped clay mugs. I'd snuck in extra panela to make the tea sweet for the toddlers. It worked. They guzzled it down, then went back to inquiring about their corn. "Da? Ga? Ba?"

Meanwhile, in broken Spanish, Grandfather told Esma about the disgusting things I'd eaten as a toddler. Kitten throw-up, chicken droppings, owl pellets.

I refused to translate, but Esma caught the gist without my help. She made faces and laughed. I was a little embarrassed, but mostly I wished she could stay forever. Or at least a few more days. But how? Especially now that I knew how her people felt about Rom and gadjé mixing. For nonbusiness reasons, at least.

After the tea, Da, Ga, and Ba curled up in the shade, sleeping in a pile like puppies.

Esma finished her tea and wandered around the courtyard. She stopped under the tree in the corner, in front of a colorful sawdust mosaic framed in wood. The flowered border was done, but the inside remained to be finished.

"Pretty," she said. "What is it?"

"It's for my sister's cabo de año. Grandfather will fill in the rest with more flowers and stars and birds and things."

Esma cocked her head. "When did you say this party was?"

"In three days. And it's not exactly a party," I admitted. "I mean, it's in honor of a dead person. But we'll have sweet tamales and cinnamon-chocolate," I added, to make it sound more cheerful.

As she stared at the picture, her mind gears were turning. "Think your grandfather could put a Romani wagon in the picture? I mean, he can still do flowers and birds, but they'd be painted on the wagon."

"I guess," I said, wondering where she was headed. "Why?"

Her eyes shone. "Think you could invite my people?"

Excitement bloomed inside me. "Maybe. But would they come? I thought they didn't approve of spending time with gadjé."

"This would be for business relationship reasons. We can call it the Romani Business Appreciation Event."

"Are we clean enough for your people to eat the food we make?" I couldn't help it; a little resentment crept into my voice.

She shrugged. "As long as the drinks are sweet enough and no one sees Thunder pooping all over your shirt, my people should be fine."

The corner of my mouth turned up. "I'll sneak extra panela in the chocolate."

"Great! Now go ahead," Esma urged. "Tell your grandfather."

I translated most of it into Mixteco, but there was no equivalent for Romani Business Appreciation Event. I wasn't sure how he'd react; he was always adamant about being honest, and this involved some . . . creative storytelling.

"Romani Business Appreciation Event?" Grandfather repeated. And then he threw his head back, and the laughter spewed out. "Yes. I think Lucita would like combining her cabo de año with this, don't you?"

I nodded. "Definitely." This was the first time in a year I'd been able to talk about Lucita with a smile.

"This evening," Grandfather said, "after the movie, I'll formally invite the Rom."

I hugged him. "Grandfather," I whispered, "you really think I'll be Esma's friend forever?"

"I can tell you this," he said in my ear. "Somehow, the Queen of Lightning put the spark of life back inside you." He looked at Esma, standing expectantly at my side. "It's true, you have the power to save each other. I'll do what I can to make your friendship last."

INVITATION

*T*hat night, moon shadows stretched long through the pines where the Rom's wagons circled a bonfire. Sweet smoke drifted and swirled above, past the golden flames and into the cool smattering of starlight. Music rose, a cascade of violin notes and hands clapping in rhythm, sticks drumming against tin buckets, and above it all, a soaring voice. It was a song without words, a kind of trilling melody, a soul cry that soared and dove and soared again.

It was Esma, I was certain.

In the darkness, Grandfather and I walked unseen to the edge of their circle, watching the young women dance, their arms raised, faces aglow, jewelry flashing, skirts and braids whirling. It felt as if we had stumbled across something secret and ancient. I put my hand over Thunder, who was trying to squirm out of the sling, as if she wanted to join in. Esma had said she'd be disowned if she befriended gadjé. And now, watching her people, I understood what a loss it would be for her to give up this life. Even if the boria did call her squash head all the time.

When one of the men noticed us, he said something to Esma's grandfather, the Duke. And the Duke said something to his wife, the Mistress of Destiny, who sat on a tree stump with her knees splayed, pipe bobbing, foot tapping in time with the music. Her nose twitched in surprise, and her eyes squinted at us, puzzled. As word spread through the group, people stopped their music and dancing one by one. To my dismay, Esma stopped singing, too, and set down her violin. But the secret look she gave me made up for it.

Grandfather and I introduced ourselves and begged pardon for interrupting them.

The Duke reintroduced himself as Ivan, Duke of the Impossible Caravan, Master of the Traveling Cinema. Ceremoniously, he twirled the tips of his enormous mustache and welcomed us into their firelit circle.

We sat on little wooden chairs. The Duke pulled another white orb from his suit pocket—maybe a peeled apple; it was hard to tell in the dim light. He bit into it and munched, then stuck it back into his pocket. Noticing our curiosity, he pulled out another one, unbitten, and offered it to us. As he leaned in, I smelled it, the sharp odor that stung my eyes. Onion.

Grandfather and I shook our heads politely.

The Duke, still munching, said something passionate in

garbled Spanish. Esma clarified, lacking his enthusiasm. "Raw onions," she sighed. "Supposedly his secret to good health. Strength. Long life. He snacks on them all day long."

Moving swiftly, she grabbed two porcelain cups from a low, round table draped with a gold-fringed cloth. On the table sat an enormous, shiny silver vessel, with a spout that Esma opened with her pinkie. Transfixed, I watched as steaming, honey-colored liquid poured out, into the cups.

"Tea," she announced, placing the cups in our hands.

I sipped. It was a strange, dusky taste—nothing like the pale yellow chamomile tea I was used to. No, sipping this was pure magic, as though I were somehow sipping a night of Romani music and dancing and films. My insides warmed, suddenly golden.

In Mixteco, Grandfather said, in his most formal voice, "Thank you for the tea. And for bringing joy into our hearts and a spark into our souls." I translated in my own most formal voice.

Duke Ivan gave a little bow. Grandfather and I bowed back.

Roza, Mistress of Destiny, just chewed on her pipe and watched us with sharp eyes.

Grandfather said, "We are planning a special occasion in your honor . . . the Romani Business Appreciation Event."

Once I translated, Ivan's eyebrows shot up. After a stunned moment, he said, "Señor, before I was born, my father came by boat across the ocean. All the way from Hungary he came, to find a safe place for his family. Back then, he did metalwork."

The Duke paused and reached over to touch his wife's coin neck-laces. "My father's art," he said proudly. "Despite his extraordinary talents, we were often refused service in the cities . . . unjustly arrested . . . spat upon." The Duke traced a jagged scar on his cheek. "Some people have even thrown stones at us."

I strained to understand his Spanish, as tangled as over-grown bean vines, past and present intertwined. But the meaning behind the scar was clear, and it set off a wave of fire in my center. I felt like a brittle, fragile twig, set aflame and tossed in a flooding river. Burning and drowning at once. Powerless.

I looked away from his scar, into my amber tea. My heart thudded. Sweat broke out. I couldn't breathe. And all the while, I tried not to think of the other time I'd felt like this, after what had happened to my father.

After a pause, the Duke continued. "So we mostly stay away from cities. Since we moved from metalwork to the traveling cinema, we only go there to rent reels and sell hats and baskets. We travel to the tiniest of tiny villages, where we are treated best." He smiled, patting the coins over his chest. "And your Hill of Dust, this is the first place to hold an event in our honor. For that, we are grateful."

I sipped the golden tea, and it calmed me just enough to sputter a translation.

Grandfather's eyes crinkled with compassion. "My people embrace you as true friends. We, too, have suffered such indignities."

I held my breath, wondering if he, in turn, would tell details of these indignities. The first, the biggest, the most terrible would be about my father. My insides began to burn and drown again. I gnawed at the inside of my cheek.

Thankfully, Grandfather moved the topic back to our invitation. "Three nights from now, we will join together in respect and gratitude. The event will occur at our house, over there, three houses west of the church."

Ivan returned his smile, then raised his shoulders and sighed. "Thank you for this great honor, my friend, but we must decline. We leave tomorrow morning. You see, we've already shown all the films we've brought. We would have no way of making money for three more days. Alas, we would lose money, as we must rent these films by the week."

Grandfather sipped his tea, unruffled. "My people would happily offer more baskets and hats to watch the same movies again."

The tips of Ivan's swirling mustache rose. "Why thank you, kind sir, but we would have nothing to eat. We've already told your fortunes in exchange for food. We have nothing else to offer."

Again, I translated, sweat pouring from my armpits. I glanced at Esma, but she didn't look concerned. And Grandfather only smiled, as if he'd expected this glitch.

"Our family," he said, "has a fruit grove not far from here. Oranges, mangoes, limes, papayas, avocados. You are welcome to eat as much as you can pick."

Ivan sighed, fingering the rim of his hat. "Thank you, friend, but we cannot live on fruit."

Again, my heart caved. Living on fruit gives you terrible stomach cramps, it's true. Lucita and I had tried it the first time our mother crumbled. After what happened to our father, we stayed in his village for months. His relatives tried to help us, but there was a drought, and the corn harvest was bad, providing hardly enough for even half the tortillas we needed. Our mother forgot to feed us, so Lucita and I scavenged for fruit, making ourselves sick. That's when Grandfather journeyed to the village and, finding us half-starved, brought us to my mother's native home on the Hill of Dust.

"True, one cannot live on fruit," Grandfather agreed, sipping his tea, "but we've had a good corn harvest, enough to share with you." His eyes twinkled. "We also have a patch of wild onions. The sweetest you've ever tasted. The biggest you've ever seen. You're welcome to as many as you like."

This caught the Duke's attention. You could almost see him drooling at the thought of pocketfuls of onions. He raised a finger, pausing to confer with the Mistress of Destiny.

I studied their expressions and movements, remembering what Grandfather always said about gestures speaking louder than words. I peered past Duke Ivan's grandiose mustache and saw the uncertainty in his eyes, the torn movements of his mouth. He looked to his wife for guidance, and she, miraculously, seemed to be convincing him to stay.

The Mistress of Destiny waved her pipe in the air, said

something bold. Then she walked over to Esma and tugged on her braid, speaking in a gruff voice melting with tenderness. Gently, she tapped the side of Esma's head. She said something to Duke Ivan, and the commanding look in her eyes made it clear that Roza, Mistress of Destiny, was the true leader.

Doing his wife's bidding, Duke Ivan turned to Grandfather. "It would be our honor to attend the Romani Business Appreciation Event."

"Thank you," Grandfather and I said at the same time.

Duke Ivan continued. "Please send your grandson tomorrow morning to show our women where to gather the food. Our granddaughter, Esma, will come along to translate."

Grandfather nodded. "My grandson, Teo, will help them gather as well."

As we bid the Rom good night, I saw Grandfather and Roza exchange glances, and I wondered if she, too, saw the world in full color, saw outside the frame that limited the rest of us. Once we left, violin notes and Esma's voice flew up into the night, far above any stones and scars and burning and drowning. Her song was free and joyful, a rising flock of birds. The magic of the tea lingered on my tongue, the taste of possibility.

SQUASH HEAD

*O*n the way to the fruit tree grove the next morning, the toddlers followed me like baby ducks, sputtering "Da? Ga? Ba?" and tugging at my clothes and reaching for Thunder, who they knew was in my sling. The Mistress of Destiny twitched her nose at me and muttered something in a low voice to Esma.

Esma eyed me cautiously. "My grandmother said she's not even going to ask how my cousins are already friends with you and your duck."

Thank goodness the toddlers couldn't talk. I met Roza's suspicious gaze and offered her an innocent smile.

When we reached the onion patch, we dug them up with sticks and knives. The women looked impressed at their size, but grumbled as they stuck the onions in sacks.

"They're not fans of my grandfather's stench," Esma whispered. "But it's true, he never gets sick."

Later, in the woods by a mostly dried riverbed, we picked low-hanging mangoes from trees and gathered the ones on the ground, stuffing them into burlap sacks. Some mangoes were already old and rotten, filling the air with a sweet scent of decay. Plenty were ripe, small but full of juicy, honeyed promise.

An hour or two passed quickly, and although I couldn't talk openly to Esma, we exchanged the secret glances of best friends. When the young women said they were tired and ready to go, I pointed out mangoes higher in the branches. "You all can rest beneath the trees while I climb up and toss more down."

"I'll help!" Esma said.

One of the young women scowled at her and said something sharply. She pointed to Esma's lame leg, her curled-up fingers. Her meaning was obvious: You can't climb trees.

Esma raised her chin and loped over to the biggest mango tree in sight. She grabbed a low limb and heaved herself up, tossing her weak leg over the branch. Panting with the effort, she paused to catch her breath. It took her a while, but she managed to climb halfway up the tree, until she was hidden in the canopy. I scampered up after her, careful with Thunder asleep in my sling.

As birds chirped in the branches, Esma and I talked softly, occasionally tossing mangoes down to the women below. Wrapped in a cocoon of leaves, I felt like it was only Esma and me, in our own green world.

After devouring three rosy-orange mangoes, Esma asked, "Why does your family let this fruit fall and rot?"

"My mother used to bring Lucita and me here to gather it and sell it at the market. But since my sister died, my mother stopped caring. About the fruit, about me, about anything. It's like she died with my sister."

Esma's face grew tender as a new leaf. "What about your father?"

Her question was a fireball that knocked me into a raging river. At least, that's what happened inside me. On the outside, my face turned stony and my fist clenched a mango.

Could I tell her the truth? It would hurt; it would burn; it would steal my breath away. Still, I had to. This was my loyal friend for eternity.

"One day," I began, "when I was little, we were selling palm hats in Mexico City—my parents and sister and me. We were crossing a really wide street. The cars were whizzing by so fast, and there were so many lanes . . . like the river flooding in the worst storm of rainy season. We were all holding hands, running across . . . then Lucita dropped her orange."

I paused. I'd never talked about this with anyone but Grandfather. But Esma was listening with her raindrop eyes wide. "The orange, it rolled backward. Lucita ripped her hand from mine. She tried to pick it up. I stopped to help her. My hand—I felt it tear out of my father's. He turned back. And his face was—it was all fear. That's when I saw the car. So close, racing toward us. My father pushed us out of the way."

Esma was leaning in close now, her face wild with concern. *She's here with me,* I realized, *right here inside this burning-drowning memory.* And her gaze was like a hand holding on to mine, tight and determined.

My voice lowered and crackled and almost didn't make it to the end. "There was a screech and a thump. The car—it hit my father. And then everything goes fuzzy. I remember blood and tears on his eyelashes. I remember that orange, round and perfect. I remember the driver standing over my father, talking to another driver. Calmly. Too calmly. And most of all, I remember their words."

Esma's head was cocked, waiting. "What?" she said finally.

The words came out of my mouth, stinging and smoking. "'It's just an indio.' Then the other man—he shrugged and said, 'What's one less indio?' They dragged my father to the side of the road. They wiped his blood from their shirts with handkerchiefs. Then they got back into their cars and drove off."

"And your father?" Esma whispered. Her voice was a rope I hung on to so I wouldn't drown.

"I tried to stop his bleeding. But I couldn't. I couldn't save him."

Once I finished, I felt something dripping over my hand. I looked down. I'd squeezed the mango so tight that juice had burst out like blood.

Esma took the scarf from her hair and wiped the nectar from my hand, gently, as if it really was blood and I really was hurt. Then she looked me straight in the eyes and said, "You couldn't save him, but you'll save other people. Lots of them."

"I'm too weak, Esma."

"Weak? Look what you did to that mango!" she said, balling up her sticky, wet scarf and tucking it in her pocket. "And you saved Thunder! Nothing is impossible for you!"

She settled back into the crook of two branches, peeled another mango, and bit into the juicy tip. With her headscarf off, her hair flew out in wild waves. "My mother's dead," she said matter-of-factly. "She died in childbirth. I was her first and only baby. My dad remarried. See that woman down there?" She poked her head through a gap in the leaves and pointed. "The one in the green dress?"

I spotted her and nodded. She was the one who whacked Esma and called her a squash head the most.

"That's my stepmother." Narrowing her eyes, Esma dropped a mango, which fell through layers of leaves, landing squarely on the woman's head.

"Ow!" came an annoyed shout. And then something like, "Watch out, squash head!"

Esma smiled, satisfied.

It was mean, but the woman deserved it. I said, "I've been watching how they act around you, Esma."

Her face darkened. "And?"

"They're jealous."

She nearly spit out her mango. "Jealous?" she said, wiping nectar from her chin.

"They wish they had lightning inside, too."

She barked a laugh. "I don't think so."

"And your grandmother, the Mistress of Destiny," I continued.

Esma looked at me, her expression suddenly vulnerable. She cared what her grandmother thought, I realized. That was whose opinion mattered.

"When she taps your head, it's like a hug. When she tugs your braid, it's like a kiss. And when she calls you squash head, it's like she's really saying 'I love you.'"

Esma's eyes shone, and she blinked quickly, then sniffed. Softly, she said, "I wish we could stay up here all day."

"Let's do it!" I said.

"Spending all day in a tree with a gadjo would definitely make me marime." Quickly, she added, "At least, that's what *they'd* say."

I remembered that word. *Unclean. Impure.* It still made blood rush to my face, hot and indignant.

"And if that happened, my grandfather could disown me, kick me out of the family. Then I'd never see my grandmother again."

I took this in. "Your grandmother's the one who's really the boss." I paused. "You know she's on our side, right, Esma?"

"Well, she did give us our true fortune," Esma admitted. "After your grandfather asked her to. But then why didn't she stand up for us? Why didn't she argue with everyone who said it was impossible?"

"She knows that if she tells you something is impossible, you'll do it."

"True." Esma plucked a few more mangoes and breathed in the flowery scent before dropping them below. She stuck out her chin. There, in our cave of fluttering leaves, her eyes met mine. "Thanks for everything, my friend for life. And I mean it. You really are. Even without the fortune, you would be."

I reached out and tugged her braid, then tapped her lightly on the head. It was the first time I'd touched her, and it felt like the opposite of burning and drowning. It felt like flying through a cool, bright, wide-open sky. "Thank *you*, squash head."

10

CURSE

*I*n the freshness of the next two mornings, I led Esma and Roza and the boria and toddlers along winding trails to more fruit trees and onion patches. The Duke was enchanted by the giant, sweet onions and eager for more. Grandfather had arranged for my cousins to cover my morning chores so that I could act as guide. Later, in the afternoons, when the Romani women were preparing peppery stews, Esma would tell them she was going to fetch fresh water and leave with the toddlers and a tin bucket. She'd find me and the goats, and together we'd all gather by the river.

On our last full day together, she dipped her feet in the water, and then I dipped in mine, and then we were up to our knees and splashing and soaking wet and laughing. The currents were gentle and sweet and cool, and afterward we lay on the boulder and watched the leaves' shifting patterns above us.

Every so often we glanced at Da and Ga and Ba to make sure they weren't indulging in more duck poo.

I'd noticed that Thunder didn't poo too much unless she'd recently eaten, so I let her crawl on me when she had an empty stomach. She waddled on top of me with her little webbed feet, over my chest, then nibbled at the collar of my shirt and hair and earlobe. Her personality had been coming out, more and more—feisty, demanding, and fiercely loyal.

"She really thinks you're her mamma," Esma said. "I bet she'll still be following you around when we come back."

"Next year?"

She nodded. "Listen, Teo, we have to make it happen."

I agreed, but I didn't know how. The onions would be a big draw, but they weren't enough.

On the way back into town, we took a detour so I could show her a cluster of rock mounds. "Look, Esma. These are ruins from our ancestors, the ancient Mixtecos."

"It's like buried treasure!" she cried.

I scanned the ground, found small bits of obsidian knives and pottery. Archaeologists from Mexico City had taken the biggest statues away to put in a museum where folks from the Hill of Dust would never see them again. When I was little and we'd sell baskets in the city, I'd seen people lined up at the giant museum, eagerly paying to see our ancestors' crafts. Yet on the street, these same people wouldn't meet our eyes across the woven baskets we sold. And they would warn their children not to play with the dirty indio kids.

Now that burning-drowning feeling was coming back, so I looked up at Esma's face, all lit up with delight. It made me feel better and breathe better. I dropped the pieces of glassy obsidian and red pottery into her hand. "You can keep them," I told her, knowing there were thousands more pieces just like them around here.

Excited, she tucked the little treasures into her pockets. Biting her bottom lip in concentration, she dug around with a stick, overturning small rocks, searching for more. From underneath one, a scorpion skittered out, and I jumped back, pulling her with me.

But it didn't bother her. Bravely, she kept digging and, minutes later, uncovered part of a carved stone face.

"Look, Teo!" Brushing away more dirt, she carefully pulled out an entire statue, unbroken.

It was small enough for her to cradle in her palm. It looked like a raccoon wearing a giant crown of corncobs. "What is this?" she asked in awe, blowing off the dust.

"We call them *diositos*—little gods. People say they're good luck. Most of us have one or two at home. But don't tell the priest about it," I added with a smile. He wasn't a fan of our diositos. "You should keep it, Esma."

Suddenly, her face blazed with an idea. "I've got it!" she shouted. "You and your grandfather can present this to our people. Tell them it's a good luck gift from your village."

I eyed the statue, doubtful. "You think it will make them come back?"

"Oh, we'll add . . . some creative storytelling."

I tilted my head, waiting.

"We Rom are experts at it. Of course, we usually use it on you gadjé."

I gave her a look.

She bit her lip, thinking hard. "So, Teo, you'll give them the diosito and here's what you'll say." She climbed onto a rock mound—what was once part of an ancient temple. She held up the statue, threw back her shoulders, and boomed, "Dear Romani friends, please accept our gift to you. If you return in one year, this diosito will bring you the best of luck. Your food will taste especially delicious. Your movies will have extra magic to entrance your audiences. People will flock to your shows like ants to honey. You will be showered with money like a rainstorm."

I climbed up beside her on the rock and straightened tall. I shouted, "Good fortune will follow you like a baby duck follows its mother. The largest and sweetest onions will be yours."

She grinned. "But if you don't return, dear Romani friends, your entire family will be cursed."

"Cursed?" I recoiled. Grandfather always warned that healers never use their powers for evil.

"It's just pretend!" Esma assured me. "Listen, tell them this." Her voice grew ominous, and her eyes shifted like shadows. "If you do not return within a year, your voices will change into croaks of mournful toads."

She let out a belch. I stifled a laugh.

"Your hair will turn into spikes, like a cactus." She stretched out her braids, widening her eyes.

I couldn't resist adding, in my spookiest voice, "Your tongue will shrivel like a worm in a desert."

Her voice rose in a creepy howl. "Your sweat will smell like an angry skunk."

I widened my own eyes. "Your poo will turn greenish yellow and goopy."

At this, she collapsed into laughter, and once she recovered, gasped, "Oh, they'll do anything to avoid that curse. I know it."

ROMANI BUSINESS APPRECIATION EVENT

*T*he night air was thick with the promise of rain, rich with the smells of sweet tamales and cinnamon-chocolate, smoky with a hundred flames of beeswax candles. Everyone in town, Mixteco and Romani alike, had gathered at our home for Lucita's cabo de año. People overflowed from the courtyard, spilling into every corner of our huts, out past our squash and bean patch, to the edge of our milpa and the fringes of our herb garden. An expanse of stars hung over the fields and mountains around us, with my home at the warm, golden center.

The Rom seemed to be genuinely enjoying our refreshments. At first they kept to themselves in a cluster, but then the chocolate and sugar and candle smoke and mist conspired to make everyone light, happy, brave enough to mingle with strangers . . . who were no longer strangers after a week here. In broken Spanish, Rom chatted with Mixteco, and Mixteco with Rom, and the language was just broken enough that the Rom didn't realize this was actually an event for my sister, and the Mixteco didn't realize that the Rom thought they were honored guests for a Romani Business Appreciation Event.

Grandfather put his hand on my shoulder and said, "They are like us, outsiders in Mexico. Both of our people have little voice in the government. City folk consider us backward. We live on the fringes, the wilds of our country. So it is with the Rom."

He nodded to himself, watching our guests. "Duke Ivan told me the Rom have traveled for many centuries and scattered around the world, yet they speak the same language and keep their traditions strong. Our people, the Mixteco, were here before the Spaniards came, before this place was even called Mexico. We too survived, our language survived, our customs survived. And perhaps that is why our village welcomes these Rom with open arms, because we see ourselves in them."

I looked at Esma and her grandparents, who were admiring the sawdust mosaic of the flowered caravan. And I wondered if the key to her people surviving had been separating themselves from outsiders—gadjé. Maybe that's what bonded them together as they danced around their bonfires, night after night for hundreds of years.

Esma and her grandparents met our eyes and ambled over. In his flowery speech, Duke Ivan thanked us, offered us some of the onions—which we all politely refused—and bid us good night as he took an enormous bite of one.

Esma shot me a pointed look.

The statue! I had to give it to them before they left. Esma and I had decided this would be the perfect time to give the gift. The curse would seem spookier in the flickering candlelight and ghostly mist.

I pulled the little diosito from my pocket, my palms damp. I tried to channel Pedro Infante and all the other bold actors I'd seen on-screen the past week. I said, "Dear Romani friends, my sister died a year ago today. She would have loved the movies you've shown. She would have loved the aliveness you've brought. She would have loved . . . you."

I placed the statue in the Duke's free hand, the one that wasn't occupied by an onion. "Please take this ancient diosito that our ancestors made many years ago."

Glancing at Esma's eager face, I launched into the speech I'd memorized, about the good luck the statue would bring. By now my cousins had gathered, sensing something exciting was happening. Lalo understood enough Spanish from his year at school to do a rough Mixteco translation—a word here and a word there.

Esma translated to her own people while Duke Ivan nodded and smiled, extra big at the mention of onions. In return, Grandfather nodded and smiled.

I'd told him about this part. But not the next.

I took a deep breath and, trying to make my eyes scary and my voice haunting, explained the curse that would befall them if they didn't return.

On hearing Lalo's choppy translation, Grandfather gave me a strange look, but I kept going.

Duke Ivan must have understood some of my ranting; I could tell from the way his mustache fell into an upside-down arc over a deep frown. And as Esma translated, making her voice eerie, Duke Ivan's face darkened more with every gory detail. With effort, he swallowed his mouthful of onion and put the remaining half onion in his jacket pocket, looking woozy.

Here was a man who did not like curses. His hand went to his throat at the part about the toads, to his mustache at the part about the spiky hair, and to his paunch at the part about the duck poo. He now held the statue at arm's length, thoroughly disturbed.

Maybe we'd overdone it. Maybe we'd ruined everything.

Roza, on the other hand, wore an expression of skeptical amusement, at least when Duke Ivan wasn't looking at her. While she watched Esma's theatrical translation, the Mistress of Destiny's nose twitched, as if trying to hold back laughter. It was like a volcano, bubbling up and threatening to explode. Finally it gushed out, this lava rush of laughter, but she covered it up, feigning a coughing fit.

She made such a commotion that Ivan patted her back, concerned. Eventually, she calmed down and wiped her eyes and sniffed. Beyond the giant nose, her moist eyes crinkled in enjoyment. She tapped Esma's head, tugged her braid, and whispered something to her, which I could only guess involved the word *squash head*.

Then the Mistress of Destiny turned to her husband. I figured they must be debating whether to accept the statue. With a sigh of exasperation, she grabbed the statue, kissed it, pressed it to her bosom, then issued a firm and unshakeable order.

Duke Ivan grimaced, sighed, and turned to Grandfather and me. "Thank you for the gift, my friends." He shook our hands, leaving sharp traces of onion juice. "We will be certain to return next year to avoid the unpleasantness of the curse."

His wife elbowed him. He added, "And of course, we look forward to enjoying your company once again."

Esma brightened and declared, "I would like to play a song in honor of Lucita."

She wedged her violin beneath her chin and eked out a melody, mournful and beautiful, something that brought to mind caves and candles, beams of light cutting through the night, white sheets waving like magic in the breeze. Her voice rose in an open-mouthed, wordless song, as though she'd converted lightning and stars into spiraling notes, waves of sorrow and waves of joy, waves of losses and waves of wishes.

I looked at my mother, sitting with my aunts outside the kitchen, and wished she could feel it, too, this aliveness all around us. I wished she could feel my sister's presence in the music and mist. I could. It was a soft and whispery presence, something comforting that would always be with me.

STORM

The next day, beneath a heavy white sky, the Rom packed up their camp and loaded their wagons. Everyone on the Hill of Dust came to see them off.

Esma walked over to me and Grandfather, under the guise of thanking us for the Romani Business Appreciation Event. "Well, my friend for life, this is it. The roots of our friendship are planted deep."

I nodded, my lip quivering. If I opened my mouth, I might crumble to bits.

She looked furtively behind her, and seeing that her family was busy packing, she leaned toward me. For one heart-thrumming moment, I thought she might hug me good-bye. Instead, she bent toward my sling, cupped her hands over Thunder, and kissed her downy head. In return, Thunder peeped and nibbled at her ear.

Esma giggled. Still standing close, she stared at me, as if memorizing my face. And then, "Teo, before we leave, can you ask your grandfather something important?"

"Sure. What?"

"Ask him if I'm going to be a famous singer one day."

Confused, I said, "Why don't you ask the Mistress of Destiny?"

Esma lowered her voice. "Here's a Romani secret, never to be divulged. Promise?"

"Promise."

"As far as I can tell, most Romani women aren't true fortune-tellers. They just pay close attention, make good guesses, tell the gadjé whatever they want to hear."

I swallowed hard. So this whole friends-for-life thing was invented? Crushed, I asked, "The Mistress of Destiny made up my true fortune?"

"No!" Esma cried vehemently. "Here's the strange thing! After paying so much attention, my grandmother sometimes sees glimpses of real things, real fortunes. Like she did with you." Esma paused. "Once she told me my true fortune."

"What was it?"

"She said I'd be a famous singer. That was a long time ago, when I was little, before—before the lightning strike. I asked her about it later and she said, 'No, squash head, you imagined it.' But, Teo, I remember, I remember she had that same look in her eyes that she did when she saw your true fortune."

"Why would she lie?"

She lowered her head. "Because if I become a famous singer—it means I'll be marime. I'd have to leave my family forever."

After spending a week with Esma and her people, the gravity of this decision sank into me. Becoming a famous singer would get her disowned. Becoming my friend for life would get her disowned. I remembered how joyful she looked, dancing and singing and playing music around the fire with her people.

"Esma, do you really want to make these fortunes come true? Do you really want to be a famous singer?" I forced myself to continue, my voice raw. "Do you really want to be my friend for life?"

"Yes," she said, without hesitation, her chin jutting, determined, in the air. She glanced at Grandfather. "Your grandfather, he has powers like my grandmother. That's how he knew she was hiding your true fortune. So please, ask him, will I be a famous singer?"

Once I translated, my grandfather regarded her. Then he took her hand—the one with the curled-up fingers—and gave a deep bow, a gesture of true admiration. "Queen Esma," he said, "it doesn't take a divination to see that whatever it is you want, you will make it happen."

And then, Esma's stepmother called out for her and stomped over, smacking her head, then pulled her away by the ear.

Moments later, the horses were hooked to the wagons, and the Rom were walking beside them, loaded with packs of their own. They waved good-bye, and we bid them farewell. The

Mistress of Destiny pulled something from her pocket—the diosito—and held it up as she waved, looking directly into my eyes. In broken Spanish, she said something along the lines of, "Here's hoping none of us is croaking like a toad or pooping like a duck next year."

Somehow Grandfather caught the gist of her words and laughed a deep belly laugh.

The caravan began its descent down the mountain, with Esma bringing up the rear, carrying a satchel in front and Da on her back and holding Ga's and Ba's hands. "Good-bye, my friend for life! Until next year!"

"Good-bye, Queen of Lightning!" I called after her.

As she grew smaller, loping away in that crooked dance of hers, my eyes burned and my chin trembled. Once she turned the curve, I ran up into the hills, into el monte. I perched on a high lookout, where I could watch the caravan wind down into the valley, on to their next village. At the horizon, clumps of stone-gray clouds were rolling in, and a deep rumble sounded in the distance.

Lightning illuminated the entire sky. I tucked myself farther back against the rocks, under the overhang, watching the first storm of rainy season draw near. The rain came, first a few drops, then walls of water. Safely under the overhang I sat, feeling the air's new coolness. Bolt after bolt of lightning crackled against the dark sky, flashes of wild energy.

Water slid down the mountains, gushing mud, and far below, the river swelled and roared. Tucked far above in my mountaintop nook, I imagined Esma and her people taking refuge inside their wagons, sheltered from the howling and pounding. I heard Esma's shouts in the crashes of thunder, her screams in the wind, alive and whirling with possibility.

And I screamed, at first wordless, open-mouthed screams. Dozens, maybe hundreds that I'd swallowed over the past year. Then, when I was all screamed out, words formed, words for Esma. "I will see you again. And one day, I will save you, too."

DROP

Mateo

THE HILL OF DUST,
OAXACA, MEXICO
Present Day

13

FIRST INTERMISSION

*M*ateo, how about some food?" The question comes from a distant place, some other world.

"Huh?" My voice sounds strange and hoarse.

I blink and focus on Grandpa's head, which is tilted in concern. "Food?" he repeats, making an eating gesture.

It's like a spell has been broken, like there's a glitch in the movie I'm watching and it's suddenly just . . . stopped.

"Food," I echo, staring down at the coin necklace in my hand. It feels almost alive, something with a heartbeat. "Why food?"

He grins. "Thought I heard your belly rumbling."

"Oh." I listen, embarrassed. Yup. My gut's making a storm of its own.

"And, mijo," he says, "there are some strange noises coming from your pocket."

"What?" Oh. Right. My phone. It's sounding message alerts in the form of my favorite guitar riff. I silence it without even seeing how many texts I've missed or what time it is. This is the longest I've gone without checking my phone. Well, at least outside of sleeping, plane rides, and school.

The weird thing is, I don't care. I still have one leg in the world of his story, and I want to climb back in. All I can think about is Esma, somewhere out there. I pool the coin necklace from one hand to another, like a deck of cards. "Did she come back, Grandpa?"

He stands up slowly, without a word. Then he takes some new candles from his altar, lights them, and smushes them over the ones that have burned out. The room brightens.

He sits down again, and his eyes shine with reflections of flame, like tiny mirrors. And my stomach grumbles fade and he starts talking and the movie plays on . . .

GUST

Teo

THE HILL OF DUST,
OAXACA, MEXICO

Long, Long Ago

14

SPARK AND FLASH

*O*ne year later, the Rom came at sunrise, when the sky was a riot of pink and gold, when the air was fresh and cool and full of hope. For months, I'd been glancing at that bend in the road, far down the valley, at the foot of the Hill of Dust, waiting, waiting, waiting. And at the moment their trail of wagons and horses and scarves and coins rounded the curve, the sun peeked above the mountains and shone long rays across the valley, through wisps of hearth smoke, onto their caravan.

I'd been crossing the courtyard for breakfast, but at the sight of the Rom, I sprinted down the road.

Until a flurry of whistles flew at me.

Months earlier, Thunder's cute peeps had changed to piercing whistles. Her beak had bloomed bright pink with a yellow patch, like a slice of rosy mango. Her feathers had grown in a rich coppery brown on her neck and back. Black feathers had sprouted on her belly, and a patch of white feathers spotted her now-black wings. Her neck stretched long and proud, and she strutted around on tall legs as though she were boss of the world, even though she barely reached my knee.

Her high-pitched twitters were easy to translate. *Slow down, Teo!*

Reluctantly, I slowed down.

In her whistle language, she scolded me as she waddled up. *Don't you dare leave us behind!*

Yes, *us*. There were two new members of my rescued-animal club.

Spark, a baby goat born blind, whose *baah* of protest was barely audible over Thunder's scolding. *Please slow down, please?* Spark was saying in her timid voice. *What about little me?* She meandered along, her nose and ears quivering in the breeze, trying to compensate for her lack of vision. She was white with honey speckles and the softest ears I'd ever felt, a tender velvet that your fingers couldn't resist smoothing.

And then there was Flash, the newest member: a three-legged skunk, just a few months old, who I'd found as a baby caught in a trap. When it was clear he'd never survive in the wild, Grandfather removed the skunk's stink glands so that he could live with us. Now, Flash scampered back and forth along the road, curious about every twig, every bug. He was a slippery, roly-poly thing, always on the move, devilishly weaseling here and there. He was only still when sleeping, and only then could you fully appreciate the beauty of his shiny, coal-black fur with the perfect, milk-white stripe running down the center of his back to the tip of his bushy tail.

Relenting, I slowed even more, letting all the animals catch up. Sometimes it felt as if each of them held a little piece of Lucita's soul—Thunder's bossiness, Flash's playfulness, and Spark's tenderness. I was bound to them, and we were as loyal to each other as family.

But slowing down for the animals meant my cousins had time to catch up, too. "Hey, wait for me!" Lalo shouted. He was just a couple years younger but still whined like a little kid when he felt left out. "Where are you going, Teo?"

"Nowhere," I called back. I wanted to greet Esma and her people first, have them to myself for a bit. Soon enough they'd be mobbed.

Of course, Lalo followed me anyway, and then little red-faced Chucho caught up, too. When they caught sight of the caravan, Chucho yelled so loudly the entire village must have heard. "THE GYPSIES!"

For someone so small, he had a giant mouth. Within moments, children appeared like bees on sweet rolls. They ran ahead to the Rom, as I hurried my animals along. The adults soon abandoned their chores and followed, too, jostling past. I picked up Flash so he wouldn't get stepped on. Thunder shot warning whistles at anyone too close to the goat—her own large, furred, four-legged baby.

Now the nervousness set in. What if Esma had changed? Gotten a new best friend for life? Forgotten about our fortune altogether? Or what if she needed to be saved? Could I do it? Maybe rescuing animals was practice for saving the Queen herself one day.

I continued down the dirt road, trying to calm my thudding heart. But even the morning birds were chirping with the thrill of the Rom coming. What would I say to Esma? She was just minutes away now, three more switchbacks down the road. I peered at the valley where the villagers had already reached her caravan. They were petting the horses, running their hands over the carved swirls of the wagons, reaching out to shake the Rom's hands.

I was squinting, searching for Esma, when I noticed footsteps and the pungent smell of shoe polish. A rough voice said, "*Hola*, Nephew." It was my uncle Paco, who'd recently returned from working for three years in Mexico City. The way he talked about it, you'd think he was mayor of that place.

He'd had a round paunch before but now was thin, almost caved-in looking, with bloodshot eyes. He claimed it was lack of sleep from the ruckus out here in the boondocks—roosters and crickets and dogs. Supposedly he'd gotten used to sleeping to the civilized sounds of buses and automobiles and streetcars out the window. *Real glass* windows, he was quick to point out. He rejected farm chores and spent most of the day polishing his shoes, which was another reason for not working—he didn't want to dull the shine.

Thunder didn't like him. When Uncle thumped me on my back—a little too hard—she spewed out a string of disapproving whistles. He gave a vague kick in her direction, which only served to sharpen her whistles to a shrill siren.

"Shh, Thunder," I said. If Uncle didn't calm down soon, she might bite his ankle. You didn't want to get on Thunder's bad side, especially when she was protecting her little family.

"So, Nephew," he said, walking stiffly in his shiny shoes. They were so small and pointy, I had to wonder how he crammed his feet into them. "What's all the fuss about?"

I answered softly. "The Rom are here. The Gypsies."

He reeled. "You all permit them in our village?"

I blinked. Why wouldn't we? "They're our friends," I said. "We welcome them."

Uncle shook his head. "You all really are as ignorant as city folk say."

My muscles tensed. Why had he even come back to the Hill of Dust, only to insult us?

"In the city, we scorn the Gypsies." He spit on the ground, a yellow glob of phlegm. "They're all dirty beggars. Sneaky, out to steal kids and every last centavo."

I swallowed hard, wishing I could pick up the pace and leave Uncle behind, but then I'd also be leaving behind Spark and Thunder. I patted Flash as he wriggled around in my shirt, patches of black-and-white fur peeking out here and there.

"Well, Uncle," I said finally. "I don't know about the Rom in the city, but this caravan is good and honest. They show us movies in exchange for hats and baskets. And they tell our fortunes. You'll see."

"Right, and they pick your pockets while you're busy watching. Or ransack the houses you leave empty. Now in the city . . ."

I blocked him out, tired of hearing about the wonders of the city—electricity, phones, radio, television. But it pained me to hear him insult my friend for life and her people. I racked my mind for an excuse to get away from him.

As I thought, I stroked Flash, who was creeping around my neck now, nibbling at my collar with sharp, tiny teeth.

Uncle stopped his ranting and said, "Is that a skunk on your neck?"

I gave him a bewildered look. "You've never noticed Flash before?" But as I said it, I realized that of course he hadn't. He was so absorbed in his own complaints, he barely noticed the goings-on of daily life around him. "Yes," I said. "He's a skunk. Only three legs, but he manages."

Unaware that Flash's stink glands were no longer intact, Uncle took a step away and wavered there, watching my skunk warily and muttering about backward villagers like me.

Thunder took advantage of his distraction to waddle over to Uncle's left shoe and let out a goopy, greenish-yellow stream of poo on the freshly polished leather.

She half-flew, half-waddled away before he could kick her. She sat at the edge of the road, fluffing her tail feathers, indignant, watching Uncle's reaction from the corner of her eye. He was livid, jumping around and cursing, and finally stormed off toward our home, probably to spend the morning removing every last trace of duck poo from his precious shoe. Once he disappeared around the bend, a satisfied Thunder strutted back to my side.

Through the mesquite leaves, a breeze rippled, like the light sound of Lucita laughing at my duck's antics. Grateful that Thunder had freed me of Uncle, I rounded the last curve and found myself at the edge of the crowd swarming the Rom—practically the entire village. This time, everyone greeted our visitors warmly, eager for the wonders they'd brought. My people spoke with the Rom in broken Spanish, asking what they'd seen in their travels over the past year.

I breathed in the rich horse smells, the scents of amber tea and fringed carpets and far-off lands that clung to the wagons. The acrid scent of the Duke's onions cut through the dusty haze. My eyes lingered on the wagons' golden spirals, the deep red and turquoise flowers, all of it more ornate than even the gilded, angel-speckled ceiling of our village cathedral. I tried to glimpse inside one of the wagons, through the blue curtains, but it was too dark and stayed hidden in mystery.

Searching for Esma, I wove through the throng, eyes skimming over the flower-clad boria with babies strapped to their backs. There were Da and Ga, whose hair had sprouted out in waves, like agave leaves. There were the men with gold jewelry sparkling in the sun. There was the nose of Roza, Mistress of Destiny, twitching and dancing with delight over her pipe. And there was the Duke's mustache, prancing around as he smiled and laughed and munched his onion. The warmth of familiarity filled me, and I hugged Flash tightly as I took it all in.

Finally, I spotted Esma. She looked the same as I remembered, only taller, and with a different dress and scarf—all royal ruby reds, poppies and roses and dahlias. And more necklaces of beads and shells and coins; it looked like a thousand jewels had spilled from a treasure chest hidden beneath her scarf.

On seeing me, a smile lit up her face like a sunrise, more dazzling than in my memories. On her hip, she held Ba, who sputtered off words in Romani, his sounds now broadened beyond *ba*.

As she set him down and loped toward me, I drank her in like a glimmering red glass of *agua de jamaica*. She came close, and for a moment I thought she'd throw her arms around me. But she said, "My friend for life! I missed you!"

I nodded, overcome with the miracle of Esma in front of me, in the flesh. This was the moment I'd dreamed of all year. She stood so close I could smell the spice of her breath— cinnamon and sweet tea and unknown scents.

"Me, too," I whispered. And then I added with a shy smile, "Queen Esma."

She stared at me for a while, a huge grin on her face, and I tried to look back but it was too much, like looking at the sun. "Your eyelashes grew," she observed.

I blushed, stared at my feet.

She spotted Thunder, who was prissily preening herself. "Your duck grew up! And look at your new little creatures!" She petted Spark's soft ears, watching Flash wriggle in my arms.

Then she took Ba's hand and smoothed it over the silk of Spark's fur, murmuring something in Romani.

Then, like a dark shadow, her stepmother closed in, frowned, and snatched up Ba. She bonked Esma's head and dragged her away by her elbow.

I sighed. That was one thing that hadn't changed.

With her other hand, Esma waved vigorously. "See you tonight, Teo!" she called back. "I have a surprise!"

SURPRISE

*A*s the projector beam illuminated moths and bats, I knelt on the dusty ground with Spark's head in my lap. Thunder settled at my side, her beak resting drowsily on my knee. In front of me, Flash played with a bit of string, pouncing on it like a cat. When he got too rowdy, Thunder let out a grumpy barrage of whistles.

I kept glancing over my shoulder, searching for Esma, wondering what her surprise could be.

Excitement hung in the plaza like electricity, even more so than last year. Most everyone on the Hill of Dust had been looking forward to this day all year. As the Duke and his sons fiddled with the projector, spooling spirals of film, nearly all of my village sat on the edge of our little wooden chairs. In eager voices, people speculated on what this new movie might be, and mused over questions they'd ask tomorrow at the fortune-telling.

My cousins Lalo and Chucho insisted on sitting beside me, vying for a prime place to rub Spark's ears. Nearby sat Aunt Perla and her new husband and my other aunts and uncles and cousins, each with freshly woven hats on their laps. My mother was at home, as usual, shrouded in her shawl, huddled over her cardboard box of treasures.

This was something new she'd started this past year. She'd place the worn box on her lap like a baby, then carefully pick up a necklace, admire it, put it back. Next, she'd choose a fancy spoon, which she'd admire, then tenderly set down. And on it went with a silver candlestick, a tin box, a picture frame, gold earrings, and a random smattering of other shiny possessions. Grandfather suspected my mother deemed it safer to love things she could keep protected in a box. He gave her healing teas and did cleansing ceremonies for her, but she only cared about the contents of her box.

And Grandfather, he rarely left home now, claiming he wanted to keep an eye on my mother and the animals. But there was more to it. I tried not to notice how just crossing the courtyard left him breathless and limping.

The movie started, and everyone hushed. When the star actress came on-screen, I gasped. A stab of recognition shot through me. Those heart-shaped lips, those impossibly long, curved eyebrows, that soft, dark cloud of wavy hair. The sight made my legs quake, my stomach churn, a cold panic grip me.

This was Maestra María, the teacher I'd had during my stint in first grade. Or at least the spitting image of her.

Six years earlier, on that first morning of school, I'd thought, *Oh, how beautiful!* But before the first lesson was over, I'd witnessed the evil hidden beneath all that beauty. And by the afternoon, I'd fallen victim to her wrath, and trudged home in tears. It had been the same day after day: One of us students offended her somehow. In retaliation, Maestra María would raise a long, curved eyebrow like the bow of an arrow, just before her attack. Her weapon of choice was not an arrow but a wooden ruler, an innocent tool until you saw how ruthlessly she wielded it. To this day, her memory struck an instinctive fear, a reflex to cower and flee. I suspected a gaping hole where her heart was supposed to be.

Wincing, I forced myself to watch the film, noting that this actress wasn't quite identical to Maestra María. I was somewhat reassured by the slight difference in nose length and chin width and curve of her shoulders. Yes, it must have been a different woman altogether, but she proved just as heartless, and moved her eyebrows in a similarly vicious manner.

La Mujer Sin Alma—the Woman Without a Soul—the Heartless Woman. This was the name of the movie and the main character. She was a beautiful and evil lady who made rich men fall in love with her. Compared to my teacher, she was sneakier with her evildoing, and targeted grown men rather than innocent children, yet both she and Maestra María lacked a soul.

Afterward, everyone was still shivering and marveling over the horrid, gorgeous movie star—whose real name, someone said, was María Félix. Another María, I noted. Although, in fairness, half the women I knew had María as one of their names.

I was relieved when the movie ended. I liked the funny ones with songs and silly mustached men better. While the others were picking up their chairs and bidding each other good night, I spotted Esma at the edge of the cornfield. I hoped she would sing and play violin while her people packed up the film, as she had last year.

But no, she was standing there, staring at me. Silver eyes glittering, she motioned for me to join her. And she disappeared into the tall stalks.

Heart pounding, I stood up and strolled over to the milpa, as casually as I could with three animals at my heels. A bossy duck, three-legged skunk, and blind goat usually attract attention, but everyone else was still under the movie's spell and didn't notice me slip into the cornstalks.

A few rows back, I stumbled right into Esma. Embarrassed, I staggered backward.

With a grin, she grabbed my hand and steadied me. She led me deeper into the shadows of the field, where no one could hear or see us. Her hand was warm, and I could feel her lightning pass into my palm and spread through my body.

When she released my hand, I was breathing hard.

"Teo, my friend for life!"

"Esma, my queen," I whispered, my voice soft beneath the crickets' chorus.

She greeted my animals, cooing and fussing over them, and then stood up to smile at me. Her teeth glowed as white as a crescent moon.

I swallowed hard. "What's your surprise?"

She pulled a small card from her pocket. "Look!"

I held it up, out of the shadows, against the sky. There were letters and swirls and stars. I could sound out a few short words, thanks to my time in school six years earlier. *Of, the, a . . .* words that didn't tell me anything useful. "What does it say?"

Her shoulders fell. "You can't read, Teo?"

I looked away, ashamed. "No." And feeling the need to defend myself, I added, "Hardly anyone can read in my village. The kids work all day." I didn't say that the beautiful and evil Maestra María had terrified me—and most of the others who had dared go—into quitting school.

Esma tapped her finger to her chin. "Then we'll have to find another way."

"But what is it, Esma?"

"A business card." Eyes flashing, she tossed a shell-laced braid over her shoulder. "See, Teo, one night my family was showing films near Mexico City, and I was singing and playing violin after the movie, just fooling around. I didn't think anyone was paying attention. And when I stopped, a man and his wife came up to me, clapping."

Esma's eyes were wide as she spoke, her hands and arms making sweeping gestures, painting pictures of her words. After a dramatic pause, she continued. "Teo, the man was a music agent! He said I could be a star! A famous singer!"

I was speechless. Of course, *I* knew she could be a famous star. But it was something else altogether to hear about another person recognizing her talent. Someone who could make a difference in her life. I wanted to be the one to save her. Or at least help her.

This was her dream. Yet I remembered what it would mean for her—leaving her family forever. And for me—if she left her family and settled in the city, I'd probably never see her again. But she had to leave. If she stayed with her people, she'd have a life full of squash-head insults and bops to the head. I kept my thoughts to myself and said only, "That's your dream."

"Yes!" Esma's chin jutted out in that fierce way. "Then the Duke came over, and when the man asked him about training me for a professional career, he said, 'Absolutely not' and walked away. But the woman slipped me this card and whispered that if I ever decided to try, I could live with them until I made enough money to put me on my feet."

Esma cradled the card against her cheek. "I was hoping you'd read it," she said.

"Well," I said, "we'll find someone who can. My uncle just got back from working in Mexico City. Maybe he can read a little."

She paused, shook her head. "I wanted you to teach me to read."

I furrowed my eyebrows. She wanted my help, yet I couldn't give it. "Why, Esma?"

She raised her arms, palms upward, as though channeling celestial light. "Reading is like lightning."

I tilted my head. "Lightning?"

"Power, Teo. If I'm going to be out on my own in the gadjé world, I need to know how to read. So no one takes advantage of me."

"Doesn't anyone in your family know how to read?"

She shook her head, adamant. "My people don't read, don't approve of their kids reading. They say we'd become marime, part of the gadjé world."

That word again, *marime*. Impure. My gaze fell to the ground, where Flash was nibbling on Spark's ear. "Well, I can't help you, Esma. I'm sorry."

She looked at me wildly. "Nothing is impossible."

Cringing inside, I thought of Maestra María, that terrible, elegant eyebrow arching upward.

"I know!" Esma said. "Why don't you start going to school now? Then next year when I come back, you can teach me."

I rubbed my temple, remembering Maestra María's ruler, the sting, the hot, humiliating tears, the bruise that lasted days afterward. "But who would herd the goats and do my chores?"

"You'll find a way."

And then she dropped to the ground and held her palm out to Thunder, who crawled right into her lap. She started petting Spark, letting the goat nuzzle against her. She reached out to Flash, unafraid of the possibility of stink.

"He can't spray," I assured her. "My grandfather removed his stink glands."

"*Pobrecito*," she said, touching his nose to hers. "Poor little guy. Three legs and no stink. You'll just have to find a new weapon, huh?"

"He has one," I said, motioning to my duck. "Thunder. Our grumpy guard duck."

Esma's laughter rang out, a melody like raindrops on leaves. "Think she could guard me from the boria?" she joked. "Next time my stepmother tries to whack me, Thunder can fly up and bite her hand."

"Actually, ankles are her specialty." I grinned. "And greenish-yellow poo on shoes."

As we talked, I settled beside her, only a sliver of space between us. I breathed in the smell of earth and corn and leaves and night, and the spice and wood smoke that clung to her. She smelled like the promise of distant lands, of adventure, of possibility. I reached over and stroked the animals' fur and feathers, and our fingers brushed, and more lightning passed into me.

"My powers flare up when I'm with you," she said.

"I know," I said softly. "I feel it in your fingertips."

And there in the dappled moonlight, with creatures warm and breathing, and lightning passing between the places our skin touched, we told each other all the things that best friends share.

She showed me her new beads and shells and coins, like blooms on vines winding around her neck, her wrists, in and out of locks of her hair. Some she'd found at the sea, she said, and some in the jungle, and some in pine forests, and some in deserts.

She told me how her stepmother wouldn't let her sleep in the wagon anymore and made her sleep outside instead, even during storms. It was a good thing, too, because thanks to her lightning powers, one night, camping beside a river, she awoke hours before dawn, knowing something bad was about to happen. Then she saw the river rising, fast, and using her talent for screaming at the top of her lungs, she woke the others. They moved to higher land just before the water flooded the valley.

Another night, they were camped in a field with some other Romani caravans near Mexico City, when Esma woke up smelling gasoline and smoke. She saw that someone had lit fire to the dried grasses, and the flames were zipping toward their wagons. Again, her screaming skills paid off, and within two seconds, she'd woken up everyone in camp. They moved their wagons just before the flames could engulf them. Esma narrowed her eyes and said, "I knew who set the fire—I saw him—a man who'd fought with my father earlier that evening. But later that night, there was a storm, and the man's house was struck by lightning." She grinned, triumphant. "Lightning avenged me!"

And on and on we went, exchanging stories. Hers were more exciting than mine, and mostly involved her saving herself and her entire caravan from doom. She definitely didn't need anyone to save her, not with lightning powers on her side.

At first I was nervous, and my words came out stuttering, but soon they flowed between us like warm honey. I told her about my animals' antics, how when Flash got grumpy, he'd raise his tail in anger, assuming he was spraying his offender, then strut smugly away. I told her how I saw Lucita in my animals, in starlight, in sunlit clouds, in the paths of hummingbirds . . . and how happy, mixed with sad, it made me.

Esma told me she'd composed secret songs about missing me and Thunder. She sang them lightly, under her breath, and shivers and sparks danced over my skin, through my blood.

In whispers, we talked until the church bell struck midnight. And then she said, "Alas, my friend for life, I must bid you farewell. The boria will be wondering why there's no squash head around to whack."

"What'll you tell them?"

She thought for a moment, cradling Flash in her arms. "That I encountered a vicious skunk and had to stay perfectly still so it wouldn't spray me."

"Creative storytelling," I said.

"Well, Flash *is* pretty vicious," she laughed, as the skunk ran up her arm and nibbled at a red ribbon woven into her braid. She handed me Flash and stood up, adjusting her head-scarf. "Until tomorrow, Teo."

Esma left first, just in case anyone was still in the plaza, and I stayed with my animals, warm in the afterglow of her light-ning. I wondered if I could face the beautiful, evil Maestra María again, in order to make Esma's dream come true. It wasn't exactly saving her, but it was close. And as I thought, a question took shape in my mind—the perfect question for tomorrow's visit from Roza, Mistress of Destiny.

Back home, I poked my head into Grandfather's room. He'd waited up for me. I was touched; lately he'd been going to sleep earlier and earlier, sometimes before twilight, skipping supper altogether.

"Teo! Come in!"

He sat on his petate, leaning against the adobe wall, smil-ing with tired eyes. He looked small, huddled in his poncho; lately he'd gotten chilled so easily. His room smelled of earth and incense and herbs and wool and beeswax—Grandfather's unique combination of scents.

"Tell me about the movie, Teo," he said, reaching out to smooth Spark's ears. Once you started petting her ears, it was hard to stop.

I told him about the beautiful, heartless woman with the alluring eyebrows. "She looked just like that teacher I had," I added, then fell quiet, remembering Esma's request.

Grandfather stroked Flash's fur for a long moment. "Is there something more?"

It was as if he could peer into my mind, the spaces between words.

"Esma wants me to go back to school."

He tilted his head, surprised. "And?"

"Well," I said, looking away. "I don't know. I have the goats and my chores."

He studied my face. "Your cousins could help. Lalo could take over your chores, and Chucho could do Lalo's. They're old enough now."

I looked down. "People like us—we're not welcome in school. I can't stand how the teacher treats us."

For a moment, he was quiet. Then he said, "You already speak Spanish. This gives you a voice. And when you learn to read, your voice will be stronger. So strong you will be able to demand the teacher's respect. Not just for yourself, but for others."

"Maybe," I said, unconvinced. My voice felt like a dusty whisper now. I made a last grasp at an excuse. "But what about helping with your patients?"

He shrugged. "I only have energy for a few patients a day anyway. And since Paco is back in town, he can help translate."

I didn't like the idea of Uncle Paco in the healing hut instead of me.

Reluctantly, I asked, "You think the patients would feel comfortable with him?"

"No, but I think sometimes if you give a person a role, he steps up to it. And anyway, you learning to read is more important." His eyes twinkled. "And Esma is still your friend for life, isn't she?"

I nodded quickly. I thought of Esma and Maestra María. At the heart of it, my loyalty to Esma was greater than my fear of the *maestra*. I wasn't so much of a coward to be scared of a teacher, was I? I was twelve years old now. What could she do to me?

16

SOMETHING STUPID

*I*n the angled morning sunlight, I was scattering corn for the turkeys when a cluster of Romani women and children strutted up our path. Roza's nose did a happy jig as my entire family gathered in the courtyard, eager for their fortunes. "Buenos días," she said in her choppy accent, and then something that Esma translated as, "It's marvelous to be back!"

Aunt Perla stepped forward, holding her new husband's hand. Before their marriage, he'd been a widower for years. Now they lived just a few houses down, but she made sure to be here bright and early so she could show him off to the Rom. "Look!" she squealed. "My husband. Strong and handsome, with brown eyes and black hair." She squeezed his bicep, ruffled his hair. "Just like you said!"

The others looked doubtfully at her husband. True, his eyes were brown, but his hair was more gray than black, and his predominant feature was not muscle but a large gut hanging over his waistband. And handsome? Well, that was stretching it. His teeth looked stolen from a horse, so big that his mouth never quite closed. And then there was his chronically stuffed nose, certainly not mentioned in the fortune. Yet my aunt believed he was handsome, and he doted on her like she was a princess.

She patted her round belly. "And you were right! A baby!"

Roza nodded, twitching her nose, unsurprised but obviously pleased. Esma translated the boria's polite murmurs of congratulations.

My grandfather hobbled out. "Welcome, Mistress of Destiny. We hope your people will come again to our . . . special yearly event. It's in three days."

Upon hearing the translation, Roza nodded, let her hand linger in his, patted it with her other one. "It would be our honor."

Grandfather led us all into the healing hut, and as I unstacked chairs for our guests, he lit candles.

The fortunes were similar to last year—marriages, babies, bouts of good luck, bouts of bad luck, things lost and found. When my turn came, I perched on the wooden seat across from Roza and Esma, twisting the hem of my shirt.

"And what is your question, Teo, my friend for life?" Esma asked, exuberant.

Softly, I translated. My relatives raised their eyebrows, curious about my friendship with this Romani girl. My cousins giggled and made jokes and low whistles.

A blush warmed my face. I looked at Esma for a moment, then flicked my eyes to Roza. "Mistress of Destiny," I asked, "should I go to school?"

There was another flurry of murmurs and baffled whispers.

Roza looked amused at the question, her mouth widening into a five-toothed smile. "That's a new one. Haven't heard that before."

As Esma translated back and forth, her eyes glittered with hope.

I dealt the cards as Roza instructed and watched her nose flutter as her gaze swept over the cards—a jumble of swords and cauldrons and goblets and royalty and suns and moons that meant nothing to me.

She shook her head and muttered something.

Esma's shoulders sank, and a shadow passed over her face. She took a deep breath and began arguing with Roza. After a storm of impassioned words flew between them, Roza smacked Esma's head lightly and tugged her braid and gave her a command.

Esma hesitated before translating, her voice bitter. "No, you shouldn't go to school. It's a . . . it's a waste of time." She blinked back angry tears.

Pipe bobbing, Roza studied her granddaughter. Her nostrils expanded to nearly double their size as she sucked in a long breath. After a moment, her nose calmed and her eyes softened. She spoke again, resigning herself to something.

A smile broke out over Esma's face. She translated, giddy. "You shouldn't go to school. No child should. But the fact is, you will! You will go to school! For reasons more noble than most. You will learn to read. And it will change your life. And the lives of others!"

Roza narrowed her eyes and pursed her lips and added something else.

Esma suppressed a smile as she said, "The Mistress of Destiny would like to make it very clear that in her own opinion, however, school is not recommended."

With a glint in his eye, Grandfather nodded at Roza and said, "Thank you for that true fortune."

"You go next," Lalo said, urging my grandfather forward.

I stood up to offer the seat.

He shook his head. "I'm an old man. Fortunes are for the young."

But Chucho and my other cousins pushed. "Come on, come on, Grandfather."

With a sigh, he consented and sat down, looking almost sadly at Roza. With trembling hands, he dealt the cards.

Roza gazed at the cards, then at his face, deep creases at the corners of his eyes from years of smiles, and between his brows from years of compassion for others' pain. And lately, from some of his own pain.

Her nose held perfectly still, motionless as a statue. Something passed between the two of them. Something beyond words, something that remained unspoken. She laid her hand over his. "Your grandson will bring you great joy."

Grandfather appeared relieved. "He already does." He added, "He also brings me three-legged skunks and baby ducks and blind goats."

Laughter filled the room, and as if on cue, Flash squirmed out of my arms and onto the table, attempting to gnaw at the fortune cards. Then Thunder spewed out a wave of curmud-geonly whistles, as if to say, *Quiet down, now!* She didn't like crowds or closed-up spaces or noise . . . unless she was making it herself. With all the ruckus, Spark the goat began to *baah* and stumble around, confused.

Embarrassed, I scooped up Flash and set him firmly in my lap, then drew Spark in close, stroking her ear.

As my cousins joked about my animals, Grandfather and Roza continued to stare at each other, in silent conversation. Despite the commotion, her nose remained still as a leaf on a windless day.

And then Uncle Paco entered the room, limping slightly from his too-tight footwear. "What's going on here?" he bellowed in Spanish.

Thunder gave him an unwelcoming whistle and stood between me and my uncle, protectively.

Roza broke her gaze with Grandfather. Like the hair on the back of a dog, her nose stood up, tall and ready for a fight.

I groaned inside. I'd been hoping Uncle had slept in late this morning, as he did most mornings, lost in dreams of sewage pipes and television.

"Well?" he demanded. And again, louder now, "What are these people doing in my home?"

My relatives didn't answer, simply looked the other way as if that could make him disappear. The odor of shoe polish oozed through the room.

"Answer me!" he shouted in Mixteco first, then in Spanish. He swung his arms around wildly, nearly hitting Aunt Perla in the face. Her husband pulled her in close, gaping at Uncle.

Esma cracked the silence, her head high. "We're reading fortunes, señor."

He glared at her, then at the others. "I'll tell you what they're doing! They're getting you in a crowded space and distracting you so these little Gypsy brats can pick your pockets." He pointed to Da, Ga, and Ba, who were more interested in picking their noses than any pockets.

His rant continued, a furious mix of Spanish and Mixteco. "Criminals, all of them. I've seen Gypsies in the city, how they work, like sneaky foxes. They'll even steal your kids."

Esma kept her chin jutting bravely out, and translated not a word. But her people's offended expressions made it clear they understood the gist.

My stomach was in knots. We'd worked so hard to forge a friendship, not just between me and Esma but between our people. What if my uncle ruined it all?

Grandfather spoke. His voice sounded more fragile than ever but had a calmness that commanded attention. "Son," he said to Uncle, "these are honored guests. There is a respect among us. I ask you to show them this same respect."

This, Esma did translate, with a flash of pride.

Uncle barged through the crowd to the table. "So read my fortune," he challenged. "Do it now."

Esma whispered words to her grandmother. Roza seemed unruffled. The tip of her nose had somehow turned up, as if it were looking down on Uncle. If a nose could be indignant, this was it.

Tapping her pipe against her teeth, she instructed him to shuffle and deal the cards. He did so, roughly, banging them on the table.

She stared at the cards, then at him. Her words were slow and solemn.

Esma translated, "Your insides are torn up, broken."

Uncle shifted uncomfortably in the chair. All my relatives listened carefully, watching his reaction.

Esma's translation continued. "Beware of doing something very"—and here Esma paused and seemed to hold back a smile, but then she rearranged her face into something solemn—"very stupid."

At that, Uncle erupted, all rage and clumsiness. He flipped the table over. Cards scattered. Roza held her ground like a mountain, with Esma at her side, but the other Romani women gasped and skittered backward with the toddlers. My aunts pulled away, against the wall, holding their own children. My uncles lunged toward Uncle Paco, trying to restrain him.

But he shook off their hands.

Anger rippled through the room. Even Flash the skunk was arching his back and stamping his feet in outrage. Fists were clenching, eyes narrowing. Someone would get hurt if this wasn't stopped. And the Rom might leave forever. I had to do something.

I looked at Esma for inspiration, at her gleaming silver eyes, at her fierce, proud jaw framed by braids and shells and coins. And I thought about what she would do in my place. I felt her lightning in my blood.

I righted the chair, stepped onto it, and held up my skunk, whose bushy tail was already raised and ready. I spoke loudly, from my belly, staring straight at my uncle. And I aimed Flash's bottom right at him.

My cousins and other uncles and aunts were surprised but unafraid, knowing that except for his penchant for nibbling at clothes and grain sacks, my skunk was harmless. Esma murmured something to her relatives, which made them relax. Now only Uncle Paco looked wary.

My voice thundered, low and strangely commanding in Mixteco. "Uncle, my skunk has no patience for . . . stupid things. He's just about to spray."

That was like a bucket of cold water on Uncle's head. He fled the room.

I lowered Flash, who promptly began biting at a loose thread on my sleeve.

Over the next hour, my relatives fetched payments of eggs, vegetables, and corn for their fortunes and chatted with the Romani women. The children picked up the cards from the floor, eager to touch their magic. Eventually, my aunts and uncles and cousins trickled out to return to their chores, and the Romani women and children headed outside and down the path, leaving only Roza and Esma and Grandfather and me. We lingered at the doorway, half in the sunshine.

A tiny snort of laughter escaped from Roza. Esma pressed her lips together to keep her own laughter from bursting out.

Grandfather said, "Your fortunes appear true, Mistress. My son did something very stupid indeed. And as a result, my grandson has given me great joy."

"And school?" Esma asked, looking at me hopefully.

Bolts of lightning were still flowing through my blood, making me brave . . . for the moment at least. I glanced at the Mistress of Destiny, chomping on her pipe, awaiting my response. Maybe this could be my way to save Esma. And maybe, if Grandfather was right, to save my future self.

"Looks like I'm going," I said. "Even if it's not recommended."

THE HEARTLESS WOMAN

*I*n the half light of dawn, sneezing and rooting through dusty junk in our storeroom, I found a yellowed notebook with only a few warped and water-stained pages left. A search through more odds and ends revealed a pencil stub, shorter than my thumb, which I sharpened with a knife.

The church bell rang six chimes. Time to leave for my first day of school. I rubbed my eyes, still groggy from staying up late after last night's movie with Esma. We'd met again in the shadows of the cornfield, whispering stories from our year apart. My body felt exhausted, but the precious hours with Esma were worth it, especially since I couldn't see her again till later this afternoon.

Quickly, I tossed my supplies into a small satchel along with a few tortillas and a lime and goat cheese for lunch. Still sipping their morning atole, my aunts and uncles waved and wished me well, while my cousins skulked, annoyed they had to take over my chores. And my mother—she slept, shutting out the world.

On the walk over the caked-brown hills, I tugged at my clothes, uncomfortably small. These were the pants and shirt I wore to weddings and baptisms, since they had only a few patched holes. I'd washed the shirt yesterday, and it hadn't dried completely. I shivered in the cool morning air. My mother used to wash and patch my clothes, but she barely left her room now, either sleeping or rifling through valuables in her cardboard box.

I'd tried to make Thunder and Spark and Flash stay home with Grandfather, but five minutes into the walk, they'd appeared at my side. Little did they know they had an hour's trek ahead of them—narrow pathways through patches of prickly trees, across dried riverbeds, around spiky palm fans. Little did they know a heartless woman would be waiting at our destination.

Even though they slowed me down—Spark with her blind meandering, Flash with his lopsided darting, and Thunder stopping to groom at every trickle of water—I was glad for the company. I needed their support. Not a single kid from my village had even stayed in school till Christmas. Now it was May, late in the school year. Would anyone even be there besides me and Maestra María? What if all her fury was focused on me alone?

But as I approached the one-room adobe building perched on a hill, I spotted a cluster of students under a tree.

"Buenos días," they murmured in Spanish, friendly enough.

"*Yo'o naa yo*," I said, greeting them in Mixteco. "*Nixi yo'o?*"
How are you?

With a furtive glance at the schoolhouse, they mumbled
answers in Spanish. "*Más o menos.*"

So-so.

A little boy whispered in Mixteco, so softly I could barely
hear, "She doesn't like us speaking our language."

I glanced at the others, who nodded gravely. Their weary
faces made it clear: They were dreading another school day.
There were twelve of us in total, all boys from other villages,
mostly six or seven years old. I was the oldest, over a head taller
than the rest.

From a safe distance, I peeked inside the classroom. There,
writing on the blackboard, was Maestra María. She looked just
as I'd remembered, just as stunning as the Heartless Woman
herself.

Last night, the Rom had shown another María Félix film—
La Devoradora. The Devourer. And now, I was on the verge of
being devoured. My insides twisted.

Yet the maestra was so pretty it took my breath away. Her
waist was small, her skirt full and powder blue, reaching just
past her knees. She wore shiny patent-leather shoes with little
heels that made her ankles look as graceful as a deer's. Her
creamy sweater was trimmed with pearls and looked feathery
soft, so unlike the coarse cotton and wool the women of my
village wore. Silky brown curls fell around her shoulders.

"Hey," one of the older boys said to me. "Why are these animals with you?"

I told them about rescuing Flash and Spark and Thunder, and they listened, curious, but when Maestra María rang the bell, they fell silent and marched inside like a funeral procession.

I followed them, so nervous about the teacher that I didn't notice my animals following me.

Not until I saw Maestra María's horrified expression. "Get those foul creatures out of my school," she hissed.

"Sorry, Maestra," I stuttered. I was already rattled, and the school day hadn't even started yet. Breathless, I settled my animals outside.

"Please, please be good," I begged them. "Thunder, keep an eye on Flash." In response, she gave an irritated series of whistles.

I kissed Flash's nose. "Just sleep, all right?" I pleaded. He was nocturnal, at his craziest at night, and took catnaps throughout the day.

I gave Spark's ears a final rub, which instantly calmed me. I didn't have to worry about her; she'd just lie there, docile, obeying Thunder's orders.

Pausing, I watched Flash wriggle in and out of Spark's legs, entertained for the moment. It was my last chance to grab my creatures and run home. But Esma's silver eyes and golden coins flashed before me, and I forced my legs to walk back into the classroom.

Maestra María strode up to me, placing a manicured hand on her hip. Her eyebrow shot up. And her red-stained, heart-shaped lips twisted into a frown. "Aren't you old enough to know not to bring filthy animals into school? In fact, aren't you too old for school?"

I felt suddenly self-conscious. She didn't seem to remember me from six years earlier. Probably for the best—this way I didn't have to explain why I'd quit.

"I need to learn to read, Maestra," I said, looking at the packed dirt floor.

"Why now?"

My mind was a blank, so I told her the truth, already kicking myself as I did. "A-a Gypsy said I was destined to come to school." Silently, I added, *Although it was not recommended.*

"A Gypsy?" the maestra spat, her elegant nose wrinkled in disgust. "They're as ignorant as indios."

My face burned. I glanced around the room. Except for her, everyone here was indio. Mixteco, specifically.

She frowned. "Sit down there."

And if I'd had any hope that she might have softened, after the morning was over it was clear that she was, if anything, more evil than ever. Minute by minute, I felt I was sinking further and further, and it grew harder and harder to breathe.

She had us copy words and letters and make the sounds. None of the students were actually reading yet, since everyone else had dropped out before they'd gotten that far along. I tried to help the younger children, but the maestra shot me the evil eye when I spoke with them. One little boy, Benito, was hopelessly confused and too scared to ask her for help, so he asked his older brother Marcos, in Mixteco, about the instructions.

Before he could answer, Maestra María had trained her evil eye on him like an arrow and arched her eyebrow like a bow. Benito couldn't have been more than six or seven; he still had all his baby teeth.

"I told you," she said, "none of that uncivilized language in my classroom. Ten smacks. Benito, put out your hand."

His eyes filled with tears as he extended his hand on his desk. It was small and pudgy with lingering baby fat, and his knuckles were still just dimples.

The maestra took a ruler from her desk and smacked the boy's hand. Once. Tears streamed down his cheeks and he cried out. Twice. Now the boy was sobbing, trembling. Three times. Snot and tears covered his face, and his eyes were wide with fear.

I watched. My blood burned while the air pressed on me like water, dark and dense and suffocating.

She held up her hand for another smack.

I couldn't stand it, this burning and drowning. I leapt up, bursting through the surface of something. Taking the boy in my arms, I held his hand gently in mine.

I breathed. My heart still galloped, but air filled my lungs and cooled my blood and cleared my head. My eyes met hers. "That's enough, Maestra."

I turned to Benito and comforted him in Mixteco. "*Taxiini, taxiini.*"

She took a menacing step toward me. "Who are you to come in here and tell me how to run my classroom?"

"He's just a little boy." I wanted to say more but stopped myself. I could just walk out, never come back. But I couldn't leave Benito here to fend for himself.

And there was Esma. What would she say if I hadn't made it through a single day?

"He has seven more smacks," Maestra María said coldly. "Go back to your seat."

I steeled myself, kept my arms firmly around Benito. "No."

"No?" Her eyebrow rose higher still, until it had nearly reached her hairline. "Shall I do *your* hand instead?"

I swallowed hard, looked at the boy's hand. Red welts were forming after only three strikes.

"Yes," I said. I pressed my cheek to his head, then led him to his seat. Then I sat down, laid my hand on the desk, squeezed my eyes shut, and breathed.

There was a crack, a bolt of pain like fire that shot through my entire body. My hand wanted, more than anything, to pull away. I forced it to stay. I blinked back hot tears, braced myself for the next blow.

And it came. I breathed. I blinked. I clenched my jaw.

Then came another. And another. I bit my tongue to hold in the cries.

I looked at Benito, still shaking, tears streaming down his plump cheeks. Better me than him.

I thought of Esma, of the moment she'd been struck by lightning, how it must have burned and ached, and how, in the end, she came out stronger. She came through with powers. And like Esma, I held my head proud and tall and jutted out my chin.

Once, on the sixth strike, I did cry out.

Immediately, a commotion of wings rustled outside the open window. Thunder fluttered up, shrieking alarm whistles. Seeing that I was in danger, she flew into the room, landed on a desk in a fury of feathers.

Her whistles were so loud and shrill that kids winced, pressing their palms against their ears in wild-eyed shock. Maestra María had been holding the ruler up, poised for the next blow. She froze. At the sight of an enraged duck hurtling toward her, her eyes widened and her jaw dropped.

Thunder was in full attack mode. Like a raging storm, she half-flew, half-waddled toward the teacher. Her bright pink beak was wide open in a savage war cry. Her spindly legs were an orange blur, her wings a streak of white and black as she swooped forward.

Maestra María was now pressed against the chalkboard, shielding her face with her arms.

Just before Thunder reached that elegant, silk-covered ankle, I grabbed her.

A few feathers floated in the air as Maestra María put her hand to her chest, speechless. Her eyebrows were too stunned to rouse themselves into an arch.

I took that opportunity to deposit my duck outside. "Shh, calm down, Thunder, I'm all right. I can handle it."

I buried my face in her feathers, reached my uninjured hand out to stroke Spark's ears, let Flash slither around my neck. For a moment, I stayed like that with my animals, my hand throbbing. *Could* I handle it? I could just grab my animals and run, right now.

But Esma's lightning had filled me, and it was here to stay. No, I couldn't run away, because she wouldn't run away.

Slowly, I walked back into the building, as a prisoner would return to his jail cell. Only, like Esma, I held my head high. I imagined I was flying.

Inside, the maestra was closing the window and latching it firmly. Just outside, Spark was *baahing*, confused, while Thunder was whistling and grumbling under her breath, and Flash was scratching at the pane, trying to find a way in.

Over her shoulder, Maestra María said, "Bring that creature back here and you'll have duck stew for dinner."

For the rest of the afternoon, my hand ached. It was red and swollen and would surely be bruised, but nothing was broken. It would heal. I didn't think it could handle more beatings like this one, though. And this had only been six strikes, not the full ten. Thunder had saved me from the last four blows.

After school, I found some aloe, sliced it open with my fingernail, and placed the sticky leaf gently over Benito's swollen knuckles.

"Thanks," said his older brother Marcos, his arm around the little boy. "Wish I'd been brave enough to stand up to the maestra."

"No problem," I said, blushing. I wasn't brave, not really. Esma was the brave one. I'd just been lucky enough to have some of her lightning rub off on me.

I pressed gooey aloe to my own aching hand as my animals and I walked home. On the way back, I stopped at every creek to dip my hand in the cool water, as my animals splashed and poked around for insects and grains to munch on.

As I walked, I had plenty of time to imagine terrible things that could befall Maestra María. She could catch a mean case of lice and bedbugs and fleas all at once. She wouldn't be able to stop itching, not even to sleep, and definitely not enough to come to school. She'd have to shave off her hair to get rid of the relentless lice and burn her mattress to get rid of the bedbugs. Still, the fleas wouldn't leave her in peace. Moths and worms would eat holes in all her clothes, so she'd have to wear brown corn sacks. There she'd be, tossing and turning on the dirt, plagued by nightmares and itchiness, bald-headed and covered in welts, wearing a corn sack. And then a skunk—with intact stink glands—would spray her. Yes, she would end up wallowing in itchy, foul-smelling misery.

Shame crept through me along with my vengeful thoughts, but they did make me feel better, for a little while at least.

As I turned the bend to my house, I examined my welted

hand. Hopefully no one at home would notice. If Grandfather knew, he might not let me return to school. He was as protective as Thunder, only less boisterous.

With every jarring step, my hand throbbed with the Mistress of Destiny's words: *School is not recommended.*

LETTERS IN THE DUST

*C*oming home, I spotted Da, Ga, and Ba chasing a turkey in our courtyard. And just past them, in the shade, stood Esma, laughing and sipping drinks with Grandfather. My heart nearly jumped out of my chest. Esma and her cousins, *here*?

Somehow, she and Grandfather were chatting despite the language difference. They were surveying the half-finished mosaic for the commemoration of the second anniversary of my sister's death—also known as the second annual Romani Business Appreciation Event.

Unseen, I watched them for a moment, mesmerized by Esma's wrist, how her bracelets clinked as she swirled her arm in conversation. I'd been planning to soak my hand in cool water, nurse it with herbs until the swelling went down. But Esma's presence here was an unexpected gift, and I couldn't waste a minute of it. I tossed the aloe into the bushes and wiped the goop from my flesh, wincing. The hand was still red and swollen, so I stuck it in my pocket as I walked toward her.

My animals reached her first and nuzzled her leg. Within seconds, Flash had wrapped himself around her shoulders, poking his nose inside her headscarf.

"Teo!" she called, loping toward me. "How was school?"

I smiled and shrugged, not up for creative storytelling, but eager to spend time with her. "I have some things to teach you."

She clasped her hands together and, unable to contain her thrill, she twirled around, letting her skirt and hair flare out.

Grandfather insisted I relax and chat with Esma while he hobbled to the kitchen to fetch milk for Spark and *agua de papaya* for me. Da, Ga, and Ba toddled over to Spark and pulled at her ears. They were steadier on their feet and stronger in their grasp this year. They shouted exclamations in Romani as Spark patiently tolerated their tugging and poking. Meanwhile, Thunder waded into the irrigation ditch, fluffing her feathers, out of the toddlers' range, but close enough to keep an eye on them.

I squatted and smoothed the dusty ground with my good hand. Keeping my wounded hand in my pocket, I picked up a stick and wrote the letter *A*. Esma found her own stick and knelt beside me, copying *A* in the dirt.

We went through the alphabet, letter by letter. She focused hard, biting her lip, memorizing the sounds. She barely noticed the children and skunk and goat pattering over the letters.

"This is like magic!" she kept murmuring. "Now I get it! It's a code for the sounds."

Although my hand throbbed, the rest of me buzzed with her contagious excitement. These moments together were bursts of electricity that would keep me lit up through our times apart.

When I wrote her name in the dirt, she let out a yelp of joy. "It's like when my people leave markers on the roadside for other caravans—twigs and branches and bones, all tied and notched in special ways. But this, the alphabet, these letters, they're amazing! You can say anything!"

As she worked on copying and practicing sounds, Grandfather put his hand on my shoulder and offered me a mug of agua de papaya.

"Thank you," I said, sipping the cool, sweet juice, feeling his kindness fill me. He'd sensed that something went wrong today, I was sure of it.

That's when Uncle Paco appeared, limping out from his room, holding shoe polish in one hand and a rag in the other. When he caught sight of Esma and the children, he glared.

I held my breath, praying he wouldn't cause another scene.

Esma stopped writing, mid-letter, and eyed him, not in fear but as a challenge. Lightning danced over her skin, and her unspoken words were *Just try me, just try and you'll see who's stronger.*

My mind scrambled for a way out of the situation, a way to avoid hurt feelings and anger. But Uncle said nothing and continued on his way to a pile of metal pipes on the hill.

Sick of hearing his complaints about the lack of plumbing, my other uncles had brought him a bunch of pipes and told him to have at it. Uncle had made a half-hearted attempt to build a sewage system but had soon given up. Now he sat on a pipe and polished his shoes, watching us like a raptor.

"Teo," Esma said, glancing at him warily, "the boria was mad about his outburst yesterday. They told my uncles. They wanted to leave town, but my grandmother convinced the Duke to stay. At least until the Romani Business Appreciation Event."

"Good," I said, relieved.

Her eyes pierced into mine. "But we have to make sure your uncle doesn't make another scene. If it happens again, we'll leave the Hill of Dust forever. We can't stay in places we're not welcome. The police look for any excuse to arrest us."

I chewed on my fingernail, glancing at Uncle atop his pile of pipes.

Grandfather shuffled over. "Look at your hand, son."

My wounded hand. I'd forgotten to hide it. Quickly, I set down my drink and tried to cover the welts. The agua de papaya spilled all over the letters we'd just traced, turning them to mud.

"What happened?" he asked.

"Nothing," I said quickly, watching the liquid absorb into the dust.

Grandfather nodded. He would have let it go. At least until I was ready to talk to him about it. That was his quiet way.

But not Esma. "Your hand?" she asked. "Are you hurt?"

Seeing my troubled expression, Grandfather said, "I'll

make a poultice for you, son." And he shuffled to the herb garden behind the kitchen.

Esma grabbed my wrist. Her eyes widened as she took in the angry welts. "What happened?"

"It's not a big deal."

"I'm your best friend for life. You have to tell me."

"This doesn't change things, Esma. I'm still going back to school tomorrow."

"This happened at school? Did you get in a fight?"

She wouldn't relent, so I told her. I told her about the teacher insulting my language and people, about her hitting the boy, about me taking his place.

Esma's face reddened; her eyes turned to fire. Her entire body was smoking, flaming. Lightning shot out of her every pore, like the sky during a ferocious storm, all wild electricity.

When Esma finally spoke, it was with unwavering certainty. "That teacher will never hurt you or any other child again. I'll make sure of it."

"Esma," I said softly, "forget it. She hates Gypsies even more than indios."

"Good. I'll use that to my advantage."

"Esma," I tried again, "you can't stop her. She's been like this for years. She's even worse than the Heartless Woman. It's hopeless."

Her eyes burned. "Nothing is impossible, my friend for life."

I eyed her hesitantly. "What do you have planned?"

"Oh, I'll come up with something."

My skunk sniffed out the spilled papaya drink and scrambled over, trying to lick it up, and then just deciding to roll in it. Da, Ga, and Ba laughed.

After that, I tried teaching Esma more sounds, but the mood was broken, and although her teeth were biting her lower lip, now her concentration wasn't on the letters but on her plot against Maestra María.

Soon, Esma said she had to go, gathered the toddlers, and called back, "See you tomorrow at sunrise, my friend for life."

"Sunrise?" I sputtered.

"Oh, yes! I'm going to go to school with you."

A tingle shot through my chest. Part of it was a jolt of happiness at the idea of walking to school with Esma. And part of it was dread over what Maestra María would do to her. I swallowed hard. "How will you get away from your family?"

She shrugged. "I'll leave before they wake up. I'll do some creative storytelling when I return. They'll probably smack me and call me squash head for it, but they do that anyway."

I watched her and her cousins leave as a muddy, sticky Flash tried climbing up my leg. Grandfather stood at my side and offered me a new glass of agua de papaya.

"That teacher of yours had better watch out," he said, chuckling. "She'll meet her match in the Queen of Lightning."

MEETING HER MATCH

 $\mathcal{S}$ o, what do you have planned?" I asked Esma nervously the next morning on the way to school. I'd tried questioning her after the movie last night, but she'd insisted I go straight home and rest up for our big day.

She grinned as she dance-walked beside me. "I'll know when I see her."

I bit my cheek and tried to focus on the simple miracle of walking over the hills with Esma in the early light. Now she was singing out the letters of her name in rhythm to our steps. I could pretend we did this every day. The only thing missing was my entourage of animals. Cringing at the thought of duck stew, I'd made them stay home with Grandfather.

But I couldn't forget what was to come, her face-off with the Heartless Woman. "Really, Esma, what are you planning?"

She swirled in a circle. "Probably I'll just give her a big whack and call her squash head."

My insides jumped. "What?"

"Kidding. I'll think of something."

"I have to admit," I said, hopping over a rock, "when she was hitting Benito, I did imagine grabbing the ruler and whacking her myself." And then I confessed all the misfortunes I'd envisioned befalling the teacher, including stinkification by skunk.

Esma plucked a leaf and smiled devilishly. "I think a curse is in order."

I frowned. "You know how I feel about curses."

"Oh, Teo, this won't be a real curse."

"But if your victim believes in them," I argued, "they're still bad."

"Teo," she said firmly, "this curse will be glorious! You'll see."

And she gave another lopsided twirl for good measure.

Little Benito was in the school yard, clinging to the tree, with his older brother Marcos patting his back. "He's scared to go inside," Marcos whispered in Mixteco, glancing warily at the maestra through the doorway.

Benito loosened his panicked grip when he saw Esma. He stared, taking in her layers of red and pink and purple flowers and beads and shells and coins and braids. "Who's that?"

By now a small, curious crowd had formed. "This is Esma," I said, "Gypsy Queen of Lightning."

"Gypsy?" the boys echoed.

"But aren't Gypsies bad?" one of them whispered.

I was conjuring an indignant response in my head, when Esma did something that took my breath away.

She opened her mouth wide and sang. She sang softly enough not to announce her presence to the maestra inside. Her song was only for us, the small crowd of boys around her, drinking in her voice, enchanted.

When she finished, the boys exchanged glances, speechless.

"My people have a saying," Esma announced, silver eyes glinting. "Bad people don't sing." She waited a moment, letting it sink in. And then, "Decide for yourselves who's bad, amigos."

At that moment, the teacher rang the bell. Immediately, the other students filed inside.

Esma waited just outside the doorway, hidden around the corner. I hovered beside her.

"Go on in," she insisted.

I had the nearly irresistible urge to tug her braid. "Be careful, Esma."

"Go," she ordered.

I did. I found my seat and pulled out the water-stained notebook and pencil stub. My heart drummed in anticipation.

We'd just finished pledging allegiance to the flag when Esma strode in like a force of nature.

"Buenos días, Maestra," she declared, as if onstage.

Standing behind her desk, Maestra María regarded her headscarf and coin necklaces with suspicion. "Who are you?"

"Esma," she responded coolly, putting her hands on her hips, "Queen of Lightning." She moved toward the maestra.

Understanding dawned over Maestra María, and she took a step backward. "Are you—are you a *Gypsy*?"

Esma nodded, enjoying this. "But we call ourselves Romani."

An uncomfortable hush had fallen over the class.

"You'll have to leave," the maestra said, raising a bow-and-arrow eyebrow.

I sucked in a breath. Maestra María had overcome her shock and was readying for attack.

Esma raised her own eyebrow, making no move to leave.

The students watched with bated breath.

Maestra María reached for the ruler on her desk, but Esma snatched it up first.

And then, the Queen of Lightning loped over to the nearest empty desk and climbed right onto it. She towered over us like a statue in a church alcove. Her headscarf grazed the ceiling. She raised her arms like bird wings. "I have come to place a Gypsy curse on you, Maestra María."

The teacher glanced around, unsettled. "Get down from there!" Her voice was shrill, laced with fear. "Get out, you horrid girl!"

Esma smiled, as if the teacher had paid her the highest of compliments. "My dear maestra, here is your curse." She narrowed her eyes and pointed the ruler at the woman.

"Lice!" Esma boomed. "Thousands of them! They will dwell in your hair, make a meal of your scalp."

The children gasped. The maestra clasped a hand to her mouth.

Esma continued. "Bedbugs! Thousands of them! They will crawl over your sleeping body, sucking your blood and leaving a red sea of bumps."

The students murmured to one another in giddy disbelief.

Her voice rose again. "Fleas! Thousands of them! They will dance over your flesh, make you scratch until you bleed, even after you've shaved your head and burned your bedclothes."

The maestra stumbled backward against her desk.

Esma kept going. "And as you are lying in the dirt, miserable and bald and itching, a skunk will wander over and spray you. Liberally! And there you will wallow in your miserable cloud of stink."

The maestra tried speaking, but she was drowned out by Esma, who raised her chin higher still. "There's more! Every tear you produce in a child will be another link chaining this curse to you."

More whispers rippled through the students.

"HOWEVER!" Esma thundered. A hush fell over the room, an electric silence.

"However," she continued, in a now eerily quiet voice, "each teardrop you *prevent* will *cut* another chain in the link. And if you prevent enough teardrops, one day, you may free yourself of the curse."

There was silence as Esma punctuated her speech with a dramatic pause. And then, dignified, she climbed down and placed the ruler on the desk. With a sideways glance at the maestra, she said, "I suggest you use this wisely."

Then she did her lopsided walk-dance out of the room.

After Esma left, the maestra locked the door and called out the window, "And don't come back!" before locking it, too.

The rest of the day was hot and stuffy in the closed-up schoolroom, but the atmosphere among the students was exuberant. All day, the maestra trembled, though she tried to appear composed. She lost her temper quickly, but checked herself before yelling too much. And she didn't smack a single child all day.

The ruler stayed exactly where Esma had left it on the desk.

20

UNEXPECTED VISITOR

$\mathcal{K}$icking up dust, whizzing past agave, I raced home from school, unencumbered by my animals, hoping Esma would be waiting for me again. But no, I saw only Grandfather in the courtyard, rubbing Spark's ear with one hand, and with the other, sprinkling colored sawdust onto the mosaic beneath the tree. Esma must be back at her camp, I figured, eating the peppery stew I'd smelled while passing her camp.

On seeing me, my animals and Grandfather hobbled and waddled and scampered toward me. "It wasn't an easy task," he said, laughing. "They kept trying to sneak away and run after you." Then he listed everything Flash had gotten his sharp little teeth into—sacks of beans and corn, junk in the storeroom, crates of fabric scraps, and even my mother's box of treasures. But no lasting harm done, he assured me.

As I petted the animals, I told Grandfather about Esma's visit to school.

"Well, son," he said slowly, "I still don't approve of curses, you know. Even pretend ones." He broke into a grin. "But this one sounds pretty glorious, all right."

I couldn't wait for night to fall, to see Esma at the movie, the last one her people would show this year. Tomorrow would be the Romani Business Appreciation Event, and the morning after that, they planned to leave.

At sunset, I was sipping chili-laced atole with my cousins in the courtyard when a car—an actual car, curvy and shiny and sky blue—wound up the Hill of Dust. I'd heard the unfamiliar hum of the motor, and then Chucho had spotted the car chugging up the mountain. Within moments, my entire family except my mother and grandfather was ogling it. Even Uncle Paco paused in his shoe shining to stand up on the abandoned sewage pipes and squint down the valley.

The car stopped at the cathedral, where the road ended in the dusty plaza. Since there were still a couple hours till the movie, the stretch of dirt was empty. But now a crowd was forming around the car, mostly kids and curious adults.

Out of the driver's seat stepped Maestra María.

Panic exploded through me. Quickly, I ducked behind a tree. What if she'd come to exact vengeance on Esma and her people? My heart thundered; sweat trickled like rivers over my skin. I gathered my animals close, made them huddle beside me, hidden.

Meanwhile, people oohed and ahhed at the maestra's beauty—surely people who'd never met her before. "She looks just like the Heartless Woman!" they murmured in Mixteco, excited. "She must be a movie star!"

As enthralled as they were, they were also too intimidated to approach her. Of course, the children who'd been to school hung back like cowering animals. A survival instinct.

I sucked in a breath and poked my head around the tree, hopefully hidden by low-hanging leaves. The maestra was looking around, probably for the Romani camp.

Of all the people to come to her aid, Uncle Paco stepped forward. "Señora, you look lost. Can I help you?" He was attempting a gentlemanly voice, but it came out sounding oily.

The maestra resisted shooting him her usual evil eye. After all, she needed his help.

"Yes, señor," she said, all business.

I strained to make out her words.

"I was told there was a"—her lips pursed—"*brujo*—a witch—of some sort in this town."

"A *brujo*?" Uncle repeated, confused.

"Yes," she said, shifting awkwardly from one foot to the other. "Someone who could remove a curse."

"You mean a *curandero*? A healer?"

"Whatever. An elderly señor by the name of Teodoro."

Uncle's face lit up. "That's my father, señora!"

"Good." She gave a quick nod. "Will you take me to him?"

Eagerly, Uncle nodded. He tried to take her elbow but she

shrugged it out of his grasp, with a threatening arch of the eyebrow. They walked slowly, thanks to her high heels and his too-pointy shoes.

This gave me time to take a back shortcut to warn Grandfather that the Heartless Woman was coming—of all places—to our home.

"You can't let her in!" I argued with Grandfather, glancing furtively over my shoulder across the courtyard. It was hard to see down the path in the twilight, but it still looked clear; thankfully, the maestra was taking a while. "You know how many kids she's terrorized? Probably hundreds over the years!"

"Oh, Teo, it takes strength to move past your hurt to help someone." Grandfather spoke calmly, unrushed. "Especially someone you think you hate. But sometimes that is the very person who needs your help the most." He paused, cocked his head. "Perhaps this teacher is ready to change. If you lift up one soul, she will lift up others. And on and on it goes. This is what you do as a healer."

"I'm not a healer," I said bitterly. "I'm just a translator."

"You'll rise to the occasion when needed, son." Grandfather patted my shoulder. "People tend to do that. Surprise you. If you give them a chance."

"But, Grandfather, she's evil!" I insisted. "There's no heart there to heal!" And then, quickly, I closed my mouth. She was walking up the path in the evening shadows beside Uncle.

Grandfather invited Maestra María into the healing hut and lit some candles. Uncle followed her in like a devoted puppy. I hovered at the door, about to slip away, when Grandfather said, "Stay, Teo. Translate."

Reluctantly, I walked inside, folded my arms tight across my chest.

In the flickering light, the maestra eyed me uneasily. "You're the new boy at school."

I breathed in the beeswax and herb scents that always calmed me and tried to meet her gaze. It was like looking into the eyes of a snake. "I'm Teo," I said flatly. "I'll be the translator. My grandfather speaks Mixteco."

She hesitated, wringing her hands. "I don't know about this . . ."

"I'll translate," Uncle said, stepping closer to the maestra.

She recoiled, even less enthused about that option. "I'll go with Teo."

Uncle's shoulders fell and he glared at me. "I'll just watch, then."

"We can handle it, son," Grandfather said, ushering him outside and shutting the door.

"Have a seat," I told the maestra and motioned to a wooden chair. She sat on the front of the seat, ready to hop up and run out at the last minute.

I positioned chairs for Grandfather and me across from her. She wore a sour expression, as though she smelled something bad. *Leave*, I wanted to hiss at her. *Get out of my home.*

"Señor," she said to Grandfather, "I came to ask you to remove a curse."

He nodded as I translated. "Tell me more about this curse."

She shrank down, embarrassed. "Go ahead, Teo, tell him."

Of course, he already knew every gory detail of the glorious curse, but I repeated it anyway, relishing the stinky, itchy details.

Grandfather watched her with sympathy, and when I finished, he patted her shoulder.

At his touch, she buried her face in her hands and crumbled into tears.

Sudden bursts of tears were common in Grandfather's healing hut, so I shouldn't have been so stunned. There was something about this safe, candlelit place that had created a well-worn path for long-hidden tears. Most of all, it was Grandfather's gentle words, his compassionate touch, his way of gazing *into* people. He coaxed out their vulnerable side.

I'd had no idea Maestra María even had a vulnerable side.

Sniffing, she opened her purse and dabbed at her ruined makeup with a handkerchief. "Please, señor, can you remove it?"

He kept his hand on her shoulder and spoke kindly. "My daughter, they say no one but a Gypsy can remove a Gypsy curse."

As I translated, I made a half-hearted effort to capture his kindness in my voice, even though my hand still ached from her beating.

At the news, she murmured, "Oh, no, I was afraid of that." A new round of tears leaked out.

"But have you considered another option, daughter?" he said with smiling eyes.

"What?"

"Severing the curse by preventing children's tears."

She blinked. "How on earth would I do that?"

"Simply offer them kindness."

"You don't understand, señor. I have a class of little wild animals that I have to train and they can't even speak a civilized . . ." Her voice trailed off. She was probably remembering that I was one of those wild animals and that my grandfather couldn't speak a so-called civilized language.

"Perhaps," Grandfather said tenderly, "I can teach you some kind words in our tongue so that you may comfort the children."

She shook her head. "I can't speak that language. Not at school. The whole point is to teach them Spanish, the language of our country."

Grandfather tilted his head. "Their young minds are clever enough to learn both, so why not give them that gift?"

Rubbing her face, she said in a low voice, "My instructions are to beat their language out of them if I have to. I could be fired for allowing it in my class."

"Be brave," Grandfather said quietly. "Do what feels right in your heart, my daughter."

Again, she wiped her eyes, leaving dark smears of makeup, as if a mask were melting off. "You think if I use these words I'll break the curse?"

"Yes, my daughter. Of course, you'll need to keep using them so that the curse will not reattach. It will take practice to develop this new habit."

She let out a quivery breath. "All right."

Over the next hour, my grandfather and I taught her how to say words in Mixteco—*please, thank you, love, good, hug. Ñamani, tatsavini, kuu ini, yeu, sikita'an.*

Her pronunciation was horrible. I winced, hearing how she butchered our language. Yet as she struggled, Grandfather put his hand on her shoulder and told her in Mixteco, "Yeu. Good job, daughter. Clever student."

She laughed. But when she repeated his words, they came out harsh and choppy and without feeling.

"Imagine each word is a petal, daughter," Grandfather said. "A feather, something soft and light and tender."

She repeated the words, now in the same soothing tone as Grandfather's, and although her face was a mess of tear-smeared makeup, it looked pretty in a whole new way.

The words floated around like petals and feathers, until she smiled and said, "I think I can remember now. Thank you." She stood up, opening her purse. "How much do I owe you, señor?"

He shook his head. "You are my grandson's teacher. This is a gift to you."

I murmured the translation.

A few more tears slipped out. Still, she didn't leave.

He touched her shoulder again. "Is there something else, Daughter?"

She glanced at me and back at him. "I—I wasn't always like this. So bitter." Her words came from a deep place.

Sometimes words come from near the surface, and they sound flat and wispy. Then there are words that come from the caves of a person's soul—at least that's how Grandfather explained it. And these words were coming from a hidden place inside the maestra. They smelled musty and damp and true.

She sank back down into the chair. "My husband and I dreamed of having lots of children. But the years passed, and none came. We had a nice house, a nice car, nice clothes. But it wasn't enough. I needed a child. Then my husband died. I was grieving, but I had to work to keep my lifestyle. So I took this job, but it's torture spending all day with these children who aren't mine."

I translated under my breath as she spoke, trying to keep the shock from my voice. So there was a heart inside her after all—a shattered heart, its pieces encased in steel, but a heart all the same. I reminded myself she was the same evil woman who had beaten my hand just yesterday.

Maybe evil was simply pain in disguise.

"Pobrecita," Grandfather said. "Poor thing, you've been through so much. But I will help you. I'll give you soul cleansings and herbs that will sweeten and soften your heart, melt the wall around it."

The maestra nodded, sniffling and wiping her eyes.

We followed him into the smoke-filled kitchen, where my aunts were busy cooking beans over the hearth fire, grinding chile for salsa, patting *maza* into circles for tortillas. As Grandfather gathered the herbs, I introduced the maestra. She stood awkwardly, too tall for the squat kitchen. But she looked better now, refreshed after all her crying.

Politely, she greeted my aunts and asked, "Are one of you Teo's mother?"

My aunts looked at one another, shook their heads. "She's in there," Aunt Perla said, pointing with a spoon across the courtyard.

Maestra María smiled at me. "Perhaps I should say hello, tell her what a fine translator of a son she has." She was trying to be kind. But how could she know that meeting my mother would just lead to discomfort at best, misery at worst?

I took a breath. "Please, go ahead, Maestra," I said. "I'll help Grandfather finish with the herbs."

She gave me a strange look, and I glanced away. I couldn't bear to see people try to talk with my mother. I could forget about her craziness, let her dissolve into shadows, but when new eyes saw her, I had to remember.

The maestra bid my aunts good night, then walked across to the doorway of my mother's room. I turned away, unable to watch.

I focused on getting the dried herbs together, and by the time Grandfather and I had tied them with twine—all eight varieties—we went into the courtyard. Several minutes had passed, and I couldn't imagine what she'd been doing. My mother wasn't a conversationalist.

Sure enough, when Maestra María emerged from the room, she looked shaken. Sadly, she said to me in Mixteco, "Tatsavini." Thank you. The words floated to me like petals, strangely comforting.

She reached into her bag and pulled out a small notebook, brand-new, and a long, freshly sharpened pencil. "Since your grandfather won't accept payment, I hope you will accept a gift."

Holding the present gingerly, I thanked her. "Tatsavini."

Grandfather handed her the bundle of herbs. I translated his instructions to drink the tea twice a day, and to return to see him every evening for a week for spiritual cleanings to sweep away her bitterness.

She took his hand, held it in hers. "Tatsavini," she said, like the brush of a feather.

After Grandfather and I bid her farewell, and he disappeared into his room to rest, Uncle appeared from the shadows, reeking of shoe polish. The maestra was just teetering down the path when he took her elbow. "I'll walk you back to your car," he said.

"Oh, I'm fine," she said, continuing past the moonlit agave.

But Uncle followed her, insisting, "It's dangerous to walk by yourself. There are Gypsies lurking about."

As they walked into the darkness, I pressed my nose to the open notebook, breathed in the new-paper-and-glue scent. Even after she vanished, ghosts of rose petals lingered all around me.

21

STOLEN

*L*ater that night, laughter filled the plaza, rising into the night air above the Hill of Dust. Beside me, my cousins were rolling around in the dirt, clutching their bellies, shaking with laughter. The adults were laughing so hard they were crying. And I was laughing with more abandon than I had since Lucita and I would tickle each other as kids.

The audience was bigger than ever. Some of the other students had come with their families, a long walk from their villages. Little Benito and his brother Marcos were here with their own entourage of cousins and brothers and sisters.

The film was about a man named Cantinflas, whose mustache was short and missing the middle part, so it was just two ridiculous patches of hair on either side of his lips. He was a *pobre,* poor like us, but he found hilarious ways to put the powerful and rich in their place.

All was happy until an hour into the movie, when a man's shadow suddenly appeared in front of the screen.

He was just a silhouette. Who was it? He raised his hands and shouted something, something I couldn't hear well over the voices and music blaring from the speakers. He spoke in Spanish, and cursed often—that much I could tell.

From the audience came shouts of *Boo* and *Go away!*

But the man stayed, pacing and ranting before the screen. With a start, I recognized his telltale pointy-shoe limp and smug voice. Uncle Paco.

Nausea spread over me. I took hold of Flash and stroked him, in case I'd have to use him as a weapon again. I glanced back at the Duke, saw him grimly stick his half-eaten onion in his pocket, stop the projector, turn off the speakers.

The image paused on a close-up of Cantinflas's face cocked in a funny, sidelong expression beneath his pointy hat. But no one laughed now. The only sounds were the hum of the generator, the chirp of crickets.

Finally, Uncle Paco left the screen area, and I breathed out in relief. But now he was dragging someone—a woman—up there with him. She shielded her eyes from the projector beam.

My mother! She looked small and lost, helpless as he gripped her elbow.

A prickly heat filled me. Part of me wanted to run up and protect her, lead her back home to her safe little room. Another part wanted to shrink down and hide in embarrassment.

Instead, I hugged my animals and stayed seated.

"There is a thief here," Uncle shouted. "Someone stole this woman's prized earrings."

My mother's earrings? Stolen? I could picture them vividly—large, dangling half moons made of delicate, spiraling gold threads. A gift from her own mother on her wedding day. Who would take them from her box?

Grandfather appeared, panting, and touched Uncle's shoulder. In a low voice, in Mixteco, he spoke to his son.

Uncle shrugged him off, nearly knocking him over.

That did it. I leapt up and bolted forward. I held Grandfather steady and then carefully sat him down on my chair. Next, I retrieved my mother, slipping her arm from Uncle's hand, and led her to sit beside Grandfather.

Oblivious, Uncle was still ranting. "The Gypsy thieves stole it! They robbed a poor, vulnerable woman, my own sister!"

"What's going on?" I whispered to Grandfather.

He was still breathing hard from the walk over. "After you and the others left for the movie, son, your mother came to me, crying. She was checking her box like she always does and noticed the earrings were missing." Grandfather shook his head sadly. "Paco heard her and immediately accused the Rom."

Now Uncle was flailing his arms toward the Duke and Esma and Roza, all standing back near the projector. "That girl there! The lame girl! She was sneaking around our home."

He pointed directly to Esma.

Her eyes widened in shock, but she kept her head high. Once she translated for her grandparents, the Duke's chest puffed out angrily. His mustache leapt in indignation, the tips cocked back like fists ready to punch. He waved a large, threatening onion in the air, as if he might hurl it at Uncle. Roza bristled, shouting what I could only imagine were Gypsy curses as she pointed a finger at Uncle Paco.

My heartbeat filled my ears, along with the hot rush of blood. What could I do? The Duke had said if there was another scene, he would leave with his people and never come back. How could I stop this?

Esma stepped into the projector beam, suddenly illuminated, like a ghost. She was entirely lit up—her hair, her headscarf, her skirt, the coins and beads on her necklace. She declared, "I did not steal from this family. They are my friends." She raised her chin even higher in defiance. "And I am not the Lame Girl. I am Esma, Queen of Lightning."

Uncle took a menacing step toward her. She held her ground.

Now her uncles and the Duke came to her side. He had an onion in each hand now, grasping each so tightly his knuckles were white. His mustache twitched as if it could barely hold itself back.

A fight? If there was a fight, my friendship with Esma would be severed forever. My insides were sinking down, down. But I forced myself to stand tall, holding Flash ready.

And then, Benito walked to Esma's side. His brother followed. Each took her hand in a gesture of solidarity. In Mixteco, Benito belted out, so everyone could hear, "She's good. She helped us. And anyway, bad people don't sing!"

Then the other students emerged from the audience to stand at her side. Inspired, people from my village came to her side, until nearly everyone on the Hill of Dust was facing Uncle Paco. Heart swelling, I joined them with my animals.

My relatives stood up, their loyalty split, but finally walked to Esma's side. Everyone except for two uncles, who firmly took hold of Uncle Paco and led him away.

He struggled, red-faced. "I'm bringing the police tomorrow!" Uncle yelled. "They'll be happy for an excuse to put this trash behind bars."

After he was gone, people found their seats and quieted down, and the Duke smoothed his mustache and started the movie again. Yet I couldn't pay attention, couldn't rouse any laughter at the funny parts. I put my hand on my mother's. She sat, transfixed, not laughing at the jokes either, simply watching Cantinflas's antics in a slack-jawed daze.

Grandfather, looking exhausted, rested his hand on her other hand.

"You think she misplaced the earrings?" I whispered.

He shook his head. "I don't know, Teo. I don't know what to think."

I stroked Spark's ears and glanced back at Esma, who was standing with the Duke by the projector. "You think the Rom will leave? Before our gathering tomorrow night?"

"Who knows." He stood up shakily, casting a small shadow on the screen. "Let's get your mother home."

"We have to do something, Grandfather!"

He looked at me for a long moment. "All right, Teo. After your mother's settled back home, we'll pay the Rom a visit."

Later that night, Grandfather and I walked down the deserted, dark street toward the Rom camp. There was a distinct lack of music and dancing and singing, a stark contrast from our visit to their camp last year. And last year, Grandfather hadn't paused to catch his breath every few steps.

At the edge of the ring of wagons, I called out, "¡Buenas noches!" And then, peering inside the circle, I noticed the bustle of activity. By the light of the bonfire, the Rom were rolling up carpets and filling sacks with pots and utensils. Packing up?

When they caught sight of us, chatter rippled through them. Soon the Duke appeared, and then Roza and Esma. Her hair was disheveled, her face tearstained, her shoulders slumped, as if all the lightning had drained out of her.

Something was wrong, very wrong.

"Come in, friends," the Duke said in heavily accented Spanish, his mustache hanging down, forlorn. He gestured at tree stumps by the fire. "Please, sit down."

The table and chairs must have been stashed inside a wagon already. I sat, and a plume of smoke blew right into my face, stinging my eyes.

"I'm sorry we have no tea ready to offer, but as you can—" Esma's voice cracked as she translated. "As you can see, we're leaving at dawn."

"We have to avoid the police," Roza said apologetically, turning her pipe over in her thick hands. "They don't treat us fairly. That's why we stick to villages like yours, out here in the mountains. But now, with that man falsely accusing my granddaughter . . ."

Esma sniffled and wiped her eyes, reluctantly translating.

"Don't leave!" I said. "Please! I'll find the thief, prove Esma's innocence. Just give me another day, please!"

Grandfather added, "I will make sure my son doesn't contact the police."

The Duke looked at Roza with doubt. Esma looked at her with a last wisp of hope.

The Mistress of Destiny's nose twitched as she considered and then conferred with the Duke, shaking her head.

"My grandfather says no," Esma said softly, after her grandfather spoke. "It's not worth the risk. He's—we're sorry."

Our eyes met, and another tear slipped from hers. Her tears scared me. This was not a girl who let go of hope easily. Seeing her like this, I understood she'd begged and pleaded with her grandparents, done everything she could to convince them. I understood that if they left tomorrow morning, they would never come back.

Grandfather reached out his hand for Roza's. He locked eyes with her. In a low voice, he said, "You and I know my true fortune, Mistress. Here is my last request to you: Come to the event tomorrow."

I translated, knowing there was much below his words, things that passed between him and the Mistress of Destiny, things that unnerved me.

After a long while of gnawing on her pipe, she said something to the Duke. He protested, but she repeated it more firmly.

Finally, he nodded his head and barked out an order to his people. They stopped packing, puzzled. And then, shrugging and grumbling, they began to unpack.

Esma threw her arms around the Duke, and then around Roza. "We'll stay!" she said, doing three wild twirls. "We'll stay!"

And my heart rose with the smoke and sparks, up to the stars.

As Grandfather and I walked slowly back home, we were silent. Part of me was dancing inside at the good news; part of me felt off-balance with so many unsaid things just below the surface. *Grandfather's true fortune.* What exactly had made the Mistress of Destiny change her mind?

I didn't ask Grandfather about it. I said only, "Thank you."

He nodded, rested a hand on my shoulder. "You know, Teo. That was the first movie I've seen. And it makes me think. Life is like a movie."

"How?"

"We get so involved, we think that's all there is, what's on the screen. We laugh, we cry, we love. We forget that if we only moved our eyes away, we'd see so much more."

He squeezed my shoulder, said softly, "I'm near the end of my movie, son."

My chest clenched, making it hard to breathe. "Are you scared?"

"Not a bit. I've already been glancing off-screen all my life. And after I'm gone, you can, too. Just take a little break from your own movie, turn your head, and find me there."

So this was the unspoken, true fortune. That my grandfather's final credits were rolling.

UNLIKELY THIEF

$\mathscr{F}$resh morning sunlight streamed into the classroom as Maestra María greeted the students in hesitant, broken Mixteco. At least it showed some effort. "*Yo'o naa yo.*" Good morning.

The students' eyes grew wide, and most said nothing, probably suspecting a trap. A few brave souls answered in Mixteco. "*Yo'o naa yo*, Maestra."

She offered a crooked upturn of lips, still far from a real smile.

No, she hadn't changed overnight. Throughout the day, after a few minutes of kindness, she'd forget and fall back into the usual hard-edged words. Then at some point, seeing a student's troubled face, she'd stop herself, take a breath, and say something in choppy Mixteco. She'd drop her voice, and her eyes would flick furtively toward the door, as if at any moment, her superiors would burst in and fire her on the spot.

Be brave, I silently urged her.

By the end of the day, two facts were clear to all the students. First, the ruler had not budged from its spot on the desk where Esma had laid it. And second, Maestra María, beyond all belief, was trying to be nice. Of course, not all her words were petals; not all her words were even understandable. But she was making patient baby steps toward kindness. And baby steps toward respecting our language and people.

After school, instead of racing home, or positioning themselves at a safe distance beneath the tree to talk, the students gathered just outside the door. They showered me with questions, peering at the maestra from the corners of their eyes. And their questions were in Mixteco, testing the new limits of our teacher.

Exhilarated, Marcos said, "She's changed because of the Gypsy curse, hasn't she, Teo?"

"Where did she learn Mixteco?" asked Benito.

And from the others: "Is she really different now?"

"Will she keep being nice to us?"

"How long will this last?"

I shrugged at the barrage of questions. I couldn't tell them about her visit with Grandfather; that was confidential. But my silence only drove them to further grill me.

"Hey, did your mother ever get her earrings back?"

"Did you guys find the thief?"

"It wasn't a Gypsy, was it?"

"The Gypsies are nice! No, it couldn't have been them, right?"

I stayed quiet and let them interrupt one another. I was still embarrassed that my mother had been exposed last night. It felt better with her shut in her room, involved in her own strange rituals.

"Who's the real thief?"

"Yeah, who is it?"

"Teo, come on, tell us, what do you think? Who could have broken in and stolen them?"

That, precisely, was the question that had been flitting in and out of my mind all day. If I caught the real thief, then I could prove Esma's and the Rom's innocence. Then maybe, just maybe, they'd return next year.

"My mother might have lost them," was all I said. Yet last night, after the movie, we'd looked everywhere for the earrings, with no luck. Even if my mother had misplaced them, we would have come across them.

I looked away from the kids' eager faces, inside to the maestra, packing up. And I caught a glimpse of gold poking out from the pocket on her bag. I squinted, watching carefully.

As she arranged her pens and pencils in the pocket, she removed a pair of large, dangling earrings. Lacy half moons. My mother's earrings. Just as quickly, the maestra tucked the jewelry back into the pocket with the pens.

I glanced at the other kids to see if anyone else saw. But no, they were still deeply involved in their own speculations.

Maestra María was the thief? It felt like a kick in the stomach. Before today, I would have welcomed the chance to see her carted off to prison. But today, today I'd actually started to *like* her. To *want* to come to school.

Yesterday evening, she'd disappeared into my mother's room and stayed there, alone with her for several minutes . . . supposedly to compliment my translation skills. Maybe she'd had other motives. And maybe she'd assumed my mother was too crazy to notice something was gone.

I leaned against the door frame, shaken to the core. I'd believed her heart had opened last night; I'd believed she liked using feather-soft words. But no, her kindness was only for selfish reasons, to avoid the curse. There was something even more heartless about pretending to open your heart. The betrayal was deeper.

The maestra walked toward the doorway, and we all backed up a little. The chattering stopped.

"It's fine with me if you speak your language," she said with a smile, a little less crooked than before.

The students looked relieved; they'd hoped for this, but it was good to hear from her mouth.

"So, what are you talking about?" She'd never shown any interest in our lives until today, but now she seemed genuine.

The boys looked at one another, gauging the situation. If they told her they watched a movie shown by the Rom, would she be angry? After all, it had been a Romani girl who cursed her. An older boy spoke. "We went to see the movie last night."

"A movie?" she asked, surprised. "In the city?"

"No, in Teo's village. The Gypsies showed it."

Maestra María sucked in a breath. "I see."

Encouraged that the maestra wasn't angry, the boy continued. "Teo's mother had something stolen from her last night. Earrings. In the middle of the movie, his uncle stood up and accused the Gypsies."

The maestra paled, blinked, clutched her bag. "Well, children, I must be going," she said quickly.

She glanced back at me on the way to her car. "I'll see your grandfather later this evening, all right?"

I said nothing, only stared at her climbing into her car. She dared return to our home? Was she going to steal something else from us? But why? She had enough money. She even had her own car! Maybe that car hadn't come from her dead husband. Maybe she'd stolen that, too.

Fleeing the students' next round of questions, I started running home.

Halfway there, I slowed to a walk, breathing hard. It felt good to run, to feel my blood zooming and my heart pumping. As I rested, doubled over, I remembered that this evening was the gathering for my sister, the Romani Business Appreciation Event.

My thieving teacher would show up right in the middle of a bunch of Rom, who she could easily blame for anything else she'd steal.

And this was to be my last night with Esma for a whole year. At this rate, maybe forever.

SECOND ANNUAL ROMANI
BUSINESS APPRECIATION EVENT

*J*n the silvery-blue twilight, our Romani guests stood before Grandfather's mosaic, oohing and ahhing. Beneath the tree, the rectangle of colored sawdust featured a girl with dark hair and a red skirt and purple flowers swirling around her. Golden rays surrounded her like an angel's halo—or bolts of lightning—depending on your perspective.

To the Rom, the girl was Esma, a gesture to show we didn't share in Uncle Paco's suspicions. A sign of solidarity.

To my people, it was Lucita dancing in heaven, bathed in beams of celestial light.

Soon my aunts were handing out hot cinnamon-chocolate and sweet tamales, commanding us, "Eat! Eat!"

They had spent all day cooking, and a good thing, too, because every inhabitant of the Hill of Dust was gathered here in the candlelight, together with the Rom. Words in broken

Spanish flitted around the nighttime courtyard. Feelings filled the spaces between words, between my people and our visitors. There was appreciation, as warm as steaming tamales. But there was also fear that the ugly scene from last night could repeat itself.

The villagers said, "Oh, how sad we are you're leaving tomorrow!"

And the Rom said, "How sad we are to leave!"

"You'll come back, won't you?" the villagers asked.

To this, the Rom vaguely nodded, casting nervous glances at Uncle, who was skulking around the shadowy edges of our courtyard.

Grandfather had made him promise not to contact the police and not to stir up trouble. Uncle knew he was outnumbered, but still, I cringed at the thought of him ruining this night. What if he'd disobeyed Grandfather? What if the police were on their way?

When I'd told Grandfather about the stolen earrings in Maestra María's bag, he'd nodded, eyebrows furrowed in thought, and said, "If Paco accuses the Rom again, you can tell everyone your suspicions of the maestra. Otherwise, let's keep this quiet for now."

I didn't want to keep it quiet. I wanted to shout it out to the entire Hill of Dust, clear the Rom's name for good. It was even harder to bite my tongue when, through the crowd, I caught sight of Maestra María.

She wore a pale pink skirt and a white cotton blouse, and

her hair was gathered in a girlish, pink-ribboned ponytail. She'd probably chosen her outfit to suggest innocence. And she'd brought her large white bag, perfect for stashing more stolen goods. It made my stomach turn.

Her face held a mystified expression as she looked around, her lipstick glittering in stray light from flames and stars. Her eyes landed on me.

"Buenas noches, Teo," she said, weaving through the crowd. "What's going on here?"

"I forgot to tell you," I said flatly. "It's a kind of party." I hesitated, unsure how to explain our annual event to an outsider. "A joint celebration to honor my sister's death and a Romani Business Appreciation Event."

"Romani?" she asked, confused.

"Gypsy," I said, an edge to my voice.

She squinted at the throng of Rom. She held her bag closer, as if she were afraid *they* would steal from *her*. "These are all Gypsies?" she asked in disbelief. "You invited them to your house?"

I leveled my gaze at her. I wanted to grab her bag and dump out the contents and reveal her as the thief. "You were wrong about our language," I said evenly. "You're wrong about the Rom, too." I couldn't help adding, "They're not the thieves around here."

She gave me a strange look, but before she could say anything, Aunt Perla came by and offered her a gourd full of chocolate and a sweet *tamal*.

"Tatsavini," the maestra said in awkward Mixteco. Thank you.

My muscles clenched at the sound of her speaking our language, pretending. She ate the food, drank the drink, even tried complimenting it. "Yeu." Good.

I watched her, wondering what she had planned. Because she *did* have something planned. I could tell by the way her eyes flickered around, the way she fiddled with the zipper of her bag, the way her eyebrows pressed together, the tips up like vulture wings.

Then she said, "Is your uncle here? The one who escorted me to my car last night?"

She had to be the only person in town who actually wanted to see Uncle Paco.

"Over there," I said, pointing with my chin.

The maestra headed over to Uncle. On seeing her, his face lit up. He tucked in the tail of his shirt and wiped his hands on his pants. He grabbed an empty chair and set it between them, gesturing for her to sit.

But she didn't sit. She stood tall. And in the evil voice she hadn't used all day—the Heartless Woman voice—the maestra called out, "I'd like everyone's attention, please."

Oh no oh no oh no. This could not be good.

Rom and Mixteco alike stopped talking and stared at her. There were murmurs of "la mujer sin alma" . . . "la devoradora" . . . the woman without a soul, the devourer . . . "María Félix, the movie star herself!" She was indeed a sight to behold, the flames illuminating her gorgeous face, casting dramatic shadows beneath her cheekbones, accentuating the long, curved eyebrows.

Her expression, at the moment, was as ruthless as I'd ever seen.

She kicked off her heels and climbed onto the chair. Towering over us all, she demanded, "Where is the Gypsy girl who came to my classroom yesterday?"

Oh no oh no oh no. The maestra was going to wreak vengeance on Esma. I had to do something. I had to protect her. I had to save her.

As Esma loped forward, I stepped beside her, wishing I were brave enough to hold her hand. Instead, I kept my hands on Flash, wriggling around my collar, in case I had to threaten the maestra with him.

"What is your name again, señorita?" Maestra María asked.

"Esma," she replied, chin high. "Queen of Lightning."

My heartbeat filled me like thunder. I whispered to Flash, "Get ready."

"Esma, Queen of Lightning," the maestra continued, "did your curse say anything about the tears of a grown man?"

I blinked, confused. This was not what I'd expected.

Esma tilted her head, curious, then shook it. "Only tears of a child."

The maestra smiled. She opened the side pocket of her bag and pulled out the golden crescent earrings. She raised a finger like a magic wand and pointed it at Uncle Paco in the same way that Esma had pointed at her the previous morning at school.

"I'd like to make it clear," the maestra said, "that this man gave me these earrings as a gift when he escorted me to my car yesterday."

Uncle stumbled backward as if he'd been hit.

A wave of shock, and then relief, washed over me. Once I found my voice, I translated to Mixteco, shouting so that everyone could hear.

"Is this true?" my other uncles asked.

Uncle Paco shook his head and sputtered, "She's crazy, I didn't . . ."

"Do not lie to me," the maestra commanded, pulling her ruler from the bag. Would she actually smack him with it?

Her eyes, beneath their arched brows, bored into his, until finally, he muttered, "I took them."

For several more minutes, the maestra yelled at him and shamed him. All the yelling and shaming she'd saved up in the past day of kindness burst out, straight at Uncle. On and on she raged, her words stronger and more vicious than any ruler.

And his tears came. His tears came and he sank to the ground, a salty, wet heap in the dust.

Grandfather whispered to me, "Sometimes a heart needs to be broken open, doesn't it?"

Later, after Grandfather led Uncle into the curing room, and after the earrings were safely back in my mother's box, and after Maestra María came down from the chair, she approached Esma. For a long moment the maestra stared at her. Then, with a frown, she said, "I suppose I should thank you."

"Me?" Esma's eyes widened.

"For showing me that trick of standing on chairs." The corner of Maestra María's mouth tipped up into the tiniest hint of a smile. And then, just as fast, went back to a frown.

"You're welcome, Maestra," Esma said, almost shyly.

At that moment, the maestra's ears perked up, and she turned in the direction of the toddlers. Da and Ba were stuffing their little cheeks with tamales, but Ga was looking at hers, which had just fallen to the ground. Flash scrambled over and dragged it away.

Ga's lip quivered, and her face scrunched itself into that look a face gets just before the wailing starts.

Maestra María flew over to Ga, grabbing a new tamal on the way, and just in time, stuck it in the child's hand. Ga's face rearranged itself into a smile, and she took a huge bite. The maestra stayed beside her, kneeling down, chatting with her and the other two. Tears averted. More links in the chain broken. And yes, from the way the maestra stroked the girl's tendril, she just might have been enjoying herself.

Late into the night, right before everyone left, Esma sang a song for Lucita. A song of longing and missing and hoping. I felt Lucita's presence strongly, as if she were beside me. As if Esma's voice were so powerful, it made me turn away from the movie of my life and look into the other realm where Lucita dwelled.

Esma's voice brought tears to other people's eyes, too; perhaps they felt their own loved and lost ones at their sides. I wished my mother could hear it, but she'd already disappeared into her room with the box.

No wonder Esma's songs had enchanted the music agent. No wonder he wanted to bring this voice to the rest of the world. Despite everything it would mean, I wanted other people to hear her songs, not just people on the Hill of Dust and other Mixteco villages, but people in far-off lands.

Tears streamed down Maestra María's face as she listened. Now there was no crookedness at all in her smile. It was pure and sweet and laced with salt water. And when she bid me and Esma good night, she sniffled and said, "Esma, Queen of Lightning, your voice can bring back the dead. At least for a few precious moments it can. I thank you for that gift."

24

UNCLE PACO'S STORY

*E*very tear holds a story. That's what Grandfather always said. Judging by the tears spewing from Uncle Paco, he must have been holding in a sea of stories.

Even more tears flooded out after Grandfather gave him a *limpia* to clean his spirit. That meant spitting on him with cactus liquor and beating him with bundles of herbs. And now, in the aftermath, tearstained and huddled in the corner of the healing hut, Uncle Paco looked like a half-drowned rat, soaking wet, shivering, small, and meek.

I paused at the doorway, unsure whether to enter. My animals trailed behind me, full and sluggish after so many scraps of tamales. The last of our visitors had just left, leaving ghosts of loved ones lingering among the chocolate-crusted drinking gourds and corn husks.

Grandfather sat in an exhausted heap beside Uncle, holding a limp, damp bundle of *ruda* leaves.

"Everything all right?" I asked, more concerned for Grandfather than Uncle. Grandfather was usually asleep by this time of night. It took energy to perform a limpia, more than he now had.

Grandfather nodded weakly. "Teo, will you sit with your uncle while he drinks the tea?"

I was not enthused about being alone with Uncle in his soul-shaken state. Patients could react in all kinds of strange and unexpected ways after a limpia—from sobbing to laughing to beating the ground. But Grandfather needed my help. And I remembered what he'd said about finding strength to help those you hate. Those you *think* you hate. With a sigh, I said, "All right."

After bidding Grandfather good night, I sat on his now empty chair. Spark, Thunder, and Flash curled up by my feet.

In the flickering candlelight, I watched Uncle sip his tea and wondered when I could leave to go to sleep.

My eyelids were just fluttering shut when he spoke, in slow, soft words.

"I left this village for the city three years ago, Nephew. I planned to work in construction, make money for a house, a big one, and a big piece of land." He flung out his arms in a gesture of hugeness, splashing his tea. "I was going to come back here in a big, fancy car. I was going to find a beautiful wife."

He paused, looking at his feet, which were now bare. He'd taken off his pointy shoes for the limpia, leaving them in the opposite corner, out of place in the earthen-walled, dirt-floored room.

"But you want to know a secret, Nephew?"

"What?"

"People there taunted my goat-hide sandals, said my feet were like animal claws." He flexed his toes, spotted with oozing blisters. "They called me a backward indio, said I spoke Spanish like a fool. They cheated me out of my wages on construction jobs. When I complained, no one listened."

As he spoke, he stroked Spark's velvet ears, the first time he'd given my animals any affection. The calming powers of her ears were working their magic on Uncle, tapping into his own tender spots.

He leaned in closer and whispered, "I rooted through trash cans for food. I sat on the ground begging. Then I crawled back with my tail between my legs. Worst of all, I've treated my family the way I was treated."

Uncle reached down and picked up my skunk. He held Flash in the air, pointed the bushy tail at his own, tear-streaked face. "Go ahead," he said. "Spray me, I deserve it."

Flash thought Uncle was playing. He squirmed out of his grasp, climbed onto his shoulder, and nibbled at his collar.

"Why won't he spray me?" Uncle said miserably.

"He likes you now," I observed.

Uncle gave a quiet laugh, then ran his hand over Flash's

white stripe. "When I came back, I was ashamed I had nothing, nothing at all to offer a wife or anyone else. Then I saw that beautiful teacher with her fancy car, and I thought, *Maybe it's not too late*. But I needed to offer her something, so I took my sister's earrings." He buried his face in his hands. "I didn't think she'd notice."

Silence for a few moments. I had no idea what to say, so I tried to think of what Grandfather would say. "Do you want to change, Uncle?"

He paused, stared at the ceiling as Flash nestled into his neck. "Yes."

Again, I channeled Grandfather. I'd seen him with so many patients, it was easy to imagine his responses and questions. "Will you work hard at it?"

Uncle looked me in the eyes. "Yes."

"Then I will help you. Every day I will give you limpias and teas, and you must follow my instructions."

It felt strange hearing myself talk to Uncle this way, but it was how Grandfather spoke with all his patients, firmly, asking them questions, making sure they felt committed.

After bidding Uncle good night, I walked across the courtyard toward my room. Spark and Thunder wobbled sleepily behind me, while Flash, most lively at night, darted in spirals around my feet. Inside, my mother sat in the corner, the lantern casting eerie shadows over her face. She cradled her earrings in her hands.

I swallowed. "Are you all right, Mother?"

She rocked with her earrings. I wished she would touch me with such tenderness, gaze at my face the way she gazed into the lifeless silver and gold.

Kneeling at her side, I kissed her cheek. "I can help you, Mother. If you want to get better. Do you?"

No answer.

I put Flash into her lap, hoping he might make her laugh the way he did for Uncle.

But she only shrugged off the skunk.

I put her hand on Spark's magic ears, but she quickly moved it back to the cold metal.

Still on my knees, I begged, "Please, please, Mother. Let me help you."

Silence. I scooped Flash from the ground and gathered Spark and Thunder close and felt their warm, pulsing bodies, all feathers and fur and devotion.

I hoped they would be enough.

25

SCREAM STREAM

*B*uenos días, Teo, my friend for life!" Esma's voice rang out across the courtyard, competing with the roosters' morning crows. And a moment later, she came into view on the path, waving and loping along, swinging a red bucket.

"Esma?" I sputtered. I'd been washing my face at the cistern, and now water dripped from my chin. I'd slept badly last night, knowing she'd be leaving today, Saturday. Now my grogginess vanished. I was suddenly alert and wide-eyed, as if a shooting star had just plopped in front of me.

"How did you get away?" A bewildered grin took over my face. "And where are the kids?"

"Back at camp. I'm free!" She spun in a joyful circle, and then grew serious. "I only have an hour before my caravan leaves. Let's go to the river." She tugged at my arm. "Come on!"

I wiped my face on my shirt, then grabbed some tortillas and salt and lime for breakfast. And we headed into el monte, with my animals following. Thunder whistled and huffed, annoyed that I'd interrupted her own washing routine in the irrigation ditch, but Flash scurried happily along, always up for adventure. And Spark ambled sweetly behind us, munching on weeds and shrubs.

As we walked, I couldn't help staring at Esma, memorizing every last wild lock of hair poking out from beneath her scarf, every shell woven into her braids. "How did you manage this, Esma?" I asked, breathless. "More creative storytelling?"

"Actually, no!" Her eyes lit up. "I woke up before dawn to someone hitting my head. I opened my eyes and there was my grandmother's nose looming over me. She whispered, 'Squash head, go out and fill this bucket with berries.'

"'But what about the toddlers and packing up?' I asked.

"She tugged my braid. 'I'll handle it,' she said. 'You go.'

"'But I've never even found berries before,' I said.

"'Of course you haven't, squash head. Maybe you can find a local to show you some.'

"Again, she hit my head and stared at me, like we had a secret."

Gratitude toward the Mistress of Destiny filled me. "Your grandmother wanted you to find me," I said slowly. "She wanted us to be together. She wants to help our fortune come true."

When we reached the boulder beneath the tree, Thunder resumed her preening and fluffing in the river, while the other animals curled up with us.

Esma sang a tune beneath her breath as we squeezed lime and sprinkled salt on the tortillas. The melody of water was her instrument, and her voice mingled with its currents, as though her song came from a hidden spring inside the earth.

After we ate the tortillas, Esma brushed the salt from her hands and said, "Let's write our names in the dirt."

"I have something better," I said, and pulled out the fresh pencil and notebook that Maestra María had given me, which I'd stuck in the sack with the food. "This is for you."

Esma held the gifts like precious jewels, and then opened the first pages, beaming.

"I wrote the alphabet for you, see?" I pointed. "And some words with pictures beside them. The rest of the pages you can fill up yourself with practice."

"Thank you, Teo. You don't know how much this means to me."

She put the notebook and pencil in her deep dress pocket and pulled out the business card. "I'll have to hide these well. If any of my people knew I was learning to read . . ."

"What?" I asked. "What would happen?"

"Many years ago, before I was born, there was a Romani girl, back in Eastern Europe, the land my ancestors traveled. Her name was Papusza. Doll. She was a singer and poet, and she wanted to learn to read."

Esma stood up and began spinning. She didn't sit still much. Inside her whirled the force of storms, which she had to let out. Still swirling slowly, she said, "So Papusza gave food to gadjé villagers in exchange for reading lessons and books. Then her family caught her. Beat her. Destroyed her books."

Esma paused in her spinning and gazed grimly at the horizon.

My muscles tensed. "So what did she do?"

"She kept at it anyway!" Esma said, head high. "She wrote her poetry and sang her songs, and then, one day, a famous poet, a gadjo, discovered her talent."

My heart flew. "So it was a happy ending."

Esma shook her head. Her hand reached out for Spark's ear, and she rubbed it gently. "When Papusza entered the gadjé world, our people rejected her, declared her unclean. Marime. And the gadjé took advantage of her, used her songs for their purposes. Her sorrow was so deep, she lost her mind. Now she doesn't sing or write poetry. She's alone and abandoned, forgotten by the gadjé and scorned by my people."

Now Esma was rubbing both of Spark's ears, one with each hand. Then she sank down beside me and pulled out the notebook and pencil and business card, staring at them.

I shivered in the morning light. I wanted to grab back the notebook and pencil if they would lead Esma down the same path as Papusza. "Are you sure you want to do this, Esma?"

"I'll find a way to make my ending happy."

"But is that possible?"

"Anything is possible, Teo." She paused. "And I know that even if . . . even if I have to say good-bye forever to my people, you will be my friend. My loyal friend until the end of our long lives. And that makes me brave."

I reached out and tugged her braid. And then her other. "I'll always be here for you, squash head." Lightly, I tapped her temple.

Her face softened. "When I leave, I'll never see my grandmother again. So it will be up to you to remind me of her. How she taps my head and tugs my braid. How she calls me squash head."

"Sure," I said, my heart thudding, not from fear now but from the opposite. "Just don't make me start chewing on a pipe."

She laughed and leaned in to tap the brim of my hat. "Thanks, squash head." She gave me a sad smile, leaned in farther, and said softly, "There's more, Teo."

My breath caught in my throat. "What?"

"Remember how we were camped with other caravans for a time? And I saved everyone from the fire?"

I nodded and swallowed.

"Well, it caught the attention of a horrible, old, ugly, widowed man. And he decided he wants to marry me, even with my lightning-struck hand and leg. My father made a deal with him."

My mouth grew parched. I struggled for words. "A-a deal?"

"The geezer said he'll pay a bride-price for me. He wants to marry me next year."

Black stars filled the edges of my vision, moving in. "Will you do it?"

"Of course not, squash head! That man would suck the lightning right out of me. I'll leave long before that happens." She jutted out her chin, but her voice wavered, just a little. "I *will* be a famous singer."

"Esma," I breathed. Our faces were close. "How can I save you?"

"Just by being here," she whispered. "Being you. My loyal friend for eternity."

"I promise," I said. "I always will be." I moved my face even closer, till our noses were nearly touching, and then I didn't know what to do next, so I whispered, "Let's scream."

She smiled and stood up. "Let's scream."

And so we spun and screeched and spun. Thunder let out a disapproving whistle, and Spark just sat there, puzzled in her blindness, and Flash ran excited circles around us. The creatures and Esma soon became a patchwork blur as I grew dizzier and dizzier.

Finally, breathless and hoarse, we collapsed on the ground. "You know," I admitted, "sometimes I come out here and scream alone."

She smiled. "Scaring off the stream spirits?"

"They're long gone."

She tilted her head at me. "Why do you scream, then?"

I looked at the sky. "My mother. It's like she's already gone. A ghost. I've offered to heal her, but she's refused."

Esma was rebraiding her hair, and she paused to say, "Maybe you can only put the spark of life back inside someone who wants it."

"I wish she wanted it." I hesitated. "And my grandfather . . ." I forced myself to continue. "I don't know how much longer he'll be here." I shared my deepest fear. "I'll be alone, Esma."

She adjusted her scarf, then quietly said, "You're stronger than you think, Teo."

It was an echo of her grandmother's fortune to me—the false fortune. Or maybe not so false after all. "But, Esma, you have lightning in your blood. You have powers. I'm just a regular boy."

She finished knotting her scarf at her nape. Then, matter-of-factly, she said, "Teo, I wasn't struck by lightning."

A wave of something crushed me. Something sickening and heavy. Betrayal. "You lied to me?" I sputtered.

"Creative storytelling," she said sheepishly.

It was one thing to do creative storytelling with others. Not with her supposed best friend for life. I'd shown her the deepest, most hidden pieces of me—about Lucita and my mother and father—while she'd been *lying*? I'd even told her the burning-drowning words. Why had I trusted her?

Suddenly I was steaming with humiliation. Without a

word, I stood up and walked away. My animals made scuffling sounds as they followed me. At least they were loyal friends.

"Teo, wait!" Esma called out.

I didn't turn around. But I noticed my legs slowing, just a little, as her lopsided, running footsteps grew closer.

She gripped my arm with her good hand. "Let me explain."

Her fingers dug into my flesh, as though she'd hang on forever if need be. Still, I could probably tear my arm away if I pulled hard enough.

I didn't. I didn't because even though her lightning was a lie, it was there. It was there and it was zipping through her fingertips into my arm, through my blood, swirling and blazing in my chest.

Gritting my teeth, I stopped beside a boulder and turned to face her. "So how did you get lame?" I asked, knowing she hated that word.

With a sigh, she released her grip. She tapped her leg, held up her twisted hand. "Polio."

The word struck a deep fear, this disease everyone dreaded. My rage shifted to something else. "Then why . . . ," I began.

"I couldn't bear to be weak, Teo. I couldn't bear people calling me 'the Lame Girl.'"

I swallowed hard, wishing I could take back the word. This was Esma showing me her own deepest, most hidden spots— me, of all the people in the world. It was a gift for me alone, her friend for life.

"I made myself into the Queen of Lightning," she continued, fingering the coins at her neck. "And you know, after all this time talking about lightning in my blood, I've started believing it. I've started feeling it."

"Me, too," I admitted. She could work magic. One moment, I'd felt hurt and angry. The next, honored that she'd confided in me. And now, *inspired*, as though anything were possible, if I believed it enough.

She climbed onto the rock, raised her arms. "If you believe you're weak, you'll be weak. You're cursing yourself. Yet if you believe you're strong, you'll be strong. Give yourself a fortune and make it come true."

Her words lodged inside me, the way the lightning had. It didn't matter that lightning hadn't actually struck her. It was there, illuminating everything she did, and now it had flowed into the currents of my own blood.

In the distance, thunder rolled, a rumble through my bones.

We looked to the horizon, where strange, yellowish clouds had gathered. And suddenly, Esma said, "Oh, no! I'm such a squash head. It's been an hour, hasn't it? I have to get back to my camp."

She held up the empty bucket. "Any chance we'll find berries on the way?"

"I doubt it," I said. And then, with a smile, I climbed up beside her on the rock, spread my arms, and said, "Here is your fortune, my queen: In your bucket, very soon, there will appear berries!"

BERRIES

*E*sma's bucket was still empty as we approached her camp, bustling with people packing to leave. I slowed, breathing in the smoke and spice of their morning tea, not ready to say good-bye.

But instead of stopping, Esma suddenly yanked on my arm and pulled me in a wide arc around the cluster of wagons. She ducked behind a bush and, in an urgent whisper, said, "I have to say good-bye to your grandfather."

"But your people—they're about to leave."

"This is important!" she insisted, and took off running toward my house.

Soon we'd reached the courtyard, where Grandfather was sipping chamomile tea, slumped in a chair. He straightened up and brightened when Esma came over. "Buenos días, Queen. Have a seat and some tea!"

"I only have a minute," Esma said, pulling up a chair. "I want to thank you. For helping Teo and me. For the Romani Business Appreciation Event. For everything."

"Thank you, Queen," he said tenderly.

At that moment, a squabble broke out among Thunder and the turkeys. As I went to calm them, Grandfather leaned in to Esma, speaking softly.

I grabbed Thunder from the chaos of feathers, tucked her beneath my arm, and shushed her. Secretly, I strained to over-hear Grandfather's conversation. After some mumbling, I heard, "I have a favor to ask you, Esma." His Spanish was thickly accented, barely understandable.

"Anything," she replied.

I inched closer, ears perked, looking in the opposite direction and feigning interest in Thunder.

"After I'm gone, keep an eye on Teo's spark. If it leaves, put it back. Even if it seems impossible." He spoke slowly, deliberately, searching for the right words in Spanish. "You brought him back from the dead last year, Esma. Never doubt your power. Or your fortune. You two will be friends for the rest of your long lives."

A woman's voice rang through the morning air. "¡Buenos días!" And then, a greeting in accented Mixteco, asking how I was. "Nixi yo'o?"

Maestra María.

I raised my hand in welcome, and answered, "Yo'o sunii."

She was smiling, heading toward us, carrying a cloth bag.

"I came by to thank you for last night. I picked these up for you at the market."

She opened the bag to reveal hundreds of plump, red, glistening berries.

Esma and I exchanged wide-eyed looks.

When I could find words, I said, "Let's give them to Esma's people. As a farewell gift."

Grandfather and the maestra nodded in approval, and I dumped the berries into Esma's pail.

Grandfather smiled with his eyes. "Now there will be sweetness to add to the sorrow of their parting. All partings have a hint of sweetness, if you let them."

Along with the other folks on the Hill of Dust, Grandfather insisted on seeing off the Rom. I held one elbow while Uncle held the other, and we made our way down the dusty road to their camp. The horses were already hitched to the wagons, stomping their feet, ready to go. The toddlers were strapped onto women's backs, munching on berries, their faces stained and sticky and happy.

Esma and her grandparents approached us just before leaving. The Duke's mustache shone with fresh wax, spiraling up at the tips. Warmly, they shook Grandfather's and my hands good-bye.

Uncle stared sheepishly at the ground, muttering good-bye, and then whispered, "Sorry about everything."

The Duke grasped his hand and said, "Let us offer you a gift to show there are no hard feelings."

Esma translated this, her voice suspicious, unsure what her grandparents were up to.

The Duke slipped his hand into his jacket pocket. No raw onions, I silently pleaded.

But no, it was the little diosito statue that I'd given them last year, to ensure their return. He placed it in Uncle's hands.

"This did indeed give us good luck last year, and now we're passing it to you, so that you, too, may have good luck."

I wasn't sure what to make of this. It was a kind gesture of forgiveness, but there was something more to it. He was also ridding himself of the supposed curse, ridding himself of the need to return next year.

Worried, I looked at Esma. This was a surprise to her, too, judging by her scrunched-up expression.

"Will you come back, Duke?" I asked, steadying my voice.

He shrugged, twirling the ends of his mustache. "We go where the wind takes us. Of course, we do love your village, but you never know what the wind will blow away and what new things it will bring."

Translating slowly, stretching out our last moments together, Esma locked eyes with me. *Friends for life* were the unspoken words between us. No matter what, *friends for life*.

She held up her hand in farewell, and I held up mine.

Lightning zapped from her palm across the air into my own, an electric surge of confidence that only the two of us felt.

Yet, a few minutes later, as I watched the caravan wind down the valley, doubts crept in. What if Esma's people didn't return? What if other kids taught her to read, and she didn't need me anymore? What if she left to become a famous singer? What if Uncle's rudeness had made the Rom never want to come back? What if her father forced her to marry that man? What if she ran away to escape the marriage?

I filled my mind with little what-ifs to fend off the biggest ones: What if Esma left me? And Grandfather left me? What if I couldn't save either of them? What if I were left truly alone?

More dark yellow storm clouds rolled in after the Rom left. Zigzags of light ripped at the horizon. Far-off thunder moaned, low and sad. For a long time, I waited for a raindrop, but it never came.

HUSH

Mateo

THE HILL OF DUST,
OAXACA, MEXICO
Present Day

27

SECOND INTERMISSION

*Y*ou all right, Mateo?" The voice sounds far away.

"Huh?" I clear my dried-out throat. "Yeah, fine." It takes me a second to remember where I am . . . even *who* I am. It's like when you're so absorbed in a movie that when your friend says something, you feel like he's speaking a whole different language, even like he's on a whole different planet.

I force my mouth to form words. "Why, Grandpa?"

"You're squirming."

I bring myself back into my body, feel the wooden seat beneath me, the coin necklace in my hand.

Yup, I have to pee all right. My mind's been ignoring it, but my legs are shifting around like crazy. Just like at the movies, when you gotta go, but you don't want to leave the magic, so you just sit tight and hope the pee reabsorbs.

"I'm okay, Grandpa."

"You sure, mijo?"

Rain's dripping on the roof, which isn't helping me ignore the urge to pee.

"Yeah, you can finish the story." Then a fear strikes me. "But you did see her again, right?"

His lip quivers like a leaf, and his eyes fill, and I want to look away, but I don't. Oh, man, I've never seen Grandpa like this before.

I swallow hard, clench the coins in my hand. Grandpa told me he needed my help. And in order to help him, I have to know this story. Somehow, I have a role to play here . . . I just need to find out what it is. "Then what happened, Grandpa?"

He takes off his hat and looks up at the ceiling, wood and palm woven into a giant spiderweb pattern. He gathers a breath and holds very still, like the heavy silence before a storm. A hush falls over the room. Even my stomach quiets down.

I twirl the coins around my fingers, one way and the other and back again. Softly, I say, "Grandpa, did she come back?"

Finally, he speaks, and once again, I leave my body behind and let the movie suck me back in like a tornado.

BOOM

Teo

THE HILL OF DUST, OAXACA, MEXICO

Long, Long Ago

28

CATCHING DEATH

*A*lone in the rain, I perched atop the highest point of the Hill of Dust. These days, it should have been called the Hill of Mud. In the rock shelter beneath me, my goats were huddled with Spark and Thunder and Flash, safe from the storm.

But there was nothing between me and the lightning stabbing the sky. I raised my face, willing it to strike. No such luck.

Rainy season had been here for weeks already. The third anniversary of Lucita's death had come and gone. Esma and her people had never arrived. And this year, more than any other, I needed my best friend for life.

Out of habit, my eyes went to the base of the hill, the curve where her caravan used to come into view, in all its colorful glory, at the end of dry season.

Nothing. Only the sluice of water down the mudslide of a road. No cars or horses, much less wagons, would venture through the rivers these valleys had become.

Was that why the Rom hadn't come? But they usually came before the rains started. Had Esma left them already? Had she learned to read and write, then contacted the agent? Was she already a famous singer? Or had they married her off to that old man? What had happened?

I'd let loose so many screams by the river, there were none left. Something about that scared me. Maybe that's why I was here, inviting lightning into my veins. Real, deadly lightning.

When the storm ended and the last flashes vanished and the booms faded, I was still alive. Soaked to the bone, but alive. I gathered my animals and trudged home through the mud, walking too close to the river, raging and wild.

But Thunder stopped me. She shrieked with alarm until I moved away to a safe distance.

I headed up the path toward home, past the dripping leaves, and then stopped. This was the hardest part, coming home without Grandfather to greet me. I gathered a long breath and what little strength I had, then forced my legs to walk past his closed-up healing hut. Rain drummed on the thatched roof. It had been empty and unused for five months now. Who knew if it even smelled like Grandfather anymore. I couldn't bear to open it up to find out.

Uncle Paco called to me from the edge of the bean field, where he was installing water pipes. After a year of trial and error, they actually appeared to work. "*Oye*, Teo! Want to help?"

I could barely muster energy to shake my head.

Lalo, playing ball with Chucho by the irrigation ditch, called out, "Teo! Come play soccer!"

I kept walking past Grandfather's room. That was where I'd found him that morning, five months earlier. I'd gone in his room to offer him a cup of atole. He hadn't responded to my voice, or to my gentle nudging, or to my desperate shaking.

He'd died in his sleep, a peaceful half smile lingering on his lifeless face.

"Teo!" Aunt Perla poked her head out from the kitchen, baby on her hip. "Come inside! Have some atole! You're soaking wet! You'll catch your death of cold!"

I didn't feel the cold. My belly was empty—I hadn't eaten all day—yet I didn't feel hungry or thirsty. And the idea of catching my death? Well, it didn't feel bad. It felt like relief.

My mother was inside the kitchen, an untouched cup of atole before her, its steam making her face ghostly. She studied the box of shiny things in her lap, not looking up as I entered.

Yes, catching my death would be a relief.

The next morning I woke up with a sore throat and sneezes and a cough. Aunt Perla fussed over me, the baby slung on her back. "What did I tell you about catching your death, Teo?" she

209

scolded. "Now stay inside and rest," she ordered, tucking the wool blanket around my chin.

Any other time I would have shrugged her off and gone to pasture the animals anyway, but not this time.

I didn't touch the new notebook that Maestra María had given me to use as a journal. Every page was blank. She'd helped me apply for a scholarship to the secondary school in the nearest town. During the last months of the school year, after Grandfather's death, I'd held myself together, barely. I'd focused on schoolwork, hung on to the daily comfort of Maestra María.

Over the year, she'd become a beloved teacher to all the students, especially me. After Grandfather's death, she stayed after school to talk, soothing me with the very words in Mixteco that he'd taught her. Taxiini . . . sikita'an . . . kuu ini. She even came by our house on weekends to check up on me and bring us fruit, or vegetables, or beans.

But for the past two months that school had been out, she'd been away visiting her relatives. Now every day had become an empty page of an empty book.

I picked up one of the books she'd lent me—poetry by Gabriela Mistral.

If they could, the trees would lift you
And carry you from valley to valley . . .

My eyes couldn't focus on the words. No, not even the maestra's precious books held my interest. Instead, I stared at the bits of corncobs and dried leaves poking out from the adobe walls. What a relief it would be to join Lucita and Father and Grandfather. Was this how my mother had felt for the past three years? I buried my face in the crook of my elbow and burrowed beneath the blanket.

No, I couldn't live the rest of my life like her, mostly dead.

No, death would be a relief.

I walked toward it with open arms.

The days and nights blurred together, with my aunts bringing me atole and soups and helping me walk to the outhouse, my eyes half-closed because it was too bright outside.

"Oh, Teo," they said, in worried, distant voices, "your fever's so high."

They forced me to sip teas, asking desperately, "Teo, what would your grandfather have given you for your illness? Which herbs?"

I shrugged and rolled over.

Lalo cared for Flash and Spark and Thunder, who were often at my side, whistling and *baahing* and scuttling and trying to make me play. I ignored them.

One day, Uncle Paco came in and said, "Teo, there are some people who traveled far to see your grandfather."

I kept my eyes closed, said nothing.

"Teo, talk to me."

"Turn them away," I murmured.

"I think you could take a look at the patient. It's a girl your age, Teo."

A crazy hope. My eyes flew open. "Esma?"

He shook his head slowly. "No, not the Gypsy girl. A girl from a village three days' walk west over the mountains. No other doctor has been able to help her. The journey was hard on her." He paused. "Teo, your grandfather taught you everything he knew. You can help her."

I shook my head. "I'm too weak. I'm not wise."

Uncle Paco put his hand on my forehead. "You healed me, son."

"Grandfather did."

"You did. And you can heal yourself, too. You can heal this girl."

At the door appeared Aunt Perla, leading the girl inside. She shuffled slowly, hunched over, thin and sickly, a wilted flower supported by a couple who must have been her parents.

"I'm sorry," I said. "I'm not my grandfather. I can't help you. I can't even help myself." Inside, I thought, *And I don't want to.*

I turned over and shut my eyes tight.

29

TURNING AWAY

ime passed. Snatches of conversation drifted in and out of dark dreams. It was mostly my aunts and uncles, fretting that they couldn't fetch a doctor; mudslides had blocked the roads. One voice I never heard was my mother's.

One day, a husky, elegant voice stood out from the rest. Maestra María, murmuring sweet things in Mixteco and stroking my cheek. "Taxiini, sikita'an, kuu ini."

I opened my eyes, and there she was, like an angel.

But she was swimming in and out of focus, her lovely eyebrows waving like wings of a distant bird, lost in a cloud of rose perfume. Her voice was far away, but I tried to listen.

"Teo," she said, her eyes shiny. "I had no idea you were sick . . . I'm so sorry I didn't come sooner . . . your uncle Paco came to find me . . . oh, Teo."

She kissed my forehead, then wiped away the lipstick mark with delicate fingertips. In my ear she whispered, "You need a mother, sweet boy."

She read me books as I drifted in and out of consciousness, grasping at her words like darting silver fish. But they were too slippery, and I was too far gone. I sank into darkness.

At one point, Uncle's voice said, "What do you think, Maestra?"

I struggled to catch their minnow words.

"He needs a doctor now," she said, her voice trembling. "I'm driving to the city to fetch one."

"But the roads are closed, Maestra. It's too dangerous."

"Paco, your nephew could die."

Uncle sighed. "What doctor would risk his life to come out here? What doctor cares that much about a poor family of indios?"

"I have money," she said. "I'll say Teo is my own son."

"I'm coming with you," Uncle said after a pause. "I'll bring shovels to dig out the car."

Maestra María gave me another cool kiss on my forehead. More comforting murmurs in Mixteco. "Taxiini, sikita'an, kuu ini." Grandfather's voice spoke through her, feathers and petals that floated around me like spirits, like echoes. Perhaps he'd known that one day I'd need them, and she'd give them.

More time passed. Worried whispers of uncles and aunts.

"He's not moving."

"He's burning up."

"*Dios mío*, his pulse is weak."

"Ay, no! His breathing is so slow."

And then, the voices faded, and there were hands shaking me, but not me . . . my body . . . I could see it there below. How it shook as the hands moved it, but then flopped still, as if empty.

I was drifting outside my body, near the ceiling. I could see every detail of the room, the people in it, their faces distraught in the lantern glow. The frantic eyes of Aunt Perla with her baby on her back, the child's fingers in his mouth, shiny with saliva. Aunt Perla was the one shaking my body. My other aunts and uncles were huddled around, watching, their hands on my neck, my wrist, my chest, searching for signs of life.

I turned away.

I turned away from the movie of my life.

I saw another world, a world that had always been there, if I'd only turned around. A place of greenness and lushness, a thousand colors, an infinity of petals, sparkling water, dazzling reflections off leaves and stones, a sky the deepest blue . . . music that was really water and birdsongs and violins and voices dancing together . . . and it made me think of Esma and her caravan.

I moved toward the beauty.

There was Lucita. Beautiful Lucita, with her dazzling smile and her arms outstretched as if she wanted me to come play, as if we were still little children.

Behind her appeared Father, his strong hand resting on her shoulder.

And at her other side, Grandfather, his own wrinkled hand on her other shoulder. My powerful grandfather, before he'd grown sick. He bent down, whispered something to Lucita. Her face fell and her hands lowered.

Grandfather put up a hand as if to say stop. *Wait.*

But no, I wanted nothing more than to race into his arms.

I floated toward him, and he waved his hands, insisting, "No, Teo, go back."

Still, I flew to him, taking one last glance behind at my weak little body. It grew faraway, so tiny, a sad little heap of flesh and bone beneath my sobbing aunts and uncles and cousins.

There was the thinnest, silvery, spiderweb thread connecting me to that body. It stretched thinner and thinner the closer I moved to Grandfather and Lucita and Father. In a moment, just a moment, it would snap and I would be free.

30

THE SILVER THREAD

*F*rom behind me, light glinted. It was just enough to make me look back at the little adobe room. The source: the warm glitter of candlelight on coins.

There, at the doorway of the room, was Esma.

Esma in her flowered dress, a garden spilling over with petals, a treasure chest overflowing with gold, a bolt of lightning.

Esma, loping across the room, pushing others out of the way, throwing herself over my body.

Esma, clutching my face between her hands.

Esma, shouting, "Come back, Teo! Come back! My friend for life! Come back!"

Her shrieks were ear shattering. The howl of wind during the wildest of storms. She threw back her head and opened her mouth and screamed, as if she were at the river. As if all those screams had been building up to this moment. Her howls filled the room, bounced off the walls. "COME BACK, TEO!"

There I hovered, attached to my body by the thinnest sliver of thread, looking between Lucita and Father and Grandfather and Esma.

Grandfather's voice resounded, deep and rich. "You're needed there, Teo. You need to be the healer. You need to fill my place."

"I can't."

"Look," he said. "You made a promise to Esma. Even death cannot break it, Teo."

"Life is too hard," I said. "Without you, without my mother."

"Maestra María will be your mother. Esma will be your friend forever. Your cousins and aunts and uncles will always love you. As will your animals. They all need you, son."

"But I miss you, Grandfather!" I wanted to run into his arms.

Still, he kept his distance, his palm raised to stop me. "You can visit me when you like. Simply turn away from the movie of your life for a bit. There's no need to die, dear boy."

He didn't understand the emptiness inside me. "There's nothing to live for. Nothing to look forward to."

Grandfather sighed. "In your world, you're walking along a mountain path, only seeing what's in front of you. The present moment. But in this world, I'm a bird, seeing the entire mountain range from above—past, present, future. And, Teo, I see that not only will you and Esma be friends for life. So will your grandchildren."

Our grandchildren? Something shifted inside me. Something filled my emptiness. The possibility of my future, and my grandchildren's. I couldn't imagine myself as an old man, but the idea of it made me look back again.

Now the little adobe room was emptied of everyone but Flash and Spark and Thunder, huddled in Esma's lap. My aunts and uncles and cousins must have gone to sleep. But Esma remained, aglow in the candlelight. Her hand clutched mine.

"I'm so sorry, Teo," she said softly. "So sorry we came late. My stepmother had a baby and then there were mudslides . . ." Her voice broke. "Everyone else wanted to turn back, but my grandmother insisted we come. She knew, Teo. She knew you needed me."

Silence except for small whimpers; stillness except for her shaking shoulders.

And then, "Oh, Teo! What would I do without you?" She paused, took a long breath, collecting herself, steadying her voice. "Your uncles and aunts are worried the priest can't come to bless your body before . . . before the burial. But I know you'll come back. Won't you? You have to! You promised!"

All this time, I felt the strain of the silvery thread pulling me toward my body. At the same time, I felt the tug of the other world, so easy and glittering and colorful, the promise of an eternity playing with Lucita, basking in the warmth of Grandfather and Father.

And then, into the adobe room strutted Roza, Mistress of Destiny. She set down a burlap sack and plopped beside Esma, taking in her red and tear-streaked face. Roza tugged her granddaughter's braid gently, tapped the side of her head, and said something in Romani.

"Squash head."

In this in-between place, I could understand their language. Or perhaps I could simply understand all the feelings between the words. What mattered.

"My impossible squash head," Roza said quietly. Her nose held perfectly still. "Your grandfather is making us go. There's too much rain here to show movies. Everyone wants to leave. I can't change their minds."

"I'm staying with Teo," Esma said.

Roza pulled her pipe from a deep pocket, chewed on it for a while. "I know you are, squash head," she said gently. "I've always known."

From her sack, she pulled out a bundle wrapped in twine and a worn black violin case. She set them at Esma's feet. Then she removed a necklace of gold coins that reached down to her waist and draped it over Esma's head. It mingled with Esma's own strands of beads and coins and shells, shining brighter than the rest.

"Thank you," Esma said, wrapping her fingers around the necklace.

"Go make your own fortune, child. Your future is here. Now is the time."

Esma threw her arms around her grandmother and sobbed. "I don't know if I can."

"Make sure this boy lives," Roza said. "And he'll make sure your fortune comes true."

Her words entered me, etched themselves into my spirit. This echo of a promise I'd made, to be Esma's friend for both of our long lives. A promise that only death could break . . .

Or perhaps not.

Esma moved her grandmother's hand to the forehead of my limp body. Her voice was a hoarse whisper. "He's already cold, Grandmother. No pulse, no breath."

Munching on her pipe, Roza surveyed my body. Then she tugged at Esma's braid again. "What is it you always say, child?"

"Nothing is impossible," Esma whispered.

"Well then, work your magic, Queen of Lightning." A tear streamed down Roza's mountainous nose, trickling through its valleys and nooks like a tiny river.

After a long breath, she stuck her pipe back in her pocket, stood up, and headed toward the door.

"Wait, Grandmother! How? How do I bring him back?"

Roza's nose danced to an invisible melody. "Sing, my dear squash head. Sing."

31

A Tickle, a Nibble, a Song

*M*y soul string was stretched to a single, quivering, delicate strand.

Esma took a deep breath and opened her mouth.

The song swirled out like silver ribbons.

She rose and spun and more ribbons spiraled out from her outstretched fingertips, the rippling hem of her dress, ribbons of lightning and pure, raw power.

She swirled and sang and the ribbons braided themselves into my soul string, more and more and more until the cord was solid and thick as a tree trunk.

When I remembered to look back at Grandfather and Lucita and Father, they were far off, growing smaller and fainter and dissolving until they were only hands waving in a kind of mist.

And then nothing.

I turned back to Esma, felt her song pull at me, tugging me closer and closer to my body.

As I floated downward, Flash's ears perked up. He skittered onto my chest and nibbled at my ear. I could feel the gentle little teeth that always drew out laughter.

Then there was Spark's tongue, velvety soft and licking my arm, up and down, covering every last patch of skin. It tickled.

Then there was Thunder, biting at my ankle, so hard it hurt.

In a rush, I felt the beat of my heart and the flow of my blood and the whoosh of my breath.

I opened my eyes and saw Esma, twirling, and though I could no longer see the ribbons, they were there, making my soul string stronger and stronger with every note.

And then, all at once, Flash's nibbling and Spark's tickling and Thunder's biting made me laugh. A dry, hoarse, rough cry of a laugh.

Esma heard. She slowed her spinning, paused her singing, and stood, dizzy, meeting my open eyes. Hers were the color of my soul string, raindrop silver.

As she took my hand, a bolt of lightning shot through, right into my center.

A sudden commotion broke out. Beyond the door, in the courtyard, voices and cries and sobs shattered the night.

It was Maestra María's voice, yelling, "No, no, no, it can't be! He can't be gone!"

She stumbled into the room, and when she saw me with my eyes open, she crumpled to her knees at my side.

I felt her love, something warm and real and solid that I could hold in my hand, in my heart. The love of a mother. She covered my face with kisses and sobbed prayers of thanks, and when she finally caught her breath, she said, "Oh, Teo, they told me you'd died."

By this time, the doctor—a stout, bald man in a damp suit—had taken out his black bag and was pulling out a stethoscope.

Half-asleep, my aunts and uncles and cousins rushed over, touching my face, my hair, my flesh in disbelief.

"He's warm again!"

"His heart's beating!"

"He's breathing!"

"His eyes are opened!"

"But how can this be?"

"He was dead."

"He was cold."

"He had no pulse."

"No breath."

"I came back," I said.

Everyone gasped.

"Esma called to me," I said. "She saved me."

Esma shrugged a shoulder. "He saved himself. I just gave him a little nudge."

Maestra María threw her arms around Esma. "You sang," she said. "Your song brought him back from the dead."

I nodded.

Esma reached out to stroke Spark's ears. "Really, it was his animals," she said. "They tickled him back to life."

"Well," I said with a feeble laugh, "Thunder's bite is a little more painful than a tickle." Weakly, I reached out my hand, tapped the side of her head, and added, "One day I'll save you, too, squash head."

And then, Maestra María threw her arms around me again and kissed me twenty more times.

HEAD OF A LION,
WINGS OF A BIRD

*T*he boy's in stable enough health," the doctor announced after examining me. "His vitals are strong."

"But he was dead!" Aunt Perla said, hand over her mouth.

The man scratched his hairless head, mystified. "Perhaps he fell into a coma, or a near-death state in which his organ function slowed down. You might not have detected a heartbeat or breathing. His temperature would have dropped."

As Uncle Paco translated the best he could, my relatives looked at one another, puzzled, and rested their gazes on Esma, as if she held the secret.

The doctor shrugged as he packed his equipment away. He patted the maestra's shoulder and said, "Your son should recover soon."

My relatives looked even more confused at the doctor calling me the maestra's son.

"Give him rest and plenty of food," the doctor added. "He'll be fine."

At the mention of food, my aunts scurried out to prepare me atole and soup and tea. Meanwhile, my uncles volunteered to drive the doctor home since Maestra María refused to leave my side.

She turned to Esma, eyebrows soft with compassion. "We saw your people leaving as we came here. Maybe you can ride with Teo's uncles and catch up."

Esma shook her head. "I'm going my own way now."

Maestra María's eyebrows furrowed in concern. "I don't understand, dear."

Esma raised her chin. "My grandfather always says, 'Better to be the head of a mouse than the tail of a lion.'"

"I'm not sure I follow you," said the maestra.

"Even though the Duke lives life on the outskirts, at least he's his own master. He decides where and when to travel. He answers to no one." She wrapped her grandmother's coin necklace around her wrist, then unwound it. "But if I stayed with my people, I'd always be the *tail* of a mouse."

"And what is it you want to be?" Maestra María asked.

Esma stood up and tore off her scarf, letting her shell-woven braids and waves of hair tumble wildly over her shoulders. "The head of a lion!"

Maestra María laughed. "I can see you as a lion's head."

I grinned. "Esma has the chance to be a famous singer."

"I can see that, too," the maestra said.

Esma pulled the business card from her pocket. It was well-worn, the edges soft and rounded.

"I can read it now," she said, handing it to the maestra.

From the other pocket, Esma pulled out the notebook that Maestra María had given me a year earlier.

The maestra and I took turns looking at both items, clearly precious to Esma. The notebook was filled with writing, every last space crammed with letters. In the early pages, the writing was big and uneven and the words ran together. Yet by the end, the writing was neat and small and well spaced. They were poems—maybe song lyrics—about dreaming and longing and missing. And, I noticed with a blush, the word *Teo* was on almost every page. How could I ever have thought she'd forget me?

I found I could read the business card now, too.

Antonio Reyes Salazar, Agente de la Música

Calle Morelos No. 20, Coyoacán, México, D.F.

Impressed, Maestra María asked, "He's interested in starting your singing career?"

We nodded.

Her left eyebrow arched with an idea. "Once Teo is better, we'll drive you there, make sure this man is legitimate."

"And if he is?" Esma asked tentatively.

"Why, then we'll help you settle in!"

Esma gazed adoringly at the maestra.

And I thought, *This is exactly the mother I want. The mother I need.*

The next time Maestra María drew me in for a hug, I whispered one word.

"*Mamá*."

And then, just like that, she was.

During my weeks of recovery, Esma stayed in Grandfather's old room. Her dresses and scarves and hair absorbed the scent he'd left behind—an earthy, smoky, copal scent. Sometimes, as she breezed by, I breathed in the pieces of Grandfather that lingered in her.

Every evening, she read to me from the maestra's books in a lilting singsong voice that I could have listened to forever. Sometimes she cried there in the darkness, whispering that she missed her little cousins and grandparents. She told me funny stories about them, recounted their favorite sayings, their quirks and antics. She told me how she'd convinced her old-geezer fiancé that the lightning had zapped her brain, too, and made her crazy. And her laughter turned to tears as she confided that after she'd scared the man away, her stepmother and father treated her worse than a rat.

I held her hand and tried to comfort her. I told her to look at the whole mountain range of her life, to remember that on one of the nearby peaks, she would become the head of a lion. I told her that on one of the distant peaks, our grandchildren would become friends. And as I told her this, I secretly wondered: If our grandchildren were friends, could they also be brothers and sisters and cousins? I felt her warm hand in mine, and a secret part of me imagined us getting married on one of those peaks.

During the days, Esma's spirits were higher as she loped and swirled around the Hill of Dust. She took good care of Flash and Spark and Thunder, and helped my cousins pasture the goats in el monte. With my aunts, inside the smoky kitchen, she learned to make tortillas and atole and salsa.

My relatives remained in slight awe of Esma. They were friendly toward her, and respectful, but almost too respectful, treating her like the Virgin María, a miracle worker not entirely of this earth.

Once, Esma sighed and said, "It would be good to be someone's granddaughter or daughter or sister, wouldn't it?"

I saw the longing in her eyes. I couldn't tell her she was like a sister to me. No, she was something else, something more. So I simply nodded. "It would be."

A month after my time with death, during a lull in the rains, Esma came into my room and said, "Let's take a walk today!"

Slowly, supporting me with her arm, she led me down the muddy path to my mother's abandoned fruit grove, where rotting oranges and mangoes littered the ground. We walked among the trees, picking fruit from low-hanging branches and dropping it into our sacks. Sunlight fell through the leaves, wandering over Esma's skin, gleaming off her coins. Spark and Flash poked at the fallen fruit, scavenging bits here and there, while Thunder found small puddles to splash around in.

"What are you going to do when I leave?" she asked.

"Keep pasturing the animals, I guess." I kept my voice steady, tried to ignore the pain in my chest. "Eventually plant my own fields like my uncles."

Esma squinted at me. "Maestra María told me about the scholarship. Your chance to go to secondary school. I think you should do it."

I sat down, leaned against a tree trunk, hugging my knees. I still lost my breath easily and had to rest often. Flash nestled in the space beneath my legs, and I stroked his tail, thinking. "Esma," I said finally, "I can't just go to school. I have to contribute somehow—with work or money."

She picked up an orange, tossed it from one hand to another. Then she picked up two more and juggled them. "You could be a healer, like your grandfather."

I turned an orange over in my hand, breathed in the sweet, tart scent. Broke it open and fed it to Flash. "You really think so?"

"Yes!" Oranges in midair, she spun around, caught all three, then picked out the biggest and dug her fingertips into its liquid center. She popped a few sections into her mouth, letting juice spill down her chin.

I wondered if one day, oranges would remind me not of my father's unjust death, but of Esma, juggling and spinning and licking sweet nectar from her lips. Just as her swirling screams by the river had replaced Lucita's cries.

"I *know* you can, Teo." She wiped off the drops, took another bite. "And after you graduate, you could train with doctors in hospitals, too. So you'll know how to heal in your Grandfather's way and their way, too."

I rubbed my face. "I'm not the head of a lion, Esma."

"True," she said, wiping away more trickles of juice. "You're not."

Spark settled in my lap, and I rubbed her silky ears. "What if I'm just the tail of a mouse?"

"Know what you are, Teo?" Esma looked around, probably for a boulder to stand on. Seeing none, she hoisted herself up onto a low tree branch, then climbed upward. From the topmost branch, she said again, shouting this time, "You know what you are?"

"What?" I called up.

Through hundreds of sunlit leaves, her coins flashed, and her voice sang out, "The wings of a bird, my friend! A whole flock of birds! You lift everyone up!"

The truth is, her words lifted *me* up, until I was flying inside, right up there with her.

JOURNEY

*I*n the morning sunshine, when Maestra María's light blue car reached the top of the Hill of Dust, Esma and Uncle Paco and I were waiting for her in front of the church. Now, after another couple weeks of recovery, I was strong enough to hold Esma's satchel packed with all her belongings in the world. The bundle was no bigger than a melon. Beside me, she held her violin in its case, swinging it nervously back and forth.

I tugged at the stiff new suit the maestra had bought me. Hopefully, the new shoes wouldn't get muddy, but in case they did, Uncle Paco had lent me some polish and a rag to bring along. Now he was kneeling at Esma's feet, shining the pair of heels the maestra had bought her. Without raising his head, he said, "We'll miss you, Queen." And then, still polishing, he added, "You and Teo, you changed my thinking about things. About your people and our people. You changed the maestra's thinking, too. And I bet you'll change lots of other folks' thinking."

He stood up, wiping his hands on the rag.

"Thank you," Esma said, reaching out to take his hand, even though it was stained with black.

Uncle was not the only one sad to see her go. Earlier that morning, after my other uncles and aunts had tearfully wished her well, I'd leaned over my mother's petate, kissed her forehead, and said, "Good-bye. I'm taking a trip to the city." To my amazement, her eyes opened, and she croaked, "My box." I brought it to her, and she dug around till she found the gold earrings, the swirling half moons. "For the lightning girl," she said. I held them in my hands, watching my mother in wonder.

She must have been paying attention these past years, at least a little, through her fog of sorrow. She must have known, somewhere inside, how important Esma was to me. Maybe I couldn't fix my mother, but I could love her and treasure the pieces of herself that shone through, little by little, here and there.

Now, beside the maestra's car, I held the earrings in my free hand, waiting for the right time to give them to Esma.

The maestra stepped out in a sky-blue dress that matched her car perfectly. She kissed us both. "You two ready?"

Esma took a long breath and nodded.

I forced my chin to nod. "Yes, Maestra." I usually called her Maestra when she came to visit—nearly every evening. It was only when she'd hug me good night, when her face was close to mine, when my eyes were closed, that I shyly whispered *Mamá* in her ear, and she shyly whispered *mijo* to me. My son.

Esma climbed into the front seat, and I climbed into the back and set her satchel beside me on the creamy white upholstery. The car smelled faintly of leather and the maestra's sweet perfume.

She smiled at Esma. "You look lovely!"

She did. She'd washed her best of two dresses—the one covered in roses of all shades of red—and scrubbed herself pink and washed and freshly braided her hair. She shone.

Still gazing at Esma, the maestra arched her left eyebrow, suddenly inspired. She pulled out her purse, which looked cut from the same creamy leather as the car seats, and took out a handful of makeup. "May I?"

Beaming, Esma nodded.

"Close your eyes, dear."

Esma obeyed, and the maestra outlined her lids with black, sweeping the corners upward. Gently, she traced Esma's brows, bringing the arcs into relief. Brushed more black onto the lashes with a tiny brush. Swept rosy powder over Esma's cheekbones and berry-red cream on her lips. Finished it off with puffs of powder over her nose and forehead and chin.

"Gorgeous!" the maestra said. "Let Teo see you!"

Esma turned around in her seat. "What do you think?"

I blushed right down to my toes. When I found my voice, I stammered, "Nice."

But it was more than nice. Esma had transformed into a star, in just a few minutes, right there in the car. Her face held the magic of her songs, evoked caravans trailing up mountains, candlelit fortune-telling, bonfires and violins in the moonlight, films beneath stars, mysterious spices and stories. She looked like herself . . . only *more so*.

I handed her the earrings. "From my mother."

Esma's brow rose in surprise, and stayed that way as she fastened the earrings. Then, in a kind of daze, she collected the makeup from her lap and held it out to the maestra. "Thank you . . . both. Thank you."

"You know what?" the maestra said. "Just keep the makeup, dear. Practice a lot before you wear it out anywhere. But you'll get the hang of it soon. Dios mío, you're beautiful!"

Esma stretched her neck to look in the rearview mirror. She stared and smiled in disbelief. Tears filled her eyes.

"Oh, no, no crying," the maestra scolded, dabbing at the corners of Esma's eyes with her hankie. "I won't have you messing up that makeup now!"

She spritzed a mist of perfume on Esma's neck, and then, satisfied, tilted the mirror away, stuck the key in the ignition, and drove us, ever so slowly, down the Hill of Dust.

It wasn't until we were halfway down that I noticed my skunk had somehow snuck in and hidden beneath the front seat. "Flash?" I yelped. He leapt and hopped around the car on his three little legs as I tried to catch him.

Peering into the rearview, looking puzzled and amused, Maestra María pulled to the shoulder and stopped the car.

"Sorry, Maestra," I said, opening the door. "I'll let him out here. He'll find his way back."

"No," Esma said. "What if he doesn't? What if he gets lost or eaten?"

"Oh, he can come with us," Maestra María said, laughing.

I was just closing the door when I noticed Thunder, half-flying, half-waddling down the road in a fury of feathers and whistles. Close at her heels, a frantic Spark stumbled down after her.

Maestra María's eyebrows softened in surrender. "Let them all in," she sighed.

"Really?" I asked.

She nodded. "Just keep them off the upholstery."

I settled them at my feet, and Thunder chirped some satisfied whistles, and we were off.

For most of the drive, my jaw hung open in wonder. I'd forgotten how many mountains and villages were scattered around my own humble little Hill of Dust. The world was huge beyond belief . . . and all this was less than a day's drive from home.

The last times I'd been on these roads were back when my father was alive. We used to load up the donkey cart with baskets and hats and walk alongside it to the city—a long, hot, dusty trek that spanned days and nights.

Now, as the looming buildings of Mexico City came into view, I grew nervous. Exhaust smells replaced fresh air. Cars and trucks multiplied, rushing by like a river. An old fear clutched me, and through dark puffs of exhaust, I caught a glimpse of that orange rolling across the street and Lucita's pudgy hand slipping from mine and reaching for it. I could almost hear that thud of steel against flesh, and see the blood and tears on my father's lashes. And beside him, that perfect, glistening orange that had somehow survived.

I blinked, shook myself, then let my gaze rest on Esma's hand on the open window. I wanted to hold on to it, tightly, so tightly I'd never let it go. I wanted endless days of eating oranges and mangoes with her in the cool shade of trees.

I looked past her hand, outside the window, and saw we were leaving the wide street flooded with cars and turning onto a peaceful, cobblestoned lane, as narrow as a trickling stream, and dappled with sunlight through leaves. We passed flower-filled parks and gardens and gurgling fountains. Delicious scents poured through our open windows—jasmine and rose nectar, steam from spicy sauces simmering on corner stands. Lining the streets were emerald-canopied trees and houses painted lemon yellows and rich blues and petal pinks, a rain-bow stretching before us.

This neighborhood wasn't the crushing, suffocating city that loomed in my memory, the place echoing with those words that had set me on fire years ago. *What's one less indio . . .*

I waited for the burning-drowning wave to hit me.

It didn't. Instead, I looked at Esma and the maestra in the front seat, both glowing with excitement. Both so confident in my own powers, my own future.

My spirit flew above the flames and floods, and from up here, I felt as strong as Esma and Maestra María thought I was. From up here, I knew that somehow, I could make any fortune come true. Lightning now lived in my blood, and I would use it to lift up those who needed me.

Soon, the maestra announced, "Coyoacán!" reeling my mind back into the car. "This is Señor Antonio's neighborhood. Chock-full of writers and actors and artists. He must be a bohemian type." She turned onto another street and pointed to a brilliant blue house. "Look, that's where the artists Frida Kahlo and Diego Rivera lived. Oh, and keep your eyes out for movie stars like María Félix!"

My eyes soaked in everything. Ladies strode by in skirts long and short, and even some in pants. The men wore all manner of hats—leather and reed and felt—and their shoes ranged from boots to sandals to the shiny, narrow kind Uncle Paco wore.

I peered at Esma's profile as she gazed out the window. This wasn't new to her. She'd been to the city before to stock up on supplies and rent movies. Still, she looked stunned. Her entire life was about to change, even more than it already had.

Checking her map, the maestra slowed the car and parked at the side of a quiet street. "And here we are!"

Esma glanced back at me, gave a nervous smile. We climbed out of the car, making sure my animals stayed inside with only their noses and beak poking out the window crack.

"So much for the upholstery," the maestra murmured, putting one arm around each of our shoulders.

"I'll clean it," I assured her.

She gave a slight shrug and a half grin, then kissed the top of my head.

We walked a few blocks and slowed at the sign reading 20. It was posted on a wrought-iron gate leading into a lush courtyard bursting with flowers and fruit trees and chirping birds. I'd never seen so many shades of bougainvillea—reds, oranges, yellows, pinks, purples. Beyond the courtyard was a pink three-story house, trimmed in white like icing and half-hidden by flowers and leaves.

Maestra María smoothed Esma's hair, freshened up her lipstick, dusted more powder on her face. Then she rang the bell, looking back and forth between me and Esma, smiling, excited.

An older lady in a checked apron came to the gate and gave the three of us a curious look. "May I help you?" she asked politely.

Thankfully, the maestra spoke; my mouth was too dry to say a word. Even Esma—bold, brave Esma—seemed struck silent.

Once the maestra explained that Señor Antonio had offered representation to Esma, the woman nodded with understanding. "Come inside, please."

Under the trees of the courtyard, she offered us glasses of bright-red agua de jamaica and told us to make ourselves at home and relax on the blue chairs.

She must have been a servant, because soon she returned with three elegant young women who looked to be in their teens, not much older than Esma and me. They wore pretty, fitted dresses, much like the maestra's, only more somber colors— pale gray, black, and brown.

The servant ducked back inside, excusing herself.

Extending their hands, the women introduced themselves as Margarita, Carmen, and Dolores. Their hands were cool and smooth, while mine were damp with sweat. Even after sipping the agua de jamaica, my mouth was still too dry to speak; I could only nod in greeting.

And then, Carmen spoke the words that made my heart stop. "We're so sorry," she said, "but our father—Señor Antonio— he cannot see you."

34

A Dream, Dead

I swallowed hard and glanced at Esma. Her face was frozen.

Unruffled, Maestra María smiled. "Oh, of course, señorita. He wasn't expecting us. We'd be happy to return tomorrow, or make an appointment for another day."

The girls exchanged meaningful looks. "Well, you see, señora," Dolores said softly, "our mother passed several months ago."

"Oh," Maestra María murmured. "I'm so sorry to hear that, señorita."

Dolores continued. "Our father hasn't—he hasn't been well enough to see anyone since then."

Esma spoke up, her voice trembling. "I'm sorry about your mother, señorita." She paused, gathering herself. "But we've traveled so far, and I've tried so hard, waited so long . . . given up so much. Please, is there any way we can see him?"

Carmen gave her a kind look. "I'll ask. Please wait here."

We stayed in the courtyard, holding our glasses of cool, sweet liquid. I couldn't take another sip, afraid I'd choke on it. Esma couldn't either. She was blinking back tears, trying not to smear her makeup. I was grateful for that makeup. I didn't know what I'd do if she started crying.

I strained to hear the voices coming from an open window above us. It was Carmen's voice, speaking with a lower, man's voice, grim and weak.

But I couldn't make out any words, especially not over the chattering of the other sisters' small talk. They inquired politely about where we were from and kept offering us food, insisting we must be hungry after our journey. "No, thank you," we assured them, too nervous to eat.

The women were enchanted when they discovered Esma was a real, live Gypsy. Thankfully, they showed none of the distrust that others in the city supposedly had. Perhaps as the daughters of a music agent, they'd met talented musicians from every walk of life. Perhaps they were used to all different kinds of people in this colorful neighborhood of artists. Perhaps they'd simply learned to keep their minds and hearts open.

"May I touch your jewelry?" the youngest sister, Margarita, asked, marveling at Esma's beauty, asking question after question about her people's way of life.

In any other situation I would have liked these girls, appreciated their curiosity, their warmth, their respect for Esma. Now my mind went to Señor Antonio. I couldn't help feeling angry with him . . . but also sad for him. After Grandfather had died, I'd been so lost, I couldn't imagine going on. I'd even refused to see that sick girl who'd traveled so far. I wished I could go back in time and treat her more kindly.

Back then, I didn't think I wanted to be saved, but Esma—and our fortune—showed me otherwise. I thought of Uncle, humbled and shamed last year, and how he wanted to be healed, and let me help him.

Suddenly inspired, I interrupted Margarita. "Excuse me, señorita, but perhaps I could heal your father."

"Excuse me?"

"I'm a healer. If your father would like to be healed, I could help him."

Margarita cocked her head. Hope brightened her eyes.

Dolores looked at her sister, shrugged a shoulder, as if to say, *Why not?* "Hold on, let me ask him," Dolores said.

More time passed, and now Margarita peppered me with questions about my healing rituals. I answered as best I could, trying to sound confident yet humble, as Grandfather always had.

While we spoke, dark clouds pooled in the sky and the wind picked up and moisture filled the air. I shivered, shoved my hands into my pockets to warm them.

Margarita frowned at the sky. "Oh, these afternoon storms!" she sighed. "So good for the plants, but not for much else."

"Certainly not the roads," Maestra María agreed.

"Would you care to come inside?" Margarita asked, hugging herself in the cool breeze.

But just then, the other two sisters came outside, their faces long. "We're so sorry," Carmen said. "Our father—he sends his apologies—but he's mourning, you see. He says he's not able to see you."

I thought of my mother, how she was still lost in mourning, unable to find her way back. Not *wanting* to find her way back, even though I'd tried to guide her. Maybe Señor Antonio was like her, too far gone. A deep ache filled me, heavy as a boulder.

Dolores continued, wind whipping her hair. "My sisters and I—of course we'd love you to heal him—we're desperate to get our father back. But he's not interested. I'm so sorry."

Rubbing her goose-bumped arms, Carmen beckoned us inside. "Please do come in for a bite to eat, though. Do you need a place to stay for the night?"

Maestra María was just explaining that we had to tend to the animals in her car when I noticed Esma's red lower lip tremble. Tears welled up. Suddenly, she bolted to the gate, running in that lopsided way that shot a little pain through my chest. The gate clanked, she was outside on the sidewalk, and her sobs let loose.

I ran after her as she stumbled toward the car.

Behind me, Maestra María gave quick apologies and farewells and thanks before following us out.

When I caught up with Esma, the sky opened and poured out a sudden waterfall of rain that mixed with her tears and made black rivers over her face. Her entire body shook. The only time I'd witnessed her sob this deeply, straight from her soul, was when I'd died.

That's when I understood: Her dream was dead. Her fortune, her destiny, her hope.

Dead.

There in the rain, for the first time ever, I hugged her. I wrapped my arms around her and pulled her close, and felt her sink into me. I had to save her. But how?

"Esma," I whispered into her ear. "Let's get married. We'll make a good life together, you and me. You can be my wife."

She didn't answer.

I kept talking. "Well, we wouldn't have to do it now. Maybe in a few years? But I want you to know—I love you. I—I want to marry you."

Sniffling, she pulled away to look at me. "You would want to marry me?"

I wiped her black-streaked tears away. "Of course."

Her lips turned up in a sad smile.

35

SING

A heartbeat later, lightning flashed, illuminating the entire sky.

I squeezed my eyes shut.

Behind my lids, I saw the silver glint of Esma's eyes.

I saw her swirling and flashing and singing.

I saw the head of a lion, wild and fierce.

Then it hit me with a jolt: The Queen of Lightning was too big for the Hill of Dust. She had to fulfill her destiny. And it was up to me to make sure she did. That's when the deeper truth struck me. Saving her meant losing her. Letting her go. *Helping* her go.

Yet I wanted to hold her tightly, forever. I dug down to find the strength to do just the opposite.

The sky shuddered with white electricity, and thunder roiled, and I whispered, "But first, Esma, let's make you a famous singer."

She breathed out. "Oh, Teo, the man won't even see me."

"Nothing is impossible," I said, taking her cold hands, letting lightning flow through mine into hers.

I looked up and saw Maestra María hovering beside us, face full of sorrow. She dabbed at Esma's eyes with her hankie, a kind but futile gesture in the rain. "Ready to go home?"

"No," I said, tugging at Esma's hands. "Come on."

"What?" Esma said, resisting. "Why?"

I pulled her, the way she had pulled me back to life.

Down the street, the gate was still open a crack. I pushed it open and led Esma inside.

"We can't," she protested. "He said no, Teo."

"Maybe a part of him wants to come back to the world of the living. And if anyone can bring him back, you can." I positioned her in front of the open window of Señor Antonio. "Sing, Esma."

She wrinkled her eyebrows. "I can't."

"Sing!" I shouted, tears streaming down my own face now.

Esma drew in a long breath, raised her arms, tilted back her head.

And she sang. Raindrops fell over her eyelids and lips . . . and she sang. Her voice rang out and the raindrops accompanied her and the lightning danced.

Esma sang and it was glorious. She took all the sorrow and hope and love and longing and missing inside her and transformed it into song, pure and raw and breathtaking, straight from her center, from the center of everything.

She sang and I felt Lucita and Grandfather and Father beside me, and other spirits, too—Señor Antonio's wife, the maestra's husband.

Esma sang her own fortune back from the dead.

Silver ribbons swirled around us in the rain. I felt them inside my chest, saw them from the corner of my eye.

A face appeared at the window above, a man's face, rapt with wonder.

The sisters ran outside, into the rain, and huddled there, listening, tears trickling down their cheeks with rainwater.

After Esma's song ended, there was silence. The pitter-patter of rain, the chirp of a bird.

Dolores's eyes were closed and a smile was spread over her face and she said, "I feel Mamá, right here with us."

"Esma!" Margarita cried. "Your song brought our mother here."

Moments later, Antonio appeared at the door to the court-yard, weak but joyful. Carmen took his arm, led him to a chair, wiping it off with her hankie before settling him into it.

"Please, señorita," he said hoarsely, "please sing another."

The afternoon passed, and the rain stopped as dusk came. The girls insisted on fetching my animals and feeding them kitchen scraps. They cuddled with Spark and giggled at Flash dashing around the courtyard.

Again, the sisters invited us inside. This time we accepted. The maid served a warm, filling dinner of chicken mole, rich with chocolate and chile, and as we thanked her, she said, "No, thank *you*. You've brought life back into this home."

After dinner there was more music. The sisters played instruments expertly—piano and violin—and were delighted to see that Esma, too, played violin. They offered us soft beds and even set up crates piled with rags for my animals.

The next morning, over a breakfast of *huevos estrellados* and *pan dulce* and cinnamon coffee, Antonio announced, "Esma, I would be honored to manage your career. My daughters would like to offer you a place to stay, here with us, as our guest, for as long as—"

"You can share my room!" Margarita interrupted, unable to contain her excitement.

Antonio smiled indulgently. "I can begin setting up shows for you this week, Esma. You would not only be my client, but a member of the family. Do you accept, my dear?"

Esma looked around the table, at these girls who treated her like the queen she was, and at the same time, like a sister. Then she looked at the maestra, who gave her a smile and a little nod. Finally, she looked at me, sitting beside her.

I wanted to pull her in again, hold her tightly, be with her every moment of forever.

Instead, I tapped her head. Tugged her braid. "Go make your fortune, squash head."

Beaming, she turned to Antonio, and said, "Yes!"

And just like that, Esma's destiny unfurled like a brand-new leaf; like a royal red carpet; like a ribbon, silver and strong and flying on the breeze.

Later that morning, Esma came to the maestra's car to see us off.

She gave the maestra a long hug good-bye. "Thank you for everything."

"Thank *you*, my dear girl," the maestra said, kissing both cheeks. "You were the spark that set off everything."

With a sad smile, Esma buried her face in the fur and feathers of my animals. "Take care of Teo," she told them.

The maestra took the animals and started settling them in the car, leaving Esma and me alone to say good-bye.

Esma threw her arms around me. Chin wedged onto my shoulder, she whispered, "Thank you for wanting to marry me." She held me tighter still. Her necklaces and beads pressed against my chest; her scarf brushed my cheek. "Maybe someday," she said. "Who knows. We have our whole, long lives ahead of us."

I took her hand. I never wanted to let go. "One day I'll save you, Esma."

"You already have." Her gaze swam over my face, so close to hers. "I thought I'd never need anyone to rescue me. But all along, I needed you, Teo. You've saved me . . . just by being my friend."

Her silver eyes locked with mine. She touched my cheek, lightly, her fingertips leaving a trail of sparks. Slipping her other hand from mine, she removed a coin necklace and held it up for a moment so it flashed sunshine. Then she pooled the shimmering strands into my palm and covered them with her other hand. Pressed together, our hands were alive with sparks and tingles and crackles of lightning.

I breathed, "Good-bye, my queen."

"Good-bye, my friend for life."

Our lips touched like two bird wings brushing against each other for the tiniest moment, then flying apart on their own separate journeys.

And then, I was in the car and waving and Esma was growing smaller out the window, and we turned a corner and she was gone.

My animals settled at my feet and I felt their warmth, their tiny movements of pulse and breath. A dam blocked my throat and a tightness squeezed my chest.

I didn't talk on the way back to the Hill of Dust.

But the maestra did. The whole way, she murmured the sweetest, softest words in Mixteco, words from Grandfather that floated here and there like feathers.

And as the mountains spread around us like our past, present, and future, I dangled the coin necklace in front of it all and saw Esma in every glitter of sunlight.

BURST

Mateo

THE HILL OF DUST,
OAXACA, MEXICO
Present Day

HIDDEN THINGS

*G*randpa Teo's far-off gaze focuses back on me, onto the necklace in my open palm. The old coins are still zinging in my hand, sparks shooting out.

I rub my eyes and stretch my arms and stamp my numb feet. It's that feeling you get at the end of a movie, when the credits start rolling and you take off your 3-D glasses and blink, totally shocked to return to the regular world. Only this movie hasn't finished yet, not really. Grandpa said it was up to me to make the ending. But how?

I raise the necklace in front of me. Like a ghost of Esma, it's dancing and swirling in the air, even though there's no breeze in the healing hut.

I let it fall back into my hand. My voice creaks out, rusty. "Ever see her again, Grandpa?"

He reaches into a small pine box behind the altar and pulls

out a yellowed envelope and a postcard with wavy, worn edges. I take a closer look. They're addressed to him on the Hill of Dust, in fancy, old-fashioned handwriting.

"We wrote to each other for five years," he says with a sigh. "Esma was performing for big, adoring crowds. I was so proud of her."

"Really?" I'm actually on the edge of my seat. "Then what?"

"Well," he says, "at that time I was studying in high school, then interning at a hospital."

"The one where you met Grandma?"

He nods. Very carefully, as if handling a baby animal, he takes out the letter and unfolds it. "Here, mijo, read it."

"Um, okay." I hold the crinkly paper to the candlelight and read slowly, since it's in Spanish and written in superflowery lettering that's hard to make out.

> *Dearest friend for life,*
>   *I am in America now! Oh, how I love it here! I make enough money to live in a nice little house, and I even have a car—the same color as the maestra's! The only thing missing from my life is you, Teo. Please come live with me . . . will you?*
>   *Love,*
>   *Esma*

I swallow hard, flushing, like when a romantic scene sneaks into a "family" movie I'm watching with my parents. This is a *love* letter. I mean, Esma's practically asking Grandpa to marry her. I fold up the paper, hand it back to him. Awkwardly, I ask, "You were already in love with Grandma by then, right?"

He nods. "For days I could barely eat or sleep. I didn't know what to do. And then a sick little boy came to be healed. So sick he was nearly dead. I stayed up all night, tended to him for days with teas and herbs. And he recovered. That's how I knew, Mateo. I belonged on the Hill of Dust. I was the head of a mouse here. If I hadn't been here, the boy would have died. I asked myself, How many animals and people would suffer if I left? Yet I couldn't ask Esma to come here. She was already the head of a lion in America." He sighs. "And then there was your grandmother. I loved her, and she was happy to live on the Hill of Dust with me. That day, I wrote Esma the hardest letter of my life."

He gets quiet, so I nudge him. "And what did she say, Grandpa?"

He takes the postcard from the altar and hands it to me. There's a photo of the New York City skyline of long ago, black and gray and cream.

On the back, there's one handwritten line.

I suppose some things are impossible after all.

My insides sink. What a gigantically massive bummer. I stare at the postcard, imagining how crushed Grandpa must have been, imagining how this letter cut their bond of friendship with a single snip. And I don't know much about girls, but it doesn't take a genius to see why Grandma didn't like hearing stories about some miraculous, beautiful Gypsy girl who was in love with Grandpa. No wonder my grandparents never talked about her before.

I remember the impossible fortune the Mistress of Destiny gave to Grandpa, something like this: *You and Esma are on the path to being friends for life. If you fulfill this destiny, you will save each other when no one else can.*

A wave of sadness rushes over me. A feeling that the fortune is *supposed* to come true. A feeling that something is wrong, very wrong.

"Grandpa," I say. "You said you needed my help."

He looks at me closely in the darting candlelight. "Will you look for her?"

The necklace jolts and leaps in my hand. "Yeah. Of course."

"Gracias." He tilts his head, smiles. "It won't be easy, but if anyone can help me, you can, Mateo."

I have a zillion questions, but I'm growing more desperate for food and a bathroom by the second. I settle on, "Why now, Grandpa?"

"Lately I've been hearing Esma's voice . . . in crackles of lightning, rumbles and booms of thunder, gusts of wind, bursts of rain. She needs me, Mateo. Now."

And in the pocket of silence that follows, I swear I hear a whisper in the rain drumming outside.

"You know," Grandpa continues, "a few months ago I spoke with your grandma's spirit. She offered me her blessing to find Esma. So I gave your cousins her name and had them search online. They found nothing." Suddenly, Grandpa looks vulnerable, like a lost little boy. "Mateo, don't feel bad if you can't find her either."

I hold up the coin necklace to the light, watch it swing back and forth, imagine the Romani girl's eyes flashing, the lightning zipping through her veins, and her words: *Nothing is impossible!*

The coins buzz with electricity. Something zaps through my fingers and pumps through my blood. Esma's words echo in my head. *Give yourself a fortune and make it come true.*

"Grandpa, I'm gonna find her for you." I stand up, the force knocking my chair backward. In a voice that seems to come from outside me, or maybe from some hidden place inside me, I say, "Nothing is impossible!"

TALES FROM THE OLD PEOPLE

A knock at the door. Mom peeks her head inside. "Mateo? Papá? You guys have been in here for hours! Aren't you hungry?"

"Starving," I admit. So starving it overpowers my urge to take out my cell phone and start searching for Esma. But just barely.

Grandpa stands up. "Let's eat," he says, leaving the letter and postcard on the altar and resting his hand on my back. On the way out, he rests his other arm around Mom, his oldest daughter.

Outside, I'm startled to see it's already nighttime. I jog through the silver drizzle, across the patch of mud to the bathroom. Sweet relief. After that detour, I head to the kitchen hut, stomach growling. Bits of wet straw poke out from the adobe walls and the thatched roof. The door's open, welcoming, revealing an orange hearth fire in the corner and a little wooden table surrounded by *los viejitos*. The old people. That's what we call all the great-great-uncles and great-great-aunts who still live here in the village. I can't even keep track of how many *greats* there are.

Most of the younger relatives live in Mexico City or Chicago now, except for us in Maryland. Sometimes, my cousins come to the Hill of Dust on the weekends, and it's cool having kids my age to hang out with. But secretly, I like los viejitos the best. And now, after hearing Grandpa Teo's story, I see them in a new light. They weren't always ancient and shriveled and wise.

Grandpa and Mom and I squeeze in beside them, and his latest rescued animal—a deaf baby fox—curls at our feet. It's supercozy in here, with that fairy-tale feeling, and rain pitter-pattering the roof and chamomile tea bubbling on orange wood coals. We dig into the heap of pink-sugared sweet rolls and sip warm atole.

Everything is exactly how it's been every summer of my life, the same faces around the table, growing more wrinkled by the year. For the past two years, though, Grandma's face has been missing. Sadness gets me right in the chest, like a hole's ripped through it. I think back to her funeral, so many crying, sniffling people packed into the cathedral. Even Dad was here on that trip, comforting Mom and me.

I glance at los viejitos, glad that Grandpa wasn't left alone here on the Hill of Dust. Uncle Paco, who's technically my great-great-uncle, is shining a black shoe in his lap with a rag, and the smell of polish mixes with the wood smoke. I try to imagine him as some arrogant jerk hurling insults and stealing, and later, sniveling with shame. But I only see the gentle, funny, smart man who has offered to shine up my sneakers and flip-flops every evening of every summer I've spent here.

The Maestra—my great-grandmother—leans over and kisses my cheek, leaving a cloud of old-lady perfume. I can't help wondering if it's the same stuff she wore decades earlier. "You're getting so handsome, Mateo. Your eyelashes are just like your grandpa's when he was young, you know. Oh, the girls better watch out for you!"

I shrug and smile weakly, because what are you supposed to say to that? I have yet to see any girls stricken by my lashes.

The Maestra clasps her hands together in delight, then leans in to kiss my other cheek. Until today, I never knew why everyone calls her the Maestra; I just went along with it since I was little. When the Maestra's not looking, I wipe her lipstick from my cheeks.

I mentally erase her sags and wrinkles and age spots, and picture her as a stunning and stylish young woman. Who knows, maybe she still could be if she laid off the makeup a little. She always wears fancy dresses and heels and a perfect bun in her hair and sits up really straight. As usual, she's holding a book now, her manicured fingers smoothing the pages. Poetry, probably. She's the only one who speaks perfect Spanish besides Grandpa, and she's always trying to get me to read Spanish poetry with her, which I secretly don't mind so much.

My other great-grandmother, who I've always called *la Otra Abuela*—the Other Grandmother—hardly speaks at all, and when she does, it's in a soft mix of Mixteco and Spanish. Right now she's poking around in the cardboard box on her lap. I always figured it was like her security blanket or stuffed animal or something. I never guessed it was connected to the death of her daughter, ages ago. I just get excited that on every trip, she lets me choose a shiny old treasure as a present. Over the years, I've picked out a mirror, a knife, a picture frame . . . and this year, there are only two things left—a candlestick and a silver hairbrush.

"Choose something, Mateo," she whispers, softer than the crackle of the fire. Her voice sounds creaky and out of practice.

I take the candlestick, wondering what I'll do with it. I feel kind of bad; I mean, now the Other Grandmother only has that hairbrush to look at all day. "Thanks," I say, really looking at her for the first time, at all the sorrows behind the curtain of her eyes. "What'll you do when the hairbrush is gone?"

She moves her dried, wrinkled lips to my ear and whispers, "Why, then I'll be free."

Aunt Perla pats her shoulder, then scoops up another cup of atole for me and changes the subject. She's used to the Other Grandmother's quirks. "Teo, did you know your uncle Paco won an award for lasting contributions to the Hill of Dust?" She speaks Spanish in the choppy way of old people who spent most of their lives speaking only Mixteco. Tossing a white braid over her shoulder, she pulls out a plaque from the shelves of spices, shines it with the hem of her blue-checked apron, and holds it up proudly.

"Congratulations!" Mom says.

Uncle Paco waves away the compliments and starts in on his other shoe.

Aunt Perla explains that the award was for installing the community water system nearly single-handedly, years ago, long before any villages in the area had plumbing. Some still don't. Every time I take a shower with hot water here I feel grateful, knowing that people in nearby villages are taking cold bucket baths and peeing in an outhouse.

Grandpa Teo pats him on the back. "What would we do without you, Uncle?"

"What would we do without *you*, Doctor?" Uncle Paco says with real fondness.

It's true, Grandpa is the real celebrity around here. "El Doctor Teo," everyone calls him, with voices full of respect. Whenever people around here find out I'm Doctor Teo's grandson in *el Norte*, they tell me stories of how he saved their kid or brother or mother . . . seems like he's saved everyone in a hundred miles of the Hill of Dust. He is definitely the head of a mouse in these parts.

Modestly, Grandpa shifts the conversation to the weather—specifically, the storm today, and how Mom and I had to slip and slide up the Hill of Dust, which should be called the Hill of Mud, he jokes.

Then Aunt Perla tilts her head at Grandpa and says, "Remember the mudslide that summer you died, Teo, dear? How terrible it was?"

The other viejitos nod and murmur in agreement. Mom frowns and shifts in her seat. She's a scientist, through and through, and doesn't know how to react to these stories. But I've always soaked them up like a dried-out sponge.

For the hundredth time, they tell the story of Grandpa Teo's death, and the Gypsy Queen who sang him alive, because for her, *nothing was impossible*! And then they launch into stories about the Gypsies' fortune-telling and movies. Every summer, I've heard stories about the Gypsy Queen from the viejitos, but until my talk with Grandpa today, she just seemed like a fairy-tale heroine, not a real, live girl. I mean, I always used to picture her like some kind of superhero or goddess, living in the sky and shooting out lightning from her fingertips.

I glance at Grandpa. Usually, when the viejitos tell these tales, his face never reveals any clues. But now, he gives me a secret wink.

I keep my hand in my pocket, holding on to the electrified coins, and it's all I can do not to take them out and tell everyone, "Esma's real! Somewhere she's alive!" But Grandpa must want to keep this quiet, so I just let the necklace buzz and hum in my hand.

When Grandma was alive, she didn't like hearing these Gypsy stories, even less than Mom does. Grandma came from a town a couple hours away, where Grandpa was interning in a hospital. She was doing midwifery training there, learning how to deliver babies. I always figured that since she was from a bigger town, she just didn't believe in hocus-pocus stuff from the village. Now I get it: She felt threatened by this real, live Lightning-Queen-Goddess-Superhero, her husband's first love and supposed friend for eternity.

I used to tell my friends back home about the Queen of Lightning, and they made faces and said, "Dude, those old people are *nuuuuuts!*" Over the years, I learned to keep the mystical parts of the Hill of Dust to myself. But I wish I had someone to share them with, to *wonder* with, especially now that I've promised to find Esma, especially now that magic and real life have collided.

Once los viejitos grow too tired to continue the story-telling, they yawn and drain their last drops of atole and tea and say good night. Soon enough, I walk outside, too, where the moon is a bright, fuzzy circle, and the air is damp and cool. The mist wraps around me like a blanket.

Mom disappears into the bathroom to brush her teeth, and Grandpa brings the baby fox into his room to tuck it into its crate of rags. I linger outside, watching the cornstalks that look like people waving their leaf-arms to say good night.

A hand rests on my shoulder. It's Grandpa. I turn to face him, noticing we're the same height this year. He looks closely at me. Although his lashes have thinned and grayed, it's true we have the same eyes. Like mud puddles in reeds, he always says.

When I tell my buddies about my trips here, they get impressed with the scorpions and ancient artifacts and machetes . . . but that's not the thing that makes it so awesome. It's the hard-to-capture details—how my hair smells like wood smoke for weeks, how the tortillas taste when they're cooked over a fire, how mysterious los viejitos' voices sound when they talk about the Gypsies. And most of all, it's being with Grandpa Teo, collecting herbs by the river, wandering in el monte, and sometimes—thanks to his creature-in-trouble radar—even saving animals.

Mostly I'm okay with being an only child, but I wish there were someone back home—some *kid*—who got my new mission to find the Queen of Lightning, who got this part of my life, who got the magic of the Hill of Dust, who got that my grandpa isn't just some old geezer in the boondocks of Mexico, but more like—I don't know, a knight or king or someone really noble and important.

Someone I'd do anything for. Like find his long-lost friend for eternity.

I hug him good night, then take out my phone and start searching.

38

A PIECE OF MAGIC

A month later, on the ripped-up backseat of an ancient bus, to the annoyingly cheerful blare of *ranchera* music, I watch the Hill of Dust grow smaller. Swallowing the lump in my throat, I pull the coin necklace from my pocket and let it dangle in front of the storm clouds. Once the hill has vanished from view, I tuck the necklace back into my pocket, carefully, like a piece of magic I'm bringing home.

My forehead falls against the window. Saying good-bye to the Hill of Dust always sucks something out of me and leaves a lonely space. And now there's the added disappointment of not finding Esma. It was a bummer saying good-bye to Grandpa Teo this time, even bigger than usual, knowing something important was left unfinished.

Last month, the night of our arrival, I'd felt sure I could find out something about Esma online. I figured my cousins had spelled her name wrong when they searched for it, since it's pretty long and confusing. But when I typed in Esma's full name, I got nothing but a bunch of random links. Nothing about a singer. Dejected, I realized she probably uses her married name now, and who knows what that could be. For hours, I kept searching, but the cell connection was so spotty, it took forever and turned up nothing useful.

Then, on the second day, my phone dropped in the stream and stopped working. Even though Mom let me use her phone, it was so old and grumpy, I got nowhere. I tried a couple Internet cafés around here, but the computers were so slow I nearly bashed my head into the screens. I'd just have to wait till we got back to Maryland to make any real progress. If only Grandpa and I could get together in front of our superfast computer at home with high-speed wireless.

"Hey, Mom," I say suddenly, lifting my head from the window. "Why hasn't Grandpa ever visited us in Maryland?" It's never occurred to me to ask before; he's always seem tied to the Hill of Dust, like a kite on a string that could only go so far.

"Well," she says, glancing up from her ebook, "I used to ask him and my mom to come, but she was scared of flying and he'd never leave his animals. And he worried someone would get sick and there'd be no one to heal them."

"But now there's that new clinic nearby, right?"

"Yup. And you know, today when I was saying good-bye, he mentioned he might visit us sometime."

My eyes bug out. "No way!"

She taps her ebook screen, distracted. "I told him we'd pay for him to come with one of my cousins. Of course I wouldn't feel comfortable with him flying alone. He's never even been on a plane before."

"That'd be awesome, Mom." My heart speeds up, new possibilities exploding inside me. If I can find Esma, Grandpa could come to the United States and see her . . . and me. It would be like bringing the ultimate, giant piece of magic back home.

Mom goes back to reading, and my hand grazes the old silk string and silver coins of the necklace. *Zap.* Something's rushing in to fill the emptiness—a lightness, a liquid gold. My hands tingle and my blood screams the words: *Nothing is impossible!*

I close my hand over the necklace.

Silently, I tell myself my fortune.

I will find Esma.

ZAP!

Mateo

SUBURBAN MARYLAND

Present Day

RAINDROP, FLAME, AND ESMERALDA RAYOS

*B*ack in Maryland, a few weeks after our Mexico trip, I'm lying on my bed, covered in dried sweat from soccer camp, messing with my new phone. Esma's necklace is hanging from the end of my curtain rod, and a breeze through the window is moving the coins, making a weird, tinkling music. Most of my weekdays are filled with camp, and my weekends with the pool and Xbox with friends, but in the in-between times—like now—I search online for clues about Esma.

So far, no luck.

Last week, I mentioned Esma to my buddies because it seemed like a cool mystery, detective stuff they could get into. But they were all, "Dude, you're, like, obsessed with these old people. Give it up." And for the next few days, "Gramps" was my new nickname. Luckily they forgot about it, and I haven't reminded them.

I flip onto my back and, for the thousandth time, tap in *esma romani singer* and scroll through link after link, but it's all the same—hundreds of entries on some *other* singer named Esma, from Macedonia. I'm ready to throw my phone across the room. There has to be *something* about my Esma online, even if she ended up taking her husband's last name or failing at her career or even dying young. After all, she was on her way to fame when she wrote that letter.

Dully, I check my e-mail, eyes glazing over at the usual celebrity headlines on the home page. Musicians and actors, most of them with crazy names. In the corner of my room, the coin necklace is making a strange, light melody in the wind, like a secret song just for me. It's as if the notes seep into my brain and zap new electrical paths from cell to cell.

I'm staring at a freaky photo of Lady Gaga on my phone when it hits me—maybe Esma has a stage name. Actually, she sort of already had a stage name back when Grandpa knew her.

I type *gypsy queen of lightning*.

The results pop up.

And my mouth drops open.

No *way*.

I sit up, tuck a pillow behind my neck. My heart is thudding like crazy. The first website that comes up is a Wikipedia entry for "Esmeralda, Gypsy Queen of Lightning."

There's a black-and-white photo of a beautiful woman in some kind of coin headdress, with more coin necklaces covering her shoulders and neck. She's standing on a chair, holding a violin. Her chin is raised proudly, and her eyes are piercing, traced in black lines that curve up at the corners like Cleopatra's.

With shaking hands, I scroll down, reading more.

> ESMERALDA RAYOS, *best known as Esmeralda, Queen of Lightning, is an acclaimed singer/songwriter of Gypsy, or Romani, origin, known for her soul-searing music. Born in 1947, she spent a nomadic childhood in rural Mexico as part of the* cine ambulante, *or traveling cinema, popular in rural Mexico in the mid-20th century. At age thirteen, she left her family and signed with well-known music agent Antonio Reyes Salazar, who is credited with beginning her successful and long-lived career. She has produced seven critically acclaimed albums, and continued live performances until the early 2000s. Known for her colorful life, she has married and divorced four times, and performed internationally.*

I click on a link to hear one of her songs. The first notes are sad and fierce and beautiful, a warbling, passionate, wordless song-cry.

The air fills with a kind of electricity, speeds up my heart and tingles a place inside my chest. It's a strange feeling, deep as a cave and towering as a mountain and wide as a starry sky.

For some reason, it makes me think of Grandma.

Afternoon sunlight streams through the window, sparking off the coins, and I can almost feel my grandmother here with me, as though Esma's song has opened a path to somewhere hidden. A pathway to another world, right here in Maryland.

I have to tell Grandpa. I wipe my sweaty hands on my shorts, then scroll through my contacts, looking for his number. Hopefully he'll answer. He never set up voice mail, and couldn't care less about texting or e-mail or the Internet in general. Half the time he forgets his phone somewhere random, like the grain storehouse or the turkey coop.

But the number's not even here. Why would it be? Mom's always the one who calls him. I'm just about to text her at work for the number when my phone rings.

MOM appears on the screen.

Quickly, I answer. "Hey, Mom, this is so weird—I was just—"

"Teo, hon, are you at home?" She sounds shaken up, her voice on edge.

"Yeah. Why?"

"My dad just called me. He's at the airport."

My forehead wrinkles. "Huh?"

"I could kill him! He came all the way here, all by himself, without telling me. Said he knew I wouldn't let him come otherwise. Can you believe it? Good thing we're even in town. I mean, this isn't like the Hill of Dust, where you can just drop in and everyone's waiting for you with atole and . . ."

She rambles on for a while, and I let it sink in. Grandpa Teo . . . *here*? *Now*? Why the urgency? And so soon after we saw him? It has to have something to do with Esma. Of course, that's not something he'd tell Mom about. Too irrational.

"Listen, Mateo, I'm coming to pick you up now, then we'll go get Grandpa together, okay?"

"Sure," I say, jumping off the bed. And then, "Hey, did he say why he was coming?"

She makes a *pfft* sound. "I asked him, of course, and all he said was, 'It's time.'"

An hour later, beneath the fluorescent lights of baggage claim, I spot Grandpa Teo in his palm hat. The little kid in me escapes, and I run toward him, hurling myself into his arms.

"Careful, Mateo!" he says, laughing.

Once I loosen my grip, he sticks his hand in his suit pocket and pulls out a tiny bird. A *live* bird.

A sparrow? Now *I'm* laughing. Of course he'd have a live sparrow in his pocket.

But Mom, clicking toward us in her heels, gasps. "Papá! You brought a bird? All the way from Mexico? That's illegal! How'd you make it past customs?"

He smiles in that soothing way that makes you feel like you're sipping hot chocolate by a fire.

"Oh, mija, I found her here in the airport." He presses his cheek to her feathers. "She must've snuck in somehow. Raindrop, that's her name. Tiny as a raindrop, fallen from the sky. She hurt her wing, probably slammed into a window."

"Ay, Dios, Papá," Mom sighs. "This is so like you!" She gives him a long hug, careful about the sparrow.

On the highway, inside the car, as Raindrop lets out tiny peeps, Mom grills Grandpa about why he came, and if everything's all right back in Mexico, and whether he's going senile. Calmly, he reassures her, stroking Raindrop the entire time. His calloused fingertips ease her shivering like a magician's spell.

Mom takes the exit to our suburb, passing clusters of big gray and beige houses, interspersed with giant block stores and parking lots. I watch Grandpa Teo look out the window, sunlight flashing over his face like a strobe. I wonder what he thinks of our neighborhood with its rectangular lawns and neat hedges. His eyes don't reveal anything; they just have their same relaxed, curious expression.

We're nearing our cul-de-sac when Grandpa Teo raises a hand and says, "Stop, please."

Mom slows down, puts on her blinker, pulls to the roadside. "You okay, Papi?"

Nodding, he says, "*Momentito*," then opens the door and walks back along the curb, shaded beneath the tree canopy.

"Go see what he's doing, Mateo," Mom says, squinting at the rearview.

I hop out and see Grandpa Teo bending over something . . . a baby box turtle, mottled orange and yellow and black. It's struggling to climb up the curb. Grandpa picks it up, examines it, then searches the underbrush near the sidewalk.

"See his mother around, Mateo?"

I shake my head. For a while, we look through brambles and sticks and bushes and leaves, with no luck. The air's steamy hot, even in the shade, and within minutes, I'm sweating in my shorts and T-shirt. Grandpa's dripping in his suit.

Mom honks, impatient, and calls out the window, "Let's go!"

"*¡Ahorita vengo!*" Grandpa Teo responds. Be there in a sec. With a wink, he sticks the baby turtle in the suit pocket that's not occupied by the sparrow.

"What should we name this little guy?" he asks, wiping his forehead with a handkerchief. "How about Flame? See how his head sticks out, orange and yellow?"

"Yeah, sure," I say. And then, heart hammering, I ask, "Grandpa, why'd you decide to come here? Why now?"

"Last week," he says, "the lightning in my blood started screaming. Shouting that there was no time left. 'Find her! Save her!'" He gives a little shiver. "Any leads, mijo?"

A grin spreads over my face. "Just found her online, Grandpa." I pull out my phone, open the Wiki page, zoom in on her photo.

Grandpa fumbles with his glasses and squints at the tiny screen. For a long time he drinks in her picture, cradling the phone in his palms like a long-lost treasure. Raindrop flaps and chirps in his right pocket, and Flame tries to climb out of the left one, but Grandpa is oblivious to everything but Esma.

"She did it," he says finally, under his breath.

I take the phone and scroll down, reading the Wiki entry aloud, translating awkwardly to Spanish. When I click on the link to her song, it rises up like a wild storm over the beige houses and identical lawns. Suddenly, there's a rain shower of magic over my neighborhood.

Grandpa must feel it, too. His eyes are closed and his face is leaning back to the sky, blissed-out.

Mom honks the horn again and calls out, "What's going on, guys?"

Grandpa puts a finger to his lips, gives me a secret grin, and we return to the car as if nothing happened. Well, except for the new baby turtle in his pocket.

CONTACT

*G*randpa Teo and I don't get a chance to talk alone until the next morning after Mom and Dad have left for work. I've convinced them to let me skip soccer camp today, told them Grandpa and I would probably spend the day on nature walks. Mom frowned and said, "No more rescued creatures, okay? We're not an animal shelter here."

Grandpa promised, "We'll be good, mija."

Our real plan, of course, is to spend the whole day looking for Esma. I'm sitting with him at the sunny kitchen table, just the two of us, munching on bagels with cream cheese and feeding Flame in one cardboard box and Raindrop in another. Flame shuffles around, picking at bits of lettuce, while Raindrop peeps and pokes her tiny beak into a dish of oatmeal.

It feels comfortable with Grandpa here, even though it's weird he's never had a bagel with cream cheese before. He's brought the ancient smell of wood smoke and incense into our home, a piece of the Hill of Dust. If magic had a scent, this would be it. And he's brought the cute-magic of Flame and Raindrop, rustling and flapping around on the table.

But most of the magic is coming from Esma's music, blasting on the stereo. I've downloaded all her albums, but the one called *The Impossible Caravan* is my favorite. I keep catching the word *Teo* here and there, at least I think I do—the songs are in Romani.

Grandpa sways to the melodies, peering at an image search of Esma on my phone. In the black-and-white pictures, she's a young woman, so beautiful with those exotic eyes. The later color photos show her as a middle-aged woman with wrinkles fanning over her cheeks, decked out in bright scarves and gold jewelry and sparkling coins that make her look like a queen.

After the fourth song, Grandpa Teo closes his eyes and shouts over the music, "Is she alive?"

"I think so, Grandpa," I shout back, then turn down the stereo. "I mean, I'm not seeing a date of death anywhere."

He breathes out in relief. "Can you find out where she lives?"

"That's trickier," I admit, spreading cream cheese on a second bagel.

His face falls.

Quickly, I add, "But hey, nothing's impossible, right?"

It does require some detective work, but nothing my phone can't handle. Within an hour, I've found the number of Esma's music agency, called, and explained the situation. Thankfully, the agent's friendly, because talking to random strangers on the phone freaks me out a little. When I mention that my grandfather is the Teo in Esma's songs, the lady gets superexcited and starts talking really fast. She says that years ago Esma instructed her agency to give her phone number to Teo if he ever called.

"Awesome," I say, jotting down the number with a nearly dried-out pen.

In a hesitant voice, the agent adds, "You should know that Esma hasn't been performing for several years."

It sounds like she's about to say more, but then she stops herself and just adds, "She lives in Pennsylvania. Good luck. Send her my best."

"Where's Pennsylvania?" Grandpa asks eagerly after I recap the conversation.

"Just one state away from here," I tell him, my pulse zooming.

"Let's go, Mateo!"

"Now?"

"Yes!" He stands up, puts on his hat and suit jacket. "She needs me. It's my turn to save her."

"Um, we have to call first. To get the address."

Grandpa looks about to burst. "Go ahead!"

Bagels churning in my stomach, I call, getting ready for the weirdest phone conversation ever.

A girl answers.

"Um, hi," I begin, picking at the wood grain of the kitchen table. "Is Esma there?"

"She's still at the rehab center." A pause. "Can I ask who's calling?"

"Um, yeah, I'm Mateo. I'm Teo's grandson. He used to be friends with her and—"

"Teo!" the girl shrieks. "Did you say Teo? Her loyal friend for life?"

Ouch. I move the phone away from my ear. "Yeah."

Who knows if she hears me, though, since she's still squealing like a hyper puppy. "Really? Teo's looking for her? Oh my gosh, I've heard so much about him! She always said he'd find her one day. When he was ready. So he's ready?"

"Yeah, definitely." I try to stay cool, but I really feel like jumping up and down. "He wants to see her."

"Oh my gosh, yes! I'm there with her every afternoon during summer break. I'm her granddaughter. My name's Ruby. I'm thirteen, so I just bike over, but it's not too far. Ready? I'll give you the address, okay?"

"Uh, let me get a pen." I rush over to the junk drawer, sifting through pens for one that works. I'm actually sweating with the craziness of this, trying to wrap my head around it. *I'm talking to Esma's granddaughter. And we'll be meeting the Queen herself soon. This is it.*

The whole time, Grandpa is watching me, wide-eyed.

I find a pencil stub and copy down the room number and

address. This is all moving so fast, my hand is shaking and so sweaty I keep losing my grip on the pencil.

"Okay, cool," I say, collecting my thoughts and folding the paper into a tiny, tight square. "I don't know for sure when we'll be there—I mean, I guess my mom could drive us, maybe this weekend or next." I look at Grandpa, so hopeful. He'll want to know how she's doing. "And, uh, what do you mean, rehab center?"

Ruby gets quiet. "It's like a hospital, sort of. Sort of an old folks' home." She sighs. "My grandmom's been there a couple months now. It's like a place where people go to get better. Or to die."

Silence. "Is Esma okay?" I glance at Grandpa's beaming face, glad he doesn't understand English.

"She got cancer."

Sucking in a breath, I grip the pencil and shut my eyes. When I open them, Grandpa knows something's wrong. A dark cloud drifts over his face. He might not understand English, but he's an expert at seeing feelings in the spaces between words.

Ruby goes on. "She had chemo and it was awful, but the cancer's gone now. Or at least in remission."

The tightness in my chest lets up, but only a little, because of the somber tone of Ruby's voice. "The chemo damaged her vocal cords. She can barely even whisper now. That's why there's no point in me giving you her phone number. And . . ." Her voice grows quiet. "She can't sing."

I swallow hard. "Oh, man. Bummer." And then I flush, because what kind of stupid thing is that to say?

"It is a bummer," Ruby agrees. "The doctors said she might get her voice back with therapy, but she's been really weak and depressed and . . . I don't know. We don't know. She says she's no one without her voice." There's a pause, and then she adds, "It's like she's on the verge of giving up. On everything. On life. It scares me."

Silence. I study the pattern on the tile floor, black-and-white linoleum squares, speckled with bagel crumbs. I wish Mom were making this phone call; she'd know how to handle it.

Ruby speaks again, forcefully. "You need to come soon. Like, today!"

"Today?" I sputter. "But—"

"Nothing's impossible!"

I glance at Grandpa's stricken face and draw in a deep breath. Pennsylvania's just a state away, right? It can't take that long to get there. "Okay," I say, "um, I guess we'll be there this afternoon."

41

THE MISSION

*M*om freaks out when I text her to say we're in Dad's beat-up old truck, on the highway, halfway to Pennsylvania, on the way to see the Queen of Lightning.

She calls me immediately.

"Mateo! What the—? Does that truck even run? And is your grandpa even allowed to drive without a U.S. license?"

"Yup and yup. We looked it up. For the short-term, he can use his Mexican license."

"¡Dios mío! How on earth do you know where you're going?"

"The GPS on my phone." I finger the ripped brown vinyl seat. "We're fine, Mom."

"Mateo, put me on speaker. No wait, don't! I don't want to distract my dad and cause an accident. Has he ever driven on anything bigger than a one-lane road? Or over thirty miles an hour?"

I grin. He's grasping the steering wheel, knuckles white, eyes squinting in concentration. "Well, he's not driving much faster than that now." Cars zoom by as we chug along in the right lane.

Mom does deep yoga breathing. "Tell him to pull over to an exit. I'll pick you guys up."

I suck in a breath of sun-baked vinyl, roll down the window for fresh air. "Mom, we're fine."

"Oh, Mateo, why couldn't this wait till tomorrow?"

Unsure how to answer, I pull the coin necklace from my pocket, watch it glint and whip in the wind. I've brought it along for good luck.

"Mateo?" Mom says. "You still there?"

There's only one way to say this. "Tomorrow could be too late. Esma's been sick. She needs us now."

Silence. "She's real? You're sure of it? I mean, my dad hardly talked about her. And all the aunts and uncles made her sound like a fairy tale. And your grandma said it was just imaginary nonsense."

"Esma's real. Look her up, Mom. Esmeralda Rayos, Gypsy Queen of Lightning." Saying the words sends a little shiver up my spine. A shiver of anticipation and dread at once. Who knows how this trip will turn out? I gather the necklace into my palm, let it give me courage, then slip it back into my pocket.

More deep breathing on the other end of the phone. "Okay, be safe. Text me when you get there. You have your seat belt on, right, hon?"

From the floor by my feet, Raindrop suddenly flutters up, chirping, and I drop the phone to catch her. Grandpa swerves and then reaches out his hand for the bird. A car in the next lane over honks.

I grab the phone, which has fallen into Flame's box. Fumbling, I press it to my ear.

"What's going on there?" Mom screeches. "Are you okay?"

"Just dropped the phone for a sec."

"But what was that honking and chirping? You didn't bring that bird, did you?"

"Look, I have to give Grandpa directions. Bye, Mom. Love you." I hang up, silence the phone, stick it in the glove compartment.

"Everything all right?" Grandpa asks, stroking Raindrop's head, now happily poking out of his pocket.

"Great." I look at him, his neck straining forward like a turtle's, focused on the highway. I should prepare him for what we might find. But I still can't bring myself to tell him that Esma's giving up on life. I think that, somehow, he already knows.

According to my phone's directions, we should have arrived in two hours, at three o'clock, but since we went about thirty miles below the speed limit, we don't get there till five.

The rehab center is a low brick building with a fountain in the front and woods in the back. Not too bad from the outside, but when we step inside, I nearly gag on the mix of cleaner and pee smells. I try to hold my breath while I ask the lady at the front desk how to get to room 21. But I have to breathe as we walk down the hallways—we could be in here a while.

The patients freak me out, big-time. They're scattered in wheelchairs along the hallways, just watching us go by, some drooling, some muttering. One old lady is clutching a baby doll. Creepy. If the *opposite* of magic exists, this place is it.

Grandpa senses my discomfort and keeps one hand on my shoulder as we search for room 21. His other hand moves between Flame and Raindrop in his suit pockets. Birds and turtles have to be against the rules, but Grandpa insisted that they'd get heatstroke inside the parked truck. The nurses are too busy to notice the creatures' beaks poking out, even when the patients point and exclaim.

Grandpa Teo pats my shoulder. "Mateo, just wait till you hear Esma's voice in real life. It'll make everything better."

My gut twists around with guilt. I'm in over my head. He came all the way from the Hill of Dust, dreaming of Esma's voice, hoping to save her, and now I've brought him to this horrible, stinky place. And when he steps into room 21 and sees what's happened to her, his heart will break.

I weave my fingers through the necklace in my pocket. "Grandpa, there's something I didn't tell you. Esma—she can't talk anymore. Or sing. Cancer treatments messed up her voice."

He stops in the middle of the hallway, his hand to his mouth.

Being the bearer of bad news is the worst, but I force myself to tell him exactly what Ruby told me. I stare at the pastel pictures of sailboats and seashells on the wall because I can't meet his eyes.

Afterward, he nods grimly and pats my shoulder. "Let's go, mijo."

We start walking again and within seconds run into a girl about my age, striding down the hallway like a breath of fresh air. She has chin-length dark hair and silvery eyes lined in black. She looks a little goth, with a ripped black tank and a short black skirt. But there's a silky pink flowered scarf wrapped around her hair that makes her look like an old-time movie star.

All our eyes meet and she ventures, "Mr. Teo?"

I point with my chin to Grandpa, and she throws her arms around him.

"I'm sorry, sir, it's just that I feel like I know you. I'm Ruby. I gave up on you coming today, but look, here you are! Come in!"

I translate her words as she tugs on Grandpa's hand and pulls him into room 21.

And there, beside a hospital bed, in a wheelchair, face silhouetted against the window, is Esma, Queen of Lightning. Oxygen tubes trail like vines beneath her nostrils, over her ears, and tangle with an IV taped to her hand. She's wearing a dress covered in red roses, and necklaces of beads and shells and coins, and a scarf over her head. Just a few short wisps of hair poke out. Her face is made up, and for some reason, it makes me want to cry.

Yup, she is real, so real I want to run from the room.

"Esma?" Grandpa says.

She turns to face him, straightens up, raises her chin.

Warily, I wait to see what will happen. Will he run to her, drop to his knees, embrace her? It's been fifty years. Ruby, too, is watching expectantly.

But there's only awkwardness, the drone of the news on TV, the beeping of machines, the calls of nurses in the hallway, the rambling of patients in rooms next door.

Self-consciously, Esma tears the tubes from her nose, rips the IV from her hand. She straightens the scarf on her head. On a pad of paper on a TV tray, she writes something, passes it to Grandpa.

I look over his shoulder; I can't help it. It's in Spanish, in the same old-fashioned handwriting from the postcard and letter she wrote years ago.

> *Ruby said you'd be here a while ago. I thought*
> *you'd changed your mind.*

Grandpa Teo puts on his reading glasses and studies the paper. He seems to have lost his voice, too. And it's like he forgets she can still hear.

I answer for him, in Spanish so he can understand. "My granddad's a pretty slow driver," I say over the TV newscaster's voice. "I'm Mateo." Mustering up courage, I reach out and shake her hand, spotted purple from the IV.

"Grandmom," Ruby says, picking up the remote and muting the TV, "you should probably keep those tubes in, right?"

292

I DON'T CARE! Esma writes, pressing hard with the pen. She looks at Grandpa, then scrawls more.

Grandpa gestures for me to read the paper alongside him, leaning on my shoulder, like he needs my support. Poor guy, I'm not the right one to do this. This is a colossal mistake. Why didn't I just let Mom handle it all?

> *It's too late. I don't want you to see me like this. I wish you'd seen me onstage for thousands of people, singing my heart out. Not like this.*

Finally, Grandpa speaks. "But this is when you need me, isn't it?"

Something is passing between the two of them. Still, Grandpa seems unable to step forward and touch her.

And it's suddenly so sad and awkward, I can hardly stand it. It's painful, seeing this reunion with the mythical, miraculous girl who turns out to be real and sick and old.

Uncomfortable small talk fills the silence, started by Ruby and translated by me, the usual boring questions about marriage and children and jobs and weather. It's not the kind of conversation you'd wait fifty years for, not the kind of conversation you'd even drive a half day for on the highway at thirty miles an hour. During pauses, everyone's eyes drift toward the TV.

The small talk topics are nearly exhausted when, thankfully, a nurse pops her head in. "Last call for dinner! Should I wheel you to the dining room?"

Grandpa shifts to his other foot and says, "We'd better head back now. We should get home before dark."

As I translate, tears fill Ruby's eyes, and the black makeup smears as she wipes them. It makes me feel terrible, so terrible that I mutter to Grandpa in Spanish, "Hug Esma good-bye or something."

Tentatively, he steps toward her, bends down, and gives her a stiff pat on the shoulder.

She gives his hand an equally stiff pat in return.

Quickly, he steps back. "*Pues, adiós*, Esma," he says, not meeting her eyes.

She offers a half-hearted wave, her eyes already flicking back to the muted TV.

I'm not big on sappy scenes, but even the sappiest, pukiest scene in the world would be better than this.

Waving a limp good-bye to Ruby, Grandpa and I trudge back down the hallway.

"You can only save people if they want to be saved," he says, catching a tear from the corner of his eye. "Nearly my whole life, I tried to save my mother. Your Other Grandmother. I never could. Looks like I can't save Esma now either."

"Bummer," I say under my breath in English. "Major bummer."

"What?" he asks hoarsely.

"Nada, Grandpa." Nothing.

42

RIBBONS

*W*e're just passing the lady with the baby doll when Grandpa blows his nose, then says, "You know, Mateo, all my life I believed you'd be friends with that girl, Ruby."

I stop, turn to face him. Lite rock music trickles faintly from ceiling speakers. A nurse wheels an empty chair past us. The lady with the baby doll coos.

I find words. "Uh, what are you talking about, Grandpa?"

Leaning against the wall, he rubs his face. "You know that time I died?"

I nod, as if that's a perfectly normal question.

"Remember what my grandfather's spirit told me?" he says slowly. "The thing that made me want to live again."

I scan through that part of his story, and then, with a jolt, I remember. The thing about the grandkids! "He said Esma's and your grandkids would be friends. For life."

I nearly slap my forehead. How did I not realize this sooner? Like back when I was on the phone with Ruby? Or when we met in the hallway? I was so caught up in reuniting Esma and Grandpa, I forgot about the grandkid thing.

It hits me hard in the gut, like I've just belly-flopped off a high-dive . . . how much *sense* it makes. Ruby's the only other kid in the world who understands our grandparents' impossible fortune, who wants to bring that magic into our world, here and now. Of course I'm destined to be friends with her. It's what I've wanted all my life.

Suddenly, everything shines in a new light—the pale flowered wallpaper, the nubby purple carpet, the baby doll's plastic head. Everything is *possibility*.

The coin necklace is practically dancing in my pocket, alive with crazy electricity. I pull it out and let it wind around my fingers. And now I'm buzzing with lightning and the feeling that nothing is impossible.

"Grandpa," I begin, figuring things out as I go. "What if Esma does want to be saved? I mean, you could've tried harder back there, right? Listen, I can help you. Together—"

He pats my shoulder. "Oh, Mateo, many things happened over the past fifty years. Things—"

A sudden flutter of feathers interrupts him. Something brown and tiny flits in the air between us.

It's Raindrop. She's flown out of Grandpa's pocket. With her injured wing, she hangs crookedly above our heads for a moment, gives us a look of impatience. Then she makes a lop-sided flight back down the hallway.

No nurses notice, but the lady in the wheelchair props up her doll to give it a better view.

Grandpa and I follow the bird down the blue carpet as she darts into Esma's room. On the way in, I whisper, "Try harder this time, Grandpa."

A fresh look of determination sweeps over his face.

Inside, the bird rests on the windowsill beside Esma.

Stunned, Esma looks at the sparrow and then at Grandpa Teo, hovering in the doorway beside me.

And for the first time on our visit, Esma smiles.

"Esma, meet Raindrop," Grandpa says, laughing. "Looks like she doesn't want to leave you. Want to keep her?"

I translate for Ruby, adding in Spanish and English, "I doubt this place allows birds." Great, I sound like Mom.

Grandpa pulls Flame from his pocket. "Then how about a turtle?"

Esma smiles bigger. A hoarse whisper, like the echo of a laugh, creaks out. On her notepad, she writes, *Let's get some fresh air.*

Yes, I think. *Let's get out of here.* I translate for Ruby, who nods with relief, tucks the notepad beneath her arm, and maneuvers Esma down the hall.

Outside, I gulp the early evening air. It's still sunny and humid, and the roses give off a sweet, hopeful scent. We head down the paved path, into the woods behind the building. Ahead, Grandpa insists on pushing Esma in the wheelchair, talking to her softly in Spanish as they go.

I can't help sneaking glances at the girl destined to be my lifelong friend. That silky scarf in her hair is really cool. And she kind of bounces on her toes as she walks, like the world is her inflatable castle.

She catches me staring, and for a second, our eyes meet. I panic, because it's not every day that a pretty girl looks at me this way, so open and curious. A pretty girl I'm *destined* to be friends with.

Unsure what to do, on an impulse, I hand her the necklace from my pocket.

"Cool," she says, holding it up, staring at its silhouette against the blue sky, listening to the music of the breeze through it. Maybe it's the necklace, but something releases a river of words pent up inside her.

"Okay, Mateo, that's your name, right? Well, I have so many ideas, and none of my friends get them, but maybe you will, 'cause, well, you know . . . but listen, wouldn't it be cool to make a Romani caravan and paint it amazing colors and hook it up to a truck and drive it all the way down to the Hill of Dust? Like you and me and my grandmom and your granddad? And oh, another thing is I'm starting this Gypsy rock band and I can sing and play violin, but I need someone else, and do you play an instrument? Wouldn't that be awesome? And also, I really want to taste homemade tortillas and maybe learn how to make them, the ones ground on stone and cooked over a fire, because my grandmom always talks about them and we've been to, like, a hundred Mexican restaurants looking for them and we even went to Cancun but they're never as good as the ones on the Hill of Dust, 'cause it's, like, the Hill of Dust is pure magic, you know?"

Ruby bites her lip, suddenly embarrassed. "Oh, gosh, Mateo, I never talk this much, it's just that I've been saving up all my ideas for someone who actually cares and now you're here and I can't stop blabbing!"

She slaps her hand over her mouth. Above, her black-rimmed eyes are smiling.

I clear my throat and say quietly, "I took a woodworking class. Made a stool." I shrug. "How much harder can a wagon be?"

A happy squeal pops from behind her hand.

I keep going. "I've played drums since second grade. And I'm learning guitar."

Another squeal.

"And it's true," I say, "there's nothing like the tortillas on the Hill of Dust. They'll taste extra good after a superlong caravan ride there."

Her eyes widen to twice their normal size. If eyes could scream with laughter, that's what hers are doing now.

I feel my own eyes grow big with excitement. "My aunt Perla could teach you to make tortillas in her little kitchen hut. The best part's how your hair smells like wood smoke the whole time."

Ruby removes her hand from her mouth, revealing the world's biggest grin. Her teeth are straight and white, and her lips very pink. "That's it! That's what I want! Exactly! Tell me more about the Hill of Dust, every tiny detail."

As we walk down the path through the woods, I tell her.

And she listens.

And she gets it.

Afterward, she gives me a sideways glance. "Anyone ever tell you your eyelashes are amazing?"

Heat spreads from my cheeks to my toes. Then I whisper, "Anyone ever tell you that for fifty years we've been destined to be friends for life?"

Once we're deep in the forest, with only bits of golden sunshine sprinkled through the leaves, Esma raises her hand to say stop. We're on a bridge over a small stream. I wipe sweat from my neck and watch the water trickle by, spots of light swimming over the surface.

Shakily, Esma stands up.

Grandpa takes one elbow, and Ruby takes another. "Sure you can stand, Grandmom?"

Esma straightens up, tilts back her head, and opens her mouth. A raspy sound emerges.

Some kind of seizure? Or a stroke? I'm about to ask Ruby whether we should call 911 when Grandpa Teo throws back his own head, opens his mouth, and screams. It makes my heart jump, this thundering sound, incredibly loud for an old man.

Still screaming, he wraps his arm around Esma's shoulder. Looking strangely satisfied, Ruby sits down on a nearby log. I sit beside her, my heart beating like crazy. "What's going on?"

"Screaming at the stream!" she declares.

"Oh, right." The corner of my mouth turns up in a bewildered smile. "My grandpa told me about this."

The screaming freaks me out at first, but soon I relax. They seem so happy with their screams—Grandpa's loud, Esma's nearly silent. For a while I watch them, and then my eyes move to the reflections off the river, flashing like tiny bolts of lightning.

It's a strange thing, how their screams eventually fade into laughter, his loud, hers breathy.

Ruby turns to me. "Know what my grandmom always said? That Teo helped her discover her true power. That she owes, like, every success in life to him."

I think about this. "She helped my grandpa discover his power, too. I mean, he probably wouldn't have become the famous Doctor Teo without her."

Ruby's voice drops to a whisper. "Know something crazy? My grandmom was married and divorced four times."

I don't want to admit I already know it from Wiki, so I just say, "Wow."

"She was looking for Teo in every man. She could never find him. Not till now."

In front of us, Esma and Grandpa stand close. She leans into him, and he lets his arm settle on her hip. I can't help listening to their conversation.

"So, my friend for life," Grandpa asks, "how has life as a lion's head been?"

Pressing her lips in a girlish smile, she writes something on her paper, hands it to him, chuckling in her wheezy way.

He reads it and nods. "When you're old, you don't need to be the head of anything, do you? You can just grow like a tree, something with feet in the earth and hands in the sky and water flowing through it." Grandpa Teo pulls her closer, gives her head a light tap with his fingertip.

I can barely hear him whisper, "Oh, squash head. Let's be trees together."

Ruby elbows me, whispers, "Translate!"

I obey, and she gets a melty look in her eyes. "They do look like trees, leaning against each other, don't they?"

I nod. "It's like, even though they lived so far from each other, they were holding each other up this whole time. Like their roots were all tangled together."

"Yes!" Ruby says, giving me another sideways look that sends shivers through me, the good kind. Her arm brushes mine. It feels like there's something alive, buzzing and sparking in that tiny, warm space between our skin. "Guess we'll be seeing a lot of each other this summer," she says. Her eyes flash, silver and playful.

"Guess so," I say, feeling something big welling up inside me. "Building a caravan's a lot of work."

Suddenly, Ruby's hand flies up to my shoulder. "Look!" she whispers, her voice full of wonder.

I follow her gaze and see Esma raising her arms like branches of a tree, slowly turning in a circle.

Grandpa reaches up to take her hand and twirls her, ever so slowly, in a strange, slow dance.

Together, they spin like ancient planets.

Then Esma's song emerges, rising over the trees and into our cores. It's a single, warbling note, without words, raspy and soft.

Still, it's a song.

And as the two spin together, sunshine dances on the water, and I could swear I see two silver ribbons of light, one from her chest, the other from his, weaving together and swirling into the sky.

Author's Note

INSPIRATION

I felt fortunate to form meaningful friendships with Mixteco people when I took a teaching position in the remote mountains of Oaxaca, Mexico. For two years, I was welcomed into Mixteco communities, first as a teacher and later as an anthropologist studying their culture. During this time, I heard stories about the beloved *gitanos*, whose caravans had shown movies in this region years earlier. I knew that gitanos (also known as Rom or Gypsies) have been misunderstood throughout the world, so I was intrigued by how fondly local people spoke of them. Like the Rom, the Mixteco have also faced prejudice and racist treatment for centuries. I felt drawn to explore the fascinating relationship between these two cultures.

As I developed this story, I wove in realistic and mystical elements of oral histories I heard in Mixteco villages. The initial spark for this book came from the experiences of a ninety-six-year-old healer named María López Martinez (lovingly nicknamed María Chiquita—María the Little One). When she was a young girl, a *gitana* fortune-teller told her she would live a very long life. Shortly after her fortune, she grew ill and appeared to die. Inside their hut, her family held a candlelit vigil over her apparently dead body. At one point during the mourning, a drop of candle wax fell onto María Chiquita's body. Somehow, it woke her from death!

She told me that her time in the other realm gave her powers to become a healer. She lived to age ninety-seven, and near the end of her life, she proudly pointed out that the gitana's prediction had come true. I returned to María Chiquita's village for her cabo de año—the candlelit one-year anniversary of her death. I'm grateful to continue a friendship with her daughter, granddaughter, and great-granddaughter.

THE MIXTECO PEOPLE

In my novels, it's important to me to include not only the mystical parts of a culture, but also the tough realities that have shaped its experiences. Before living in Oaxaca, I had focused on indigenous—or native—rights issues for my anthropology studies. Once I moved there, I got a firsthand look at the injustices these cultures have faced for centuries.

As of the 2010 census, indigenous people made up 13 percent of Mexico's population. They speak a total of sixty-two different native languages. Oaxaca, the state where I lived and where this story is set, has the second-highest indigenous population (at 58 percent). (*Comisión Nacional para el Desarrollo de los Pueblos Indígenas, México, cdi.gob.mx.*)

There are over a dozen indigenous groups within Oaxaca, the Mixteco culture being most common where I lived. In rural communities, some people still speak Mixteco, close to the language spoken in pre-Hispanic times. Many of my friends have kept alive not only their ancestors' language, but also their traditions, adapting them to modern life. I studied these practices in my fieldwork on Mixtecos' ideas about illness and healing, some of which appear in this book.

In the 1500s, after the Spaniards arrived in what is now Mexico, over 90 percent of the indigenous population died from violence, forced labor, and disease. The colonial government imposed a caste—or rigid class—system. They placed the indigenous people at the bottom and those with Spanish ancestry at the top. Over the years, these groups mixed, and the ethnic category mestizo—or mixed race—was born. Mestizos, too, had more privilege and prestige than indigenous people.

During the early to mid-twentieth century, with the Mexican Revolution, the general population began to view indigenous people as the true foundation of Mexican society. Artists like Frida Kahlo and Diego Rivera honored native cultures. In the later part of the century, indigenous rights movements led the government to take more measures to respect indigenous languages and cultures. One such governmental effort was the creation of bilingual education (Spanish and the local indigenous language) in the 1970s.

Unfortunately, despite some progress, indigenous people are still marginalized—unjustly pushed to the edges of society.

In most communities, indigenous Mexicans live with higher poverty rates, much lower literacy rates, and much higher infant death rates than the general population. They have less access to quality education and health care, and often experience discrimination and racism.

During the mid-1900s—the setting of Teo's story—indigenous students could be physically punished for speaking their native language at school. Some of my middle-aged friends in Oaxaca described to me how the teacher smacked their hands with rulers when they were children. This made them feel ashamed of their native tongue, discouraging them from later speaking Mixteco as adults. Even in the late 1990s, when I lived in Mexico, I noticed that the word *indio*—Indian—was used as an insult, often together with words like *dirty, poor,* or *ignorant.* I've noticed hypocrisy in how indigenous people are treated. Pre-Hispanic cultures are highly valued, yet their modern-day descendants are marginalized.

My Mixteco friends are intelligent, hardworking, warm, fun, welcoming people who often speak several languages and hold a wealth of fascinating knowledge. Some of the stories they've told me feel enchanting—like María Chiquita's. Others upset me—like stories of being punished for speaking their native language. In writing this book, I've tried to balance the magical parts with the gritty reality. Ultimately, I want to honor the way that many indigenous people—including children—have resisted oppression and created positive change for themselves and future generations.

THE ROMANI PEOPLE

For centuries, the origin of the Rom was a mystery. Now, based on linguistic and genetic evidence, we know that about a thousand years ago, the Rom first left India and spread across Europe.

There is no accurate data for the number of Romani people in the world, in part because the Rom often choose not to register their ethnicity in official censuses. In Europe alone, Romani population estimates range from between four million and fourteen million. Several million more Rom live in the Americas.

Traditionally, the Rom traveled by caravan in groups that specialized in certain skills, from musical entertainment to metalworking. Today, some are still nomadic, and some have settled. It's remarkable that although Rom on different continents have adopted certain practices of their host countries, they have kept a core cultural identity and language for so long.

Unfortunately, over the past millennia, most Rom across the world have also suffered from misunderstanding and discrimination. Europeans thought they came from Egypt and began calling them *Gyp*sies, spreading rumors that they were thieves and child stealers. During the Middle Ages, they were enslaved, and over the past several centuries, persecuted. Many people don't know that the Rom were among the millions of people massacred in Nazi concentration camps.

In Europe today, the Romani people are still mistreated. Many are forced to move their camps or settle in substandard homes. Many have access to only poor-quality education and health care. Many face discrimination in jobs and are victims of race-related hate crimes. Meanwhile, most governments do little to protect Romani people's basic human rights.

Sadly, many non-Rom around the world aren't aware of these injustices. Instead, they have only a romantic idea of gypsies (lowercase) as simple, carefree, happy-go-lucky wanderers. International human rights movements are trying to raise awareness and promote social justice for Romani people.

Largely to escape persecution, many Rom have immigrated to the Americas over the past five hundred years. The greatest waves of Rom came between the late 1800s and mid-1900s. These subgroups of Romani people came mainly from Romania, Yugoslavia (Bosnia), Hungary, Poland, Russia, Greece, France, Turkey, and Spain. Some groups first settled in the United States or South America, and then migrated to Mexico.

Although I easily found information about the Rom in Europe, it was much harder to find sources on their presence in Mexico. The Rom have been dehistorified, as described by David Lagunas of the National School of Anthropology and History in Mexico. "They do not appear in the history of Mexico," he says. "We know very little about them." ("Gypsies, or How to be Invisible in Mexico," *IPS News Agency*.)

After much searching, I finally came across several works about the Romani culture in Mexico. I was fascinated to learn more about the traveling cinema (cine ambulante), which was popular work for the Rom in Mexico in the mid-1900s.

Since the spread of VCRs in the 1980s, few groups still practice cine ambulante (now traveling in trucks and campers). As alternatives, many Rom have turned to machine repair; buying and selling vehicles; and performing theater, magic, and clowning.

I was especially thrilled to come across several narratives by gitanos in Mexico. In one, Alfredo Yovani reminisced about his days of cine ambulante: "In the forgotten villages where nothing [new] ever came, the people would become happy [to see us]. We knew just what films they liked . . . Wherever we'd go, it was a novelty. Everyone was excited about the films. It was wonderful work . . . and we traveled around, very content." (*Piel de Carpa: Los Gitanos de México*, p. 66.)

I was happy to discover that the Mixteco villagers' fondness for the Rom was mutual. In the midst of so much prejudice, these two groups embraced each other with appreciation and respect. Now if only the rest of the world could follow their lead . . .

Mexican Spanish-English
GLOSSARY AND PRONUNCIATION GUIDE

agua de jamaica (AHG-wah day hah-MY-kah): sweet hibiscus
water

agua de papaya (AHG-wah day pah-PY-ah): sweet papaya water

ahorita vengo (ow-REE-tah VAYN-goh): I'll be there in a second

amigo (ah-MEE-goh): friend

atole (ah-TOH-lay): traditional indigenous Mexican corn drink

brujo (BROO-hoh): witch (male)

buenas noches (BWAY-nahs NOH-chays): good evening/good
night

buenos días (BWAY-nohs DEE-ahs): hello/good morning

cabo de año (CAH-boh day AHN-yoh): ceremony for the first
anniversary of a person's death

centavos (sayn-TAH-vohs): cents

chile (CHEE-lay): chili

cine ambulante (SEE-nay ahm-boo-LAHN-tay): traveling cinema

curandero (coo-rahn-DAY-roh): healer

Dios mío (dee-OHS MEE-oh): my God

diositos (dee-oh-SEE-tohs): "little gods," statues from pre-
Hispanic cultures

el monte (ayl MOHN-tay): the countryside/hilly pastures outside
of town

gracias (GRAH-see-ahs): thank you

huevos estrellados (WAY-vohs ays-tray-AH-dohs): fried eggs

huipil (WEE-peel): traditional, handmade indigenous women's tunic

indio (EEN-dee-oh): Indian. Can be an offensive term, used as an insult throughout Latin America. The respectful alternative is *indígena* (indigenous person).

La Devoradora (lah day-vohr-ah-DOHR-ah): the devourer/the man-eating woman (a classic Mexican film)

La Mujer Sin Alma (lah moo-HAYRR seen AHL-mah*): the woman without a soul / the heartless woman (a classic Mexican film)

limpia (LEEM-pee-ah): spiritual cleansing ceremony

los viejitos (lohs vee-ay-HEE-tohs): the old people (affectionate term)

maestra (mah-AYS-trah): teacher (female)

Mamá (mah-MAH): Mom

más o menos (MAHS oh MAY-nohs): so-so, more or less

maza (MAH-sah): tortilla dough

mija (MEE-hah): my daughter (contraction of "mi hija")

mijo (MEE-hoh): my son (contraction of "mi hijo")

milpa (MEEL-pah): cornfield

mole (MOH-lay): chocolate-chili sauce, a traditional food in Oaxaca, Mexico

momentito (moh-mayn-TEE-toh): just a moment

nada (NAH-dah): nothing

Nosotros los Pobres (no-SOH-trohs lohs POH-brays): We the Poor (a classic Mexican film)

oye (OH-yay): hey

pan dulce (PAHN DOOL-say): sweet roll

panela (pah-NAY-lah): raw, whole, brown cane sugar

Papá (pah-PAH): Dad

petate (pay-TAH-tay): woven palm mat

pobre (POH-bray): poor

pobrecita (poh-bray-SEE-tah): poor thing (female)

pobrecito (poh-bray-SEE-toh): poor thing (male)

por favor (pohrr fah-VOHRR*): please

pues, adiós (PWAYS ah-dee-OHS): well, good-bye

querido (kay-REE-doh): dear

ranchera (rrahn-CHAY-rah*): a traditional style of Mexican music

ruda (RROO-dah*): rue, an herb used in spiritual cleansing ceremonies

señor (sayn-YOHRR*): sir, mister

señora (sayn-YOH-rah): ma'am, lady

señorita (sayn-yohr-EE-tah): miss (young lady)

tamal (tah-MAHL): tamale (singular form)

* *"rr" represents a rolled r*

Mixteco-English

GLOSSARY AND PRONUNCIATION GUIDE

Note that Mixteco includes several dialects, and can vary even from village to village; spelling can vary as well. The dialect I've used is spoken in the village of San Agustín Atenango, in the Mixteca Baja region. Mixteco is a tonal language, so the meaning of a word can change depending on whether your voice goes up or down.

yo'o sunii* (joh-oh soo-neee): I'm fine

yo'o naa yo* (joh-oh naah joh): hello/good day/good morning (formal)

taxiini (tah-sheee-nee): calm down

kuu ini (kooo ee-nee): love

sikita'an* (see-kee-tah-ahn): hug

ñamani (nyah-mah-nee): please

nixi yo'o?* (nee-shee joh-oh): how are you?

tatsavini (taht-sah-vee-nee): thank you (formal)

yeu (jay-oo): good

* The apostrophe represents a glottal stop, similar to the sound represented by the "-" in "uh-oh." You stop airflow in your windpipe for a split second.

Romani-English
GLOSSARY AND PRONUNCIATION GUIDE

Romani dialects vary from country to country, and even from group to group within a country. Most Rom in Mexico nowadays speak Spanish and/or some form of Spanish-Romani, which includes some Spanish words interspersed in the traditional Romani language. Spelling can also vary widely; I've chosen to use the most standard.

boria (bo-ree-ah): women who have married into a family (daughters-in-law, sisters-in-law)

gadjé (ga-jay): non-Romani people

gadjo (ga-joh): non-Romani male

marime (ma-ree-may): unclean, polluted, impure, contaminated (a cultural concept)

Rom (rrom*): noun form for Gypsy**

Romani (rro-ma-nee*): adjective form for Gypsy

* "rr" represents a rolled r
** There are many different terms that the Rom use to refer to themselves, including Rrom, Řom, Roma, Rroma, Romani, Rromani, Řomani, Romany, Řomany, and Rromany. After weighing various expert opinions, I have chosen to use the term Rom as the noun form and Romani as the adjective form in this book. This was apparently the most common termi-nology among the Rom in the Americas in the mid-twentieth century, the setting of this story. Non-Romani Mexicans usually refer to the Rom as gitanos or húngaros (Hungarians), even though only one subgroup immi-grated from Hungary.

Acknowledgments

With every new book there are even more wonderful people to thank! I've been thrilled to work with the enthusiastic team at Scholastic, who have been a burst of sunshine in my life. My talented and dedicated editor, Andrea Davis Pinkney, has been the brightest sunbeam of all. Andrea, I can't tell you how honored I feel to be creating with you. I also offer a heartfelt thanks to my brilliant agent, Erin Murphy, for connecting me with Andrea, and for being so much fun to work with over the past decade, along with Tara Gonzalez, Bon Vivant Dennis, and the other shining stars at Erin Murphy Literary Agency.

Mountains of gratitude go to early readers Carrie Visintainer, Chris Resau, Dana Masden, Janet Freeman, Jeannie Mobley, Karye Cattrell, Laura Pritchett, and Tara Dairman. *Abrazos* and gracias go to Gloria García Díaz, magnificent writer friend who offered valuable feedback on Mexican culture and Spanish language elements. My spirited tribe of Colorado writer friends and my beloved EMLA gang provided me with plenty of support and laughter along the way.

Laurie McMahon, an extraordinary teacher in Half Moon Bay (who knows my books better than I do), offered me precious feedback on this manuscript. I started writing this book in my head while walking along the succulent-covered sea cliffs of Half Moon Bay, feeling elated from a visit with Laurie's students and conversations with exuberant librarian Armando Ramirez (who shared some gitano memories from his own childhood). Thank you, fantastic Half Moon Bay community!

I couldn't have written this without inspiration from Fidelina López López and the late María Chiquita López Martinez, Oaxacan women who shared tales of the queridos gitanos, welcomed me to a beautiful cabo de año, and brought magic into my life. Other generous friends in the Mixteca—Melissa Ferrin and Marcelino Ramírez Ibañez—reviewed the manuscript and offered excellent suggestions. Their extended family, including Francisco Ibáñez Martínez and the late Catalina Ibáñez Martínez, graciously shared their memories of the gitanos and answered *un montón* of detailed questions about Mixteco villages in the mid-twentieth century. I am eternally grateful for your help.

Thanks, also, to Sonia Castro Pozos and her family for Mixteco language assistance and years of friendship. A giant gracias to Baruc Cruz Blanco and my other friends in Oaxaca who have welcomed me into their families' homes and shared their stories with me over the years. This book truly would not exist without you all.

A big thank-you to Baby Goose Grape, who sparked the idea for the rescued animal characters after becoming a brief but meaningful (and very cute and poopy) part of my life. Thanks, also, to Ronald Cree and Alexis Gerard, who kindly shared some fun and quirky animal stories of their own. Rob

Sparks, birder extraordinaire, was my awesome go-to guy for Mexican waterfowl questions. And I have Les Sunde and Kathleen Pelley to thank for their words of wisdom that found their way into this story. I'm also grateful to my creative young friend Roxi for her thoughtful title feedback.

A huge thanks to Charlie Cox, who, after our serendipitous encounter at the farmers' market, took the time to show me his gorgeous vintage caravans and share his knowledge of Romani culture. I'm indebted to Matt Salo of the Gypsy Lore Society for directing me to little-known academic sources and patiently answering my many questions about Romani culture, history, and language in Mexico.

My extended family has been an essential part of my writing journey since I was a young girl. Thanks to you all for your endless encouragement, especially Mom, Dad, Mike, Aunt Liz Neal, Susan and Bruce Hansen, Wolfger Schneider, Gertrude Vuynovich, and Grandmom Winnie, who recently passed away. Thanks, also, to my wildly creative friends (since middle school)—Andrea, Megan, and the Amandas—who spent summer afternoons with me at the Scream Stream long, long ago.

As for the two biggest treasures of my life, Ian and Bran, thank you for inspiring me to laugh and love and feel so happy to be alive. As Bran says nearly every day, "This is the best day EVER!"

Finally, I want to thank you, dear reader—whether you're young or old, a teacher or student, a librarian or patron—for letting me do this job, which I love with all my soul.

About the Author

Laura Resau is the author of several highly praised novels, including *Star in the Forest*, *The Queen of Water*, *Red Glass*, and *What the Moon Saw*. She is also the author of the acclaimed Notebook series, which includes *The Indigo Notebook*, *The Ruby Notebook*, and *The Jade Notebook*. Laura's books have gathered many state and library awards as well as multiple starred reviews. *The Lightning Queen* is drawn from Laura's experience of living in rural Mexico. She now lives in Fort Collins, Colorado, and donates a portion of her royalties to indigenous rights organizations.